D09953668

the OUTER BANKS HOUSE

the OUTER BANKS HOUSE

a novel

DIANN DUCHARME

CROWN PUBLISHERS

NEW YORK

This is a work of fiction. Names, characters, places, and incidents
either are the product of the author's imagination or are used fictitiously.
Any resemblance to actual persons, living or dead, events,
or locales is entirely coincidental.

Copyright © 2010 by Diann Ducharme

Published in the United States by Crown Publishers,
an imprint of the Crown Publishing Group,
a division of Random House, Inc., New York.
www.crownpublishing.com

Crown and the Crown colophon are registered trademarks of
Random House, Inc.

Library of Congress Cataloging-in-Publication Data
Ducharme, Diann.
The Outer Banks house : a novel / Diann Ducharme. —1st ed.
p. cm.
1. Plantation owners—Fiction. 2. Fishers—North Carolina—
Outer Banks—Fiction. 3. Social classes—North Carolina—Outer Banks—
Fiction. 4. Outer Banks (N.C.)—Race relations—Fiction. 5. Ku Klux Klan
(1915–)—North Carolina—Fiction. I. Title.
PS3604.U336O87 2010
813'.6—dc22   2009027810

ISBN 978-0-307-46223-7

Printed in the United States of America

Design by Diane Hobbing of Snap-Haus Graphics

Frontispiece: From *An Outer Banks Reader* by David Stick. Copyright © 1998
by the University of North Carolina Press.
Used by permission of the publisher. www.uncpress.unc.edu

10 9 8 7 6 5 4 3 2 1

First Edition

Dedicated to Sean, Dorsey, and Katherine, my own true loves

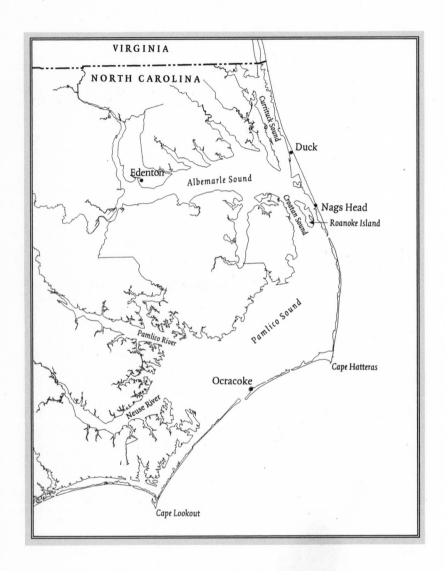

THE OUTER BANKS

CHAPTER ONE

Abigail Sinclair
Nags Head, North Carolina
June 18, 1868

I walked about on the shore lifting up my hands, and my
whole being, as I may say, wrapped up in the contem-
plation of my deliverance, making a thousand gestures
and motions that I cannot describe, reflecting upon all
my comrades that were drowned, and that there should
not be one soul saved but myself . . .

—ROBINSON CRUSOE

I WAS THE FIRST PASSENGER OFF THE STEAMBOAT. MY FELLOW TRAVELERS
had insisted, for I had spent the duration of the journey in the throes
of boatsickness. Everyone, including my own mama and daddy, had
watched me from afar, afraid to get their Sunday best too close to me.

Behind me, I could hear them all lining up, eager to disembark, but

I stood directly in the way, unable to make my way down the skinny pier toward land. Folks started to politely fuss at me, but Charlie and Martha, my younger brother and sister, began pushing on my back-side, forcing me forward.

Yet even as they jostled me along, I couldn't take my eyes from the sight of the Outer Banks of North Carolina, stretching to the left and right at the end of the pier.

Gone were the ordered, busy streets of Edenton that we had left behind. In their place was a strip of land where nature wouldn't allow such regulation.

Instead of brick buildings of commerce and law, there were giant dunes of beige sand that grew clear into the clouds. Instead of statues and lampposts, there were stunted and craggy trees that grew in the sand monsters' shadows along the shoreline. Their gnarled branches blew obligingly in the brisk wind.

Even the soundside watering town of Nags Head was unassuming, and so flat that I could see almost clear across the narrow island to the Atlantic Ocean. The hotel and surrounding white houses were tucked into the sand and foliage so nicely it was as if they had been planted there.

But beyond all this was a shimmering in the eastern sky. I knew it was the ocean there, beneath the blue. I had never seen it in my life, and my heart began to beat faster in anticipation. I took a deep breath of the salty air, picked up my skirts, and started to run. I ran the way that I used to run when I was nine years old, when nothing mattered but the day on the plantation.

Our housemaid, Winnie, hollered after me, but her voice was lost in the wind. I didn't even think about Mama and Daddy, or what they'd have to say to me later. I heard Charlie and Martha scampering after me, squealing at the game. But I didn't turn around. I just ran down the wooden pathway through the sand, my legs straining against my hoops.

Soon, from the unfamiliar exercise, I felt myself gobbling great gulps of hot air, and drops of sweat were seeping like pricks of blood into my beige traveling dress. My heavy strawberry hair baked under my bonnet, and my hands cramped with the weight of my skirts and the bunched-up parasol.

But I didn't slow until I heard a rhythmic crashing and sizzling. The wooden planks came to an end in a wide plane of sand, which met naturally and directly with the object of my affection.

"Ocean," I said breathlessly, as the wind whipped wayward strands of hair into my open mouth. Pelicans cruised like soldiers down the war zone of water, white-capped breakers marching and ebbing back, then crashing even harder. A few large ships inched along the choppy horizon.

Happy vacationers were everywhere. Gloved and bonneted women strolled with parasols, and the men splashed in the surf or even ventured out to swim in the rough water. Charlie and Martha whooped like orangutans and dashed past me to touch the shuddering water, feel with tentative hands whether it was warm or cold, but I couldn't move.

I squatted and carefully plopped down on my left hip on the sand, still sucking in the air. I must have run almost a mile from sound to sea, the entire width of the island here. My uncle Jack would have whistled his approval. To see a sight like this, he would have run along beside me, forgetting that a young lady of my seventeen years should not be running anywhere.

I had brought along a piece of Uncle Jack, a letter that he had written to me right before he died of dysentery during the war. I hadn't wanted to leave it at home, buried in the dresser where I kept a book of scraps, stuffed with dozens of Uncle Jack's letters, two tin-types, and even some of his auburn hair from a forgotten brush.

His last letter was by far the most precious to me. I tried not to handle it so much these days, because the paper was thinning out something terrible. But sometimes all I wanted to do was touch it, for I had memorized the cramped-up words long ago. And too, the letter still smelled vaguely of bark-oil tea and dirty linens, a smell that I now associated with death.

But on this day, I couldn't help myself.

Keeping one eye on the children, I wiggled my reticule from my skirts and took out the letter. It whipped in the strong wind as I read.

February 7, 1865
North Carolina Hospital, Petersburg, Virginia

My Dear Little Red Reb,

You'll have to excuse my penmanship here. I've been curled up on my right side for so long that my writing hand's gone numb. This position suits me best, though, because it quiets the sizzling in my belly a bit. I tell you, sometimes I wish I had been shot clean through the skull. This quick-step is the devil's business. You folks back home wouldn't even know me, I've lost so much flesh. I bet I'm skinnier than you are. Don't tell your daddy I said this, but I'm starting to think that he was the smart one of the both of us. I should have just stayed put. Edenton looks just like heaven in my mind, these days.

I got this cheap paper from the blue-lipped nurse that creeps around here. I don't like her much, mostly because of the sad look in her eyes. She's young, just a little older than you are now. But she isn't near as pretty as you, and like I said, she's lacking in enthusiasm. 'Course, I'd never say that about you, niece!

Which reminds me, your daddy said in his previous letter that you've been reading a lot these days. He says that you're going to drive him into bankruptcy with all of your book buying! I've been trying to picture my fiery Reb with her nose stuck in a book, just like her mama, I guess. It got me to thinking that I'd like to read one of those books myself. You're likely having a good laugh right now. But there isn't much decent to read in this hospital. I guess folks don't think sickly soldiers are the reading kind of men, and I must admit, I feel a little rusty at the exercise. Why don't you send me one of your favorites with your next letter?

It also might do you some good to get out of doors once in a while. Tell your daddy that I said to take Ace of Spades for a ride every now and then. Give the boy some sugar lumps for me, will you? I can just see you and me riding him, the way we used to. I can feel those ribbons of yours flying in my face. You never did holler, even when we were running through rivers. It's those kinds of thoughts that get me through these awful days. I don't see pretty Mary Virginia Spellman or even Annabelle Putnam in my head anymore. I picture a pair of steady green eyes and red eyelashes, and I grit my teeth and bear it. I try not to holler.

I sure hope I can get better and come on home to you and the family. I miss you all more than Winnie's butter biscuits. But if I don't make it out of this hospital, I hope you remember me kindly. Not as this run-down, sickly soldier, but as your uncle, holding you tight on the best horse I ever had.

I've got high hopes for you, so don't let me down.

As ever, your devoted uncle,
Jack Sinclair

I swallowed hard and then yelled at Charlie to pull up the legs of his trousers. My siblings were already soaked to the skin, but I couldn't muster up much of a care. I pinched Uncle Jack's letter so tightly between thumb and forefinger that I feared it would rip in the bullying wind, but I couldn't put it away just yet.

The biggest regret of my life was that I never got to send Uncle Jack a book. He died before his last letter had even reached me.

It was awful to feature someone dying from dysentery, especially Uncle Jack, who probably came out of Grandma Marian's womb with a grin on his face. I couldn't ever remember him acting low-down.

Folks liked to comment on our similar dispositions and how they made us as close as any niece and uncle could be without it seeming sinful. His big hand on my head was a constant reminder of his need to father, and of my need to be parented. We knew this about each other, but never quite said so. It was just there, hovering between us as thick as the humidity on an Edenton noon in August, this paucity of attention from my own mama and daddy. We all lived in the same house, but Mama and Daddy made their true homes inside their minds, with the front doors closed to all but themselves.

In spite of this coldness, there was a spirit in me that seeked out the heat. I'd meander through the outbuildings to find my uncle, and the slaves would point him out to me with pity on their faces. Even they knew that I was starved for affection; even they knew that Uncle Jack would welcome his niece by pulling her onto his stallion with an easy tug on her reaching arm.

It didn't feel wrong that I loved my uncle more than my own daddy. And when he died, I lost a father.

The threadbare Confederate soldiers delivered Uncle Jack to us in a coffin that needed only two skinny men to carry it. And when we looked on his embalmed body before the burial, he appeared to be a child dressed in an officer's uniform, the material bunched on him so badly. I could just imagine the disease that killed him, still hiding inside that body, nibbling and gnawing 'til there was nothing left of the once-dimpled, potbellied Uncle Jack that I'd known.

The day after his funeral we had to put his beloved stallion down. Ace was old and sickly, but he refused to die. 'Course, we all knew that he was waiting for his master to come home. When I watched the wagon bearing his huge black body make its way down the long pathway away from the house, my tears finally started to flow.

Now I shuddered slightly in the breeze and carefully placed the letter inside the reticule. Then I gazed up the beach, this beach that Daddy had just had to build a house on.

Daddy had showed us the Outer Banks on a creased United States map one day after midday dinner about a year ago. He traced the tip of his long, freckled index finger down the crooked chain of barrier islands that skipped delicately from the Virginia line down along the North Carolina coast for 175 miles.

It had always been accepted that the islands were both a blessing and a curse for North Carolina. They protected the state from all that ocean, but at the same time they hemmed it in, frustrating state commerce and travel. As such, North Carolina was an important victory for the Yankees, back during the war. When they took the state, they unlocked all the numerous waterways, giving their army access to the South and her valuables.

The fragile Banks curve eastward from the mainland, like the beak of a falcon, to an unprecedented twenty miles into the Atlantic Ocean. At the farthest eastern tip of the beak, at Cape Hatteras, two strong currents fight like cats and dogs, causing most any ship to founder helplessly on the shifting shoals. Folks affectionately refer to the area as the Graveyard of the Atlantic, due to the countless ship carcasses that have emerged from the waves.

Looking at that map by myself, I wouldn't have even noticed the islands, they were so thin. They looked as if a dull writing pencil had accidentally been left on the map, creating a snaky mark. Those islands seemed so *vulnerable*, stuck in between the hulking land mass of America and the wide-open sea.

Their stubborn reaching into the ocean, their blatant tempting of fate, captivated me, yet filled me with fear, and I took the map to bed that night, studying it by flickering candlelight.

The islands weren't far from our hometown of Edenton—just sixty or so miles due east across the Albemarle Sound. But to me they were as far away as the moon, and just as mysterious.

I had heard that the locals there descended from shipwrecked sailors and runaways who used to lure ships to their fate by tying a lantern around the neck of a horse at night. They would lead the nag up and down the shore, the bobbing lantern resembling light from another ship. The unsuspecting sailors would steer for the light, only to founder in the shallow waters near land, where the men would ransack the wrecked ship and take its contents for their own.

Hence the glorious name "Nags Head." I thought that it was a right clever trick, for such simple men.

Daddy hunted all the time back in Edenton, so much so that folks joked about Daddy's arm being a rifle instead of mere bone. I swear, he talks nicer to his pack of hounds than he does to his own children. Needless to say, most of the meat on our dining room table Daddy shot and killed himself.

He couldn't wait to explore the shallow yet wide sounds and the maze of inlets that separated the Banks from the mainland. He had already hired a local guide for the summer weekends, to show him the best spots for hooking fish.

He visited the Banks last fall to scout land for our summer cottage, and when he returned, his cart full of dead geese and ducks, he went on and on about the large numbers of waterfowl that visited the sounds on their migratory routes. And come suppertime, we all agreed that the Currituck bird meat was the most savory we had ever eaten.

⁂

My breath recovered, I clambered to my feet and looked to the north, where a handful of rustic houses sprouted from the sand. They were recently built, defying the more sensible soundside tradition, about two or three hundred flattened feet away from the ocean. These boxy cottages looked to be constructed with precaution in mind, with no thought whatsoever to opulence.

From what I had gathered from Mama and Daddy, the first cottage to be built on the ocean side was owned by the Dr. Pool family from Elizabeth City. I thought the Pool house must be the one whose wood had already darkened from its exposure to the endless barrage of salt and wind.

Word had it that Dr. Pool had already purchased a ribbon of land—about fifty acres—that stretched north from the hotel property up along the shore, and was selling the lots for a dollar apiece to his friends back home. He disliked the loneliness of ocean living, or so we had heard.

But at least those few cottages had one another for company.

Far south down the beach, I could barely see what I knew to be our cottage. It stood alone, an arrogant outcast. And the more I gaped down the shore, the more it occurred to me how eccentric, how completely *insane* the cottage appeared, all alone on an expanse of defenseless sand. It looked to be the home of a madman.

Yet at the same time it looked like some sort of miracle, a product of genius. Standing there by the sea, where nothing could live for long, it threw out a dare.

I began to walk south down the beach, faster and faster, my shoes filling with sand, until I came right up to the cottage's porch steps, unfolding like a silent welcome into the sand. It was even smaller than I'd thought it might be. It couldn't have been more different from our plantation home, which was, at the beginning of the war, one of the finest homes in Edenton.

For more than a hundred years, the Great House back home had been called, for lack of a more creative moniker, "Sinclair House." It was a three-story brick Georgian structure with fifteen high-ceilinged rooms. It had taken almost twenty years to build, back in the early eighteenth century. This beach cottage was just a little larger than our kitchen house.

The squat, two-story square, covered with cedar shingles, supported an isosceles roof that sat substantially on the second floor. Wide porches embraced the cottage on all sides, and the entire structure was perched atop numerous pilings embedded in the sand. Wood shutters yawned open with prop sticks to let the ocean breezes blow through the windows, and doors appeared to open to the interior on both the western and eastern sides.

The only thing that wasn't tight, shingled wood was the brick chimney poking obscurely from the northeastern side of the house.

The kitchen jutted out a bit from the southwestern side of the house, and the privy and an adjacent washhouse stood nearby. A little stable for our horses and cow had been built a hundred yards south, and the water pump had already been dug, down to the layer of freshwater that lay beneath the sand.

With the cotton and tobacco crops already growing strong at home, Mama, Martha, Charlie, and I would live here through the beginning of September, with Daddy tending to business in Edenton during the week and visiting every Saturday and Sunday. If the cottage didn't get washed away by the ocean, we'd return here every summer after this one. Already, I didn't think I would ever want to leave.

∂

I guessed it would take Justus a good while to load and transport our belongings in the carts. Justus was a rail-skinny, but mysteriously strong, twenty-year-old field hand from home. He was always late, always gone when needed. When he did manage to make his appearance, it was with a guilt-free expression of contentment. I personally thought it was funny, but no one else in my family got the joke.

I pictured Daddy on the docks, standing there in his finery while Justus loaded the cart with our numerous cases and cages of chickens. At least Hannah, Justus's headstrong thirteen-year-old sister, was already at the cottage, readying it for our arrival. It would mean one less thorn in Daddy's side.

I climbed the five long steps up to the porch, my hooped dress scratching the raw wood with each step. I pulled back the screen and opened the door, which still smelled of freshly cut pine.

"Hannah?" I called inside. "We're here!"

Hannah hollered her greetings from upstairs, the room where Mama and Daddy would sleep. I could hear her footsteps banging through the thin ceiling.

The sun from the windows gave an amber glow to the parlor, which was comfortably outfitted with a wide array of antique Sinclair furniture. The rug that covered the squeaky pine floor was a tread-softened blend of beige, blue, and red, and the old mahogany dining table, which matched the accompanying glass-fronted china cabinet, was draped with a white linen tablecloth and already boasted silver candlesticks and a china bowl full of shiny green apples.

Yet the walls were left unfinished, like a log cabin in the mountains, with no paint or plaster to cover the bare wood. No curtains were hung, and the raised panes of glass in the windows were already smudged with salt. I inhaled the scent of sea and freshly starched linen and smiled. Finery and rawness seemed to be everywhere.

The bedroom downstairs was much smaller than my bedroom at home, but I found the room so refreshing, with its light blue and white quilts and view of the ocean through the two windows, that it didn't seem to matter, at least for that moment, that I was sharing such a small space with my brother and sister.

With sodden clothing and salt-stiff hair, Charlie and Martha tore through the house and tumbled onto their beds while I gazed out the window. The sun reflected off the sand, so that I had to shade my eyes, even indoors. Just the change in light would take some getting used to.

"Tickle me, Abby!" ordered Charlie. I reached over to wiggle my fingers into Charlie's taut midsection. He jerked into a little ball, gasping for air and adjusting his authentic pirate eye patch, given to him by a collector friend of Daddy's. Even Martha, usually trying so hard to be a lady, tickled Charlie until he cried for mercy.

⟳

Soon I heard the creak of the oxcart and Justus's monotonous rambling. I went to greet them, and through the screen door I saw Mama ascending the front steps. Her tall, angular form darkened the doorway, blocking out the sparkling sunlight. She folded her parasol and gripped it easily in one pale, bony hand. She then walked slowly around the room, running a hand over the shiny wood of the dining chairs.

Mama, with her sunlight hair and creamy, unwrinkled complexion, could have been truly beautiful. Instead, her acidity caused her small, carved features to appear demonic and skeletal rather than aristocratic.

There was only one attribute of hers that appealed to me—her ice pick–sharp mind. Yet her big brain thought too much about everything, especially during casual conversation. Even over tea and sandwiches, she came off as socially inept and even inconsiderate, especially with well-bred women from town, who usually wanted to gossip.

Only we knew that beneath the awkward exterior coursed something much darker than poor social skills.

"What do you think you were doing, Abigail?" she seethed. "You'll be the talk of society out here for the entire summer!"

I tried to form coherent syllables for her. She expected composure and reason, especially during an argument. "I was excited to see the ocean, Mama. I wanted to compare the real thing to the image that I had in my head . . ."

She calmly stood her parasol by the door and walked over to me. "No, Abigail, you ran before you utilized the bright mind that God gave you. I ask you, daughter, why do we pay good money for your clothing, if you're going to treat it with such disrespect?"

She jerked my arms up to inspect the sweat stains that had bloomed on the linen during my unaccustomed exercise, then bent over to see the snags and sand along the hem. Charlie and Martha peered at me quietly from the bedroom doorway.

Her blue eyes flashed. "This dress is ruined," she hissed. "Winnifred, take Abigail to her room at once and remove this sordid piece of clothing. I want you to wash it and mend it and take it to a young woman of Abigail's age here on the island. A girl who will appreciate a dress of such quality, and treat it with respect."

Even though it stung, her anger was well-founded, and I hung my head in regret. Two months before our departure for Nags Head, Mama had ordered a dozen dresses for me, despite the current lack of money for such luxuries. Their ripples of silk and linen looked like mountains in springtime, with the lace like dustings of late-season snow.

Winnie hurried over, looking wild with some of her rebellious curls peeking from her scarf. She cut an I-told-you-so look at me, one of her favorite expressions. Mama then glided in her layer-cake skirts over to the narrow steps leading to the upstairs bedroom, looking as regal as she did ascending the spiral staircase back home.

Her voice had grown thin and tired, though. "Foolish girls will never become the wives of doctors. You'd better pray that Hector doesn't hear of your vulgar display of athleticism."

I should have known that it all went back to Hector Newman's courtship, a constant topic of conversation with Mama. She would never tire of it until I was finally married off.

"No more running," she said.

⚭

Winnie quickly undressed me in my bedroom and, with a few sad shakes of her head, took the dress with her when she left. Suddenly exhausted, I plopped down on the little bed, still in my corset and petticoats. The rest felt so good that I stretched out, hoping the old bed was at least somewhat comfortable. And then I couldn't help myself. I closed my eyes, even though Hannah poked fun at my belled-out hoops as she unpacked my cases.

The room had grown warm in the afternoon sun. I didn't mind the heat, though, since I was trying to shake out the early-spring chill that still encircled my bones. The Union-sent wind wanted to remind us, even these three years later, who it was that kicked our Southern faces into the dirt of our sin. Those cold blasts blew through the tall rooms and found us unrepentant rebels, bluing our lips and numbing our fingers and noses.

During the war, Mama, Martha, and I had kept close to the fireplace in cold weather, knitting socks and scarves for the soldiers. I knit so much one winter that I'm sure I left blood on some of the poor men's woolens. With Uncle Jack constantly in mind, I was one of the most active young supporters of the cause in Edenton. I recounted for him, in my countless letters, my many self-appointed responsibilities. He subsequently nicknamed me "Little Red Reb," which made me unaccountably proud.

Yet here, at this isolated cottage by the sea, the memories of those cold-needle days without Uncle Jack seemed hazy and hard to reach. Perhaps this Outer Banks house would help us *all* to forget, to wash our memories as clean as the seashells, so that we could start anew.

At first Mama had questioned the sanity of building such a house as this. She said that if God had wished for humans to build their houses next to the sea, He wouldn't have lined the beaches with sand that shifts its very nature with the changing tides.

And I saw her point. I couldn't see how a wooden house, no matter how well it was constructed, as Daddy argued it would be, would survive for long on the Atlantic Ocean's sinking sand. But Daddy was insistent, as hopeful as I'd seen him in years. Just talking about the cottage caused his cheeks to flush and his voice to soar.

Even so, the cottage had been a stretch for us. Most of our former slaves left us years ago, before the war had even ended, and Daddy had since had lots of trouble finding folks to work the land. And he preferred not to part with what was left of his money, especially if it was going to pay "lazy ingrates looking for handouts."

With no other options left for him, Daddy actually paid some of the straggling field hands to come to the island with a boat full of pine cut from our own land to construct the house according to plans that he himself drafted. Even with the nor'easters and such that hit the islands last fall and winter, the hands finished the cottage in six months flat. I wouldn't call that lazy at all.

CHAPTER TWO

Abigail Sinclair
June 19, 1868

I gave humble and hearty thanks that God had been pleased to discover to me even that it was possible I might be more happy in this solitary condition than I should have been in a liberty of society and in all the pleasures of the world.

—ROBINSON CRUSOE

OUR FIRST FULL DAY IN NAGS HEAD unfolded as thick and warm as honey from the hive. There wasn't a thing to do except eat, sleep, and daydream, and I imagined the days following like a stack of goose-down pillows, white and fluffy.

No Shakespearean sonnets to learn, no Latin lessons to strain over. No more filling my head with things that had already happened, things already written. Nags Head was a whole new language.

Anyone with warm blood in their veins would have felt the freedom, too. Charlie and Martha acted like very small jailbreaks, and Hannah was beside herself trying to keep them from sloshing into the wash too deeply. The hem of her dress was in a constant state of wetness.

In typical fashion, Daddy had risen with the sun and left the cottage on his stallion for a day of fishing. Even though he had been all the way down at the stable, giving Justus instructions for saddling his stallion, Horatio, his booming voice had woken me from a light sleep. He had missed Winnie's breakfast of ham and biscuits, though, so I felt I was doing better than he was.

Mama was the only one who hadn't taken well to the fresh air. She spent the day looking sickly and reading in a rocking chair on the porch, and I spent the day avoiding her, wearing my oldest skirt and shirtwaist. We were getting along like pie.

After a long afternoon walk down the shore and an hour of reading Mama's copy of *Moby-Dick,* I lumbered into the cottage with my hair coming loose from its pins and my forehead slick with perspiration. I couldn't wait to clean myself up with a fresh tub of water and a cake of my favorite lavender soap. But on my way inside, I heard Daddy's voice on the other side of the cottage.

He was carrying on with such jocularity that I thought his companion was a good friend of his from home who had surprised us at the cottage, to see for himself our much-debated adventure. I cringed and tried to hurry to my bedroom to wash up before anyone caught sight of me looking so wretched. But as it turned out, I shouldn't have been worried about *my* appearance; the man who accompanied Daddy inside wouldn't have been fit for entry into Sinclair House.

His deeply tanned face was disguised with streaky smudges of dirt and scruffy beard growth, and his hands and lower arms were encrusted with a layer of dark greenish grime. His hair appeared to be a shade of blond, but it was so unkempt that I couldn't even tell what it would look like in a natural state.

His brownish long-sleeved work shirt and trousers, which appeared to have never been washed or mended, hung shapelessly off his body. And he didn't even see fit to wear shoes; his bare feet were two pieces of soiled leather. My tongue curled when I caught his odor of bloody fish, mixed with the scent of stale tobacco and sweat.

Daddy, wearing his shiny riding boots, smart jacket, and top hat, didn't seem fazed in the least by the man's remarkable filth. He glanced at me as he stooped his imposing frame through the doorway and seemed not to notice either my improper appearance or my haste to escape the room.

"Abigail, I'd like you to meet my guide, Benjamin Whimble. He's showing me the best places to catch fish on the Outer Banks," Daddy bellowed. "I tell you, I've never seen such a natural!"

I guessed that this man would've been embarrassed to be seen in such a state, but he didn't seem to give it a second thought. He shifted on his filthy feet and smiled sloppily.

"Hey there, Miss Sinclair, good to meet you," he drawled. He fidgeted with a worn cap, which he at least saw fit to remove before he came into the house.

I clutched *Moby-Dick* to my chest and tried not to stare at his filthy feet. "How do you do, Mr. Whimble."

He snorted in glee. "Oh, you call me Ben. Ain't no one ever called me Mr. Whimble afore, so I ain't too used to hearing it. Fact, folks 'round here don't even call my daddy Mr. Whimble, they just call him Tremblin' Whimble, 'cause he makes men shake when he's mad. And too, he's getting on in age, so he kind of trembles when he talks now."

Daddy's guffaw caught me by surprise, so that I clean forgot my manners. "Well then. I've got to be getting ready for supper now."

I scooted toward the doorway, but I hadn't moved more than two paces when I heard him blurt, "Miss Sinclair, is that book you're holding yours? I mean, what I meant to say is, are you reading that there book?"

I gripped the book even tighter, cherishing the heavy feel of it in my hands. "Of course I am. Why else would I be carrying it?"

"Oh, right. So softheaded I am," he muttered, smacking his forehead with a dirty palm. "It's just that I ain't never met a gal that can read a book that big."

Daddy snorted. "Abigail here reads more than a young lady should, in my opinion. But her mama sets a bad example for her. Days go by and I don't see hide nor hair of her. She's out in the orchard reading books, living off the apples and a canteen of water."

Mr. Whimble grinned broadly at me, but I stood stiffly, uncomfortable with this man knowing anything that intimate about me. I made for my bedroom, leaving Daddy and Mr. Whimble talking about tomorrow's fishing expedition.

Back in my room, raking a comb through my tumbleweed hair, I was sorely distracted. I had never seen Daddy take to someone like that before. He was usually a tough old turkey to please. I supposed it was possible that Mr. Whimble had a certain way about him. And I hadn't failed to notice how his blue eyes had twinkled right through the grime.

⬥

Daddy helped all of us into the buggy and we set off for the hotel for supper. But it was slow going. The two big wheels of our buggy turned so deeply in the sand that at times old Mungo seemed to stand still, or at least wished he could. I guessed I could have walked to the hotel and eaten my meal before he had struggled through the unfamiliar sand with his load.

But of course there was my new dress to consider, and I wanted to return to Edenton at the end of the summer with at least some of my new clothing still in my possession.

Daddy told us, with a sad countenance, "The hotel that used to operate out here was burned by our boys during the war so the Yanks couldn't use it. Good thing, too, since the Fed'rals swarmed all over the Banks once it fell. Then the bastards took down the Episcopal church here, used the wood for runaway-slave houses over on Roanoke Island. As if people like that need their own houses."

Wood was still hard to come by, these days. But taking down a church for its building materials was a new low. I wondered where the church steeple had ended up. I pictured the cross sitting on top of some shack, like a weather vane.

"I can't for the life of me imagine some slave and his freeloading family squatting on my land while I was off fighting the war," Daddy huffed. "That island used to be a nice, quiet place, before the blue-bellied Yanks had their way over there."

I wasn't at all sure what he was talking about. The only thing I knew about Roanoke Island was that it was the site of the first, and doomed, English colony on American soil. But no one ever interrupted one of Daddy's tirades.

I licked my chapped lips nervously. Listening to Daddy rant about the blacks always caused my heart to shrink up inside me, like the tiny green pea under all those mattresses of puffed-up feelings—sadness, confusion, regret. I swear, I didn't know what to feel these days.

But Daddy had emotion enough for the rest of us. Almost every night at supper he barked over the sheer lunacy of black men being allowed to vote, and sit on juries, and even own farmland. And too frequently I heard Daddy and his many visitors, squirreled away in his study, discussing the sorry state of North Carolina politics, and how the white men—at least the white men who counted—were suffering at the Negro's expense. Negroes even served in Congress now. No one would have ever believed it, just three short years ago.

"So the hotel . . . Is it really that new?" I asked, with extra interest.

"Built just this year. Folks say it's just as fine as the one that burned. But no church yet, if you can believe it, so we have to have our Sunday worship at the hotel!"

I laughed along with Daddy, but Mama said with a scowl, "That doesn't seem right at all. First thing to get built is a business enterprise, and no thought given to a house of God. What kind of a place is this?"

"That's the way of the world. Money always comes first," Daddy preached. "And the folks out here have pirate's blood, anyhow. They can't help their greed. It's a perfect place for the carpetbaggers, come to think of it. Just look at all this untapped wealth."

He gestured around to the ocean and then over to the sound, like he was conducting an orchestra.

༺༄༻

The L-shaped hotel was an impressive structure for such a small island, with three rambling stories, a ten-pin alley, and a grand ballroom for nightly dancing. In the early-evening sun the white clapboard glowed like a mirage in the desert, with the brass band's tunes pumping out the open windows.

An amazing number of vacationers packed the ballroom. Big skirts and top hats bobbed and swept through the room. Even the children were smartly attired, though they were all to dine in a special part of the room designated for youngsters and overseen by servants in white aprons.

The air was perfumed with fresh paint and the floors gleamed slick with inexperience. The politician Buxton Adams and his wife, Iris, were waiting for us at a large table set with a lovely centerpiece of wild beach roses.

"Isn't this a merry gang!" exclaimed Mr. Adams, shaking hands heartily with Daddy and kissing with relish our gloved hands. "How's the ocean treating you folks? I still can't get over that cottage of yours."

His perfectly round head topped a thick body, and his mustached face glowed cherry-tomato red in the crowded warmth. Although you might not guess it at first from his large presence, Mr. Adams was dwarfed physically by Mama and Daddy both. Daddy counted this respected Conservative politician as one of his strongest allies in the fight for keeping the eastern North Carolina land, and the money and power that went with it, in the old planters' hands.

Word had it that Mr. Adams was biding his time, waiting for the radical Reconstruction pendulum to swing in the Conservatives' favor. With the recent Republican victory, however, things weren't looking so good for the Conservatives in North Carolina. But you'd never know it by Mr. Adams's jolly demeanor.

"Abigail, you are looking quite the young lady tonight. I'm not sure I would have known you from that rosy cherub of the tobacco fields! And my, my, just look at that dress—how becoming on you! You and Madeleine will have to compare notes on your dressmakers," he said, indicating his daughter, Maddie Adams, a petite sixteen-year-old girl with the serenely beautiful face of a Rembrandt subject, seated next to her mother at the table.

Maddie was no angel, though. She was known throughout the

state of North Carolina, and probably elsewhere, for her extravagant tastes and newly minted bosom, usually accentuated with inappropriately low-cut gowns. I had known her since we were small girls, although during the war we lost touch with her family and I didn't see her as often as I used to.

"Abigail, I do *so* adore your gown," purred Maddie, who wore her blond hair fashionably styled in droopy ringlets around her face. "It must be hard to find colors to go with your red hair. Lord-a-mercy, that dark green would look positively sickening on me!"

In her pink gown, with its voluminous petticoats peeking out from slits up the sides, Maddie resembled a sinfully sweet strawberry shortcake with dollops of whipped cream, carefully placed in the center of a china plate. I smiled to myself, imagining all of her drooling suitors taking tiny bites from her.

She sipped her mint tea and fanned herself with a wiggly wrist. "How is it out at that little ocean house of yours? It *is* a tiny thing— I can see it from our veranda. I can't imagine how you all stand it! I simply got *lost* in your plantation home when I was a little girl!"

"It is small, but it's refreshing to wake up to the sound of the ocean right outside my window. And we don't have to hitch a horse to a cart to get to the ocean," I tried to explain.

Maddie's big blue eyes had wandered while I was talking, and she was now waving hello to some of her friends across the room. Maddie, always more interested in having tea parties with her dollies than in exploring our land with me, wouldn't understand how the rawness of ocean living appealed to me, much more so than the Adamses' location in one of many houses clustered on the sand hills and near the homes of politicians, attorneys, doctors, and businessmen, with their constant social obligations.

Edenton, North Carolina, was its own cluster, with the neatly lined colonial streets branching out from the courthouse green. There, the Adamses' home was a pre-Revolutionary beauty on Water Street, with a view of Edenton Bay, but it was surrounded on three sides by houses owned by Mr. Adams's contemporaries. I doubted he could even venture outside without encountering a fellow judge or attorney wanting to discuss politics with him. I always thanked my lucky stars that we lived a decent carriage ride from town.

"Our cottage is like a charming Swiss chalet. It sits right on the sand hills, with the cute curly trees all around for shade, and we're up so high we have just a perfect view of the ocean *and* the sound. You should come on over after supper, to see what living in Nags Head is *really* like." She giggled.

I frowned at her, clearly recalling why we'd always ended up on opposite sides of the nursery.

Maddie giggled again. "Bless your heart, Abby, don't have a hissy fit. I'm sure your cottage is just dandy, in its own little way. I already invited Alice Monroe and George Wakefield and Red Taylor over to set on the veranda with me. You're acquainted with them, aren't you?" she said sweetly, then winked at me.

I barely smiled. Her friends were the privileged sons and daughters of Edenton society, the same people Mama and Daddy wanted me to socialize with this summer. I would have to accept the invitation.

While we dined on freshly made crab cakes, fried oysters, and corn bread, the men discussed in hushed voices the most upsetting business of the year—the election of Republican governor William Holden. The women, not to be outdone, chatted about fabrics for draperies and the newest Edenton millinery.

I had trouble following along with the men's agitated whispers, so I was somewhat forced to discuss the elegance of hats that are bedecked with a single egret feather. Apparently they were very expensive, but quite fashionable, and I imagined the women of Edenton wandering the streets looking like a flock of egrets.

I wasn't the only one at the table with a glazed expression, however. Mama, whose face had taken on a sickly yellow tinge, looked acutely miserable trying to keep up her end of the conversation with Mrs. Adams and Maddie. She hadn't the skills for lighthearted conversation, and I noticed that her food remained largely untouched. And she kept beckoning for the harried Negro servant to refill her lemonade glass, to which she subsequently added several large spoonfuls of sugar.

At one point during dessert Mrs. Adams declared, "Ingrid, I've never seen you look so poorly."

Mama said with a little shudder, "It's that ocean air. I slept with the windows open last night . . . I declare, I've never smelled such nastiness. It's made me quite sick."

Mrs. Adams laughed heartily. "That *air* is the reason everyone is here in Nags Head! Oh, you do amuse me."

Mama just reached for her glass of lemonade and took several frantic gulps.

The children's table broke up first, of course. Martha and Charlie ran out the door of the dining room with the other children, who were all itching to explore the nearby sand hills in the waning daylight.

Soon young couples rose from the tables to dance to the band, whose horns and cornets were starting to squeak after a break. Red Taylor, the handsome son of a prominent attorney in Edenton, ventured over to ask Maddie to dance with him. I could tell that he was trying hard not to stare at the bubbles of skin squeezing from the top of her gown.

Maddie took her sweet time in accepting his invitation, batting her eyelashes and looking around the room before rising from the table like a slow-to-bake yeast roll. Then Mr. and Mrs. Adams got up to make a hand-shaking tour of the room, leaving us to ourselves.

So I lingered with my parents, almost a grown woman, aware of myself in my new dress and hat, aglow in the warm light of the newly lit oil lamps.

Daddy sat back in his chair with his pipe and port. "Abigail, your mother and I have decided that you should tutor Mr. Whimble in reading and writing this summer," he said.

"Pardon me?" Surely the yelps of the children outside had somehow interfered with his communication.

He smiled at me, a smile with a warning concealed within it. "He indicated this afternoon that he would like to learn how to read and write, just rudimentary skills at best. He was crying over the fact that he had no one to teach him, and with no schools out here it's impossible for him to learn anything. So it occurred to me then that *you* are a good teacher, having taught Martha and Charlie the last few years. I told him so, and one thing led to another." He shifted his large weight, causing the new chair to cry out for mercy. "You should have seen his face. I've never seen such a display of teeth in my life. He was so grateful that he's suspending all the fees charged to me for his guide service." Then, an afterthought, he said, "It's good business, Abigail."

I stared at his sunburned nose. I couldn't even imagine a scenario in which I played tutor and dirty Mr. Whimble played student.

"Good business! I hardly think that tutoring a strange man is a wise idea. Teaching my own brother and sister is one thing, but a grimy fisherman! You don't even know this Mr. Whimble," I said desperately. "He could be dangerous! He's as filthy as an urchin! Lord knows what he does when he's not fishing and hunting and roaming around in the muck, adding clumps of dirt to his collection. I don't want to do it. I *won't* do it."

Some diners, lingering over their dessert and coffee, turned their heads toward our table.

Mama shushed me, but Daddy merely looked at me as he would a curious specimen of duck. He said, "Ben is about as dangerous as a dandelion." He shot back the last of his port. "He's smart, in his way. And patient, a hard worker. And he's a local hero, so they say," he assured me. "I like him, I really do."

"Mama, how could *you* of all people agree to this? It's not proper! What will people say?" I blurted. "He's a fisherman, for mercy's sake!"

Mama disliked fishermen as a general rule. Her daddy had been a stevedore, laboring his entire immigrant life on the fast-paced Edenton ports after he arrived from Sweden, and she had learned to dislike with a passion anything that reminded her of her previous life as a daughter of the docks. Now Mama just shrugged, not up to the fight.

In misery, I looked at the empty chairs and dirty plates and cups at our table. Me, tutor a fisherman? I snorted scornfully. But my mind wandered to Mr. Whimble's bluebird eyes, and I heard my mouth mumble, "Well, I suppose I could give it a try. Only for a little while."

Daddy said with a nod, "I'll tell him you can start tomorrow."

Mama worked hard at stifling a yawn with a vanilla hand. She said, "It will be good for your education, Abigail. *I* have found that teaching reinforces and expands our own learning. This will provide a worthy occupation for you, and keep your mind from sliding into oblivion this summer."

She removed her napkin from her lap and placed it on the table. "And I will chaperone, of course."

They rose from the table, nodding and waving at everyone in the room, as I sat numbly, my head swimming. Mercy, what had I just agreed to?

※

A pink-faced Maddie, closely circled by a flock of scavenging boys, called out to me to accompany them on her family's cart back to the house. It was dark outside, and getting late, but I agreed to go, on account of how thrilled Mama and Daddy were at the offer.

Sitting so close atop the cart, I could smell the pungent scent of alcohol on their breath as they laughed with one another. The boys then made a gallant show of assisting the ladies off the cart and helping us through the soft sand up to the little white house.

The story-and-a-half house really was charming, nestled cozily amid the bushy trees, with spectacular views of the surrounding island. Even if I couldn't see the water, I heard the Atlantic Ocean with one ear and the Roanoke Sound with the other. For once, Maddie hadn't been exaggerating.

We gathered on the eastern veranda to catch the night breeze. At the request of Mr. and Mrs. Adams, who were leaving us to ourselves, a little black boy came running to light the young men's cigars with some hot tines.

With no adult chaperones, it was too intimate there on the dark veranda. I felt as small as a mouse on a patch of moonlit sand, an easy nighttime snack for the preying owls. I crossed my arms over my chest.

Red said, "I heard about your uncle Jack a couple years ago, Abigail. I'm truly sorry for your loss. I lost a cousin in the war, too. Didn't know him very well, though. He was from down in Georgia.

He got shot straight through his skull." He puffed on a cigar, and the smoke blew quickly away into the night. "It's morbid, having a dead relative in the family."

"Yes, it is." I nodded, uncomfortable talking about my dead uncle in front of this group. I touched my reticule, buried inside my green skirts.

After an awkward silence, Red asked, "How's your plantation doing? I hear tell it's rough going for planters like your daddy these days. Bankruptcies left and right."

Alice asked, "You used to own over a hundred slaves, isn't that about right? And they all ran off, I heard."

Maddie, with a little swing of her curls, stopped her conversation with George Wakefield to eavesdrop. I heard the lonely call of a gull sliding over the ocean.

I cocked my chin out and said, "Some of our best people stayed on after the war, so we're making out. In fact, we built a cottage, over on the ocean side."

They all twittered and rustled over that like invisible birds in a bush. It got me to wondering what everyone was saying about us behind our backs. I glanced to where I thought our cottage stood, alone on the sand, but I couldn't see a single thing in the darkness.

The black boy broke the silence when he banged out the door with a tray full of silver cups. I smelled the bourbon as he stood in front of me with his offerings, and I shook my head unconvincingly. I'd never tasted alcohol in my life, but at just that moment I wanted nothing more than to guzzle a cup or two down. But the image of Daddy at breakfast, chasing his customary slice of pie with two shots of whiskey, made me think twice.

I wondered what people like the Adamses and the Taylors thought of us. I knew that our situation didn't look good. I knew that Sinclair House appeared dark and haunted, with its cobwebbed windows missing draperies, paint peeling off the moldy shutters, weeds growing in the flower beds. It resembled a sleeping giant, about to fall over with a mighty crash into the dusty earth.

Everything that my English ancestors had worked for, everything that my daddy and my uncle Jack had worked for, was disappearing. Maybe it was inevitable, the decline of our plantation. I'd like to blame its demise on the death of my uncle, but really, it was the death of the South that was to blame.

Still, the two deaths are always intertwined in my head. Uncle Jack was as much a part of the land as a tobacco leaf. He grew up in the house; he was even born, like my daddy before him, in the master bedroom, in a mahogany four-poster bed.

Even our slaves, the same ones who couldn't wait to leave us when the war ended, cried when Uncle Jack was buried, even though Daddy wouldn't let them come to the services. I could hear them late that same night, singing the saddest African songs in low, pained voices. Their singing kept me up almost the whole night, even after the songs had long ended.

Suddenly I couldn't for a moment longer bear sitting with Maddie and her friends, who were getting progressively drunker. I made an excuse about being tired, so Maddie, with a puckered smile, ordered one of their sleepy servants to drive me home on the cart.

They all called out to me as they saw me bumping along toward the ocean, "Bye now, Abigail! Don't get washed away by the waves tonight!"

I could hear Maddie's laugh spiral over and over in the wind.

CHAPTER THREE

Abigail Sinclair
June 20, 1868

I was greatly delighted with him, and made it my busi-
ness to teach him everything that was proper to make
him useful, handy, and helpful; but especially to make
him speak, and understand me when I spoke and he was
the aptest scholar that ever was, and particularly was so
merry, so constantly diligent, and so pleased, when he
could but understand me, or make me understand him,
that it was very pleasant to me to talk to him.

—Robinson Crusoe

⌘

With a belly full of pulled pork and Winnie's tasty collared greens, I sat idly on the porch, watching the beachcombers strolling up the shore. My limbs still felt like large pieces of waterlogged driftwood from my poor night's rest, and some strands of hair, having escaped a sloppily pinned knot, blew in ticklish ovals around my face.

I longed for a nap, but Mama had just leaned her head out the window to see if I had planned a lesson for Mr. Whimble. I finally went poking around in one of my trunks to find some appropriate items. I pulled out my slate and a couple pieces of chalk, which I had brought for Charlie and Martha's summer lessons, and some writing paper and my quill and ink.

Since there wasn't much wind today, I brought everything out to the porch, along with the old wooden table and chairs. I couldn't for even a minute imagine sitting indoors all summer, especially with such a smelly man.

After what seemed like a long while, I heard Winnie greet Mr. Whimble at the door on the western side of the house, but she didn't invite him in like she would a normal guest. She walked him around the outside of the house, like she would a horse.

"Here you go, Mr. Benjamin. She been waitin' on you—it ain't right to keep a lady a-settin' in the heat, you know," she said, and ambled back inside. She didn't even offer him anything to drink, which he desperately looked like he could use.

Mr. Whimble seemed not to care. He climbed up the three steps to the porch and greeted me with an easy smile. But I could see how filthy he was. I tried to conceal my distaste, since I didn't want to embarrass him. Yet even outside I could smell the fishy stench that lingered on his clothing and skin.

I was somehow disappointed that the man didn't even bother to wash before coming to sit for hours in the company of a young lady. He seemed to realize his state by the sour look on my face. "I'm afraid that I stink like a hog at slop time. I came straight from hunting with your daddy, and those largemouth bass sure gave us a hard time. I can go wash up, if you can't stand me," he offered.

I fiddled with the supplies and nibbled my lower lip. Making him wash seemed the utmost in rude hostessing. But I was spared a response by the squeaking of the screen door and Mama's appearance on the porch.

She stared at him as if waiting for an answer to an obvious question, and he shifted around in his chair, stammering out his crude introductions. I began to feel a little sorry for him, in spite of myself.

"Tell me of the schooling out here, Mr. Whimble," she ordered.

"Oh, we don't get much schooling out here, Mrs. Sinclair. We don't have a proper schoolhouse, and no teachers, neither. Every so often Shep Johnson offers up some lessons, you know, in between fishing runs and whatnot. And all the younguns drag themselves over to his house to learn their figures.

"But we all have to earn our living, ma'am, and no schooling is going to bring in the fish or build the boats. So I guess you could say we ain't too educated out here, and it don't matter that much to us, anyhow," he finished.

He seemed almost smug in his ignorance. Mama inquired the obvious: "Then why do you want to learn now? What is so important that you'd want to give up your extra wages to learn? I'm sure you could use the money . . ."

He glanced over to me and then said, with something like thought, "Well, I'll like to marry soon, and I aim to provide a good life for my family. Get a steady job, one that's not so higgledy-piggledy. I figure it's a little sacrifice for a better day later on."

He paused and smoothed his dirty hands on his cutoff trousers. "My pap thinks I'm dumber than a stump for throwing away my money on learning. I guess it does sound stupid to him. He's been a fisherman his entire life. But I know things are changing 'round these parts, and I'm not the one to get left behind."

I saw Mama's eyes appraise him with a touch more kindness. "I think that's an admirable decision. Education is vitally important. It's a new world now, and we all must adapt to it. Well, good luck to you," she said. She rose from the table to leave us alone, and went to sit on the other end of the porch to read what looked to be an anatomy textbook.

I didn't really know how to begin teaching a grown man how to read and write, so I asked cautiously, "I thought I'd start by going over the alphabet. How many letters do you know?"

"Oh, a few, I reckon . . ." he answered vaguely, looking toward the ocean.

"Can you spell your name at least?"

"Well, not exactly the entire name *Ben-ja-min* . . . but I do know that my name starts with a *B*!" he stated victoriously. "Though I ain't at all sure I could call it out from a bunch of scribblings."

An exhausted, hopeless feeling began to permeate my very bones. I could not believe that I was stuck teaching the alphabet, something that even my little brother and sister learned at the age of three, to an ignorant, uncouth fisherman for an entire summer at the beach.

Mr. Whimble ran a hand through his greasy hair. "I guess you got your work cut out for you, don't you, Miss Sinclair?"

I exhaled long and hard through my mouth, the way that Winnie sometimes did when everything was raking her nerves. Then I dragged the slate over, picked up the chalk, and began writing out the alphabet. When I finished, I asked him which letters he remembered, as I pointed to them with a finger. To my shock, he recited the entire alphabet, mixing up only *M* and *N*, and *X* and *Z*.

"Not bad," I said, surprise leaking into my voice.

He grinned and said, "Had me pegged for the village idiot, I reckon."

"It's just that you're just catching on so quickly. How much school did you say you had?"

He looked up to the porch ceiling. "Oh, 'bout a year, I reckon, give or take a couple months. It was a long while ago, though."

I peeked through lowered eyelashes at the cracked skin over his knuckles, at the meaty muscles along the length of his forearms. "So you're a fisherman. All you do is fish."

He smiled. "Yep. That's all I do. Just about every day and night. Takes a lot of time, fishing."

"How do you find the time to be a guide? And then come out here for tutoring? Do you really think you'll be able to make it over here every afternoon?" I asked skeptically. Maybe he'd get fed up with the process and stop coming altogether.

"It's the slower time of year, summer is. We long-net down in the Pamlico Sound every couple of weeks, catch spot and croaker mostly. We always have a little extra time on our hands come July and August. But things'll start ripping again in September, I reckon. Then it's back to the ocean for us."

It seemed like such a hard life. "I hope you make some money at it at least."

"Not too much. As you can see," he said, fingering his ripped shirt, "I'm lacking in niceties. But this spring Pap and me had a record catch of shad, at least for us."

"You fish with your daddy?" I asked.

"Ever since I was nothing but a babe in arms. We get sick of each other most days, but he's the only pap I got, and I love him. Plus, he's the one with the boats and the nets, so I have to stick with him," he joked.

"But you mentioned that you might want a different sort of job someday?"

He nodded, his blue eyes shifting toward the sea. "Guess time will tell. I've got my eye on some things coming down the pike."

A seagull flew to the bottom of the porch steps and stood there watching us out of the corner of its eye. We had gotten sidetracked, but I couldn't seem to stop the conversation.

"We don't eat fish very much back home. Mama's of Swedish descent, so you'd think she'd have fish for every meal. But she won't even eat salmon. Plus, Daddy's not the best fisherman in the world. We're not what you'd call water people."

"Oh, well, your pap's doing all right." His eyes lit up as he started to talk about his livelihood. "It's all a matter of knowing where they're gonna bite, and that's where I come in. But your pap's a keen observer of nature. Right clever. And I'll tell you, he is a darned good shot with the hunting rifle. Just about gave me a run for my money last fall when I took him bird-gunning up yonder in Currituck."

"I believe it. All he ever does back home is shoot animals. He's taking out his anger on the poor innocents of the world."

He looked concerned. "Is he angry? He seems even-keeled enough to me, I reckon."

I had probably said too much to the man. I didn't want him in our family's business any more than he was. "Oh, just worried is all. About the plantation."

I looked over at Mama, who seemed to be engrossed in her reading. I took up my quill and a piece of paper. "I'm going to copy out the alphabet on a piece of paper for you, and for practice, study your letters so that you can recite them all by memory. If I think you're ready, we'll start writing them soon."

"When do you think I'll be able to read books like that one you was reading the other day? Seems I'm a pretty fast learner. Shouldn't take too long, I reckon!"

I laughed a bit, then wondered if he wasn't joking. "Oh, mercy, I'm not sure you'll be able to read books like that for many—It's just that reading books like *Moby-Dick* takes many years of dedicated reading practice. And it takes a lot of learning about the world and the people in it, a lot of education."

He raised his eyebrows at me. "Well, ain't we proud? You can teach me all that, though, right? I wasn't born yesterday."

I shook my head. "Not in one summer."

He looked so downhearted that I grew bothered with myself for disappointing him. He seemed to have such high hopes for himself. "I'm not saying that you can't learn. But some of the concepts in that particular book are difficult to grasp, even for me."

I grabbed the book off the table and thumbed the pages. "See, on the surface, the novel appears to be about a whaling voyage. But it's not. There are deeper interpretations to consider."

His eyes narrowed and he scratched his head. "Huh?"

"The whale is not really a whale," I said slowly. "They're chasing knowledge, fate, the meaning of life."

He raised his eyes to the porch ceiling and drawled, "Oh, I see. Hidden meanings and all. Like a treasure map, but in a book."

I nodded enthusiastically. "That's right. Grasping those themes takes study and reflection. Maybe I could read aloud a bit of another book that I brought along for Charlie and Martha, a book about a ship-wrecked sailor living on a deserted island. I think you may like it."

"Hey now, that's a great idea! Reading out loud! I reckon I've never heard a person read a book out loud before, except the Bible, you know," he exclaimed, and grabbed the paper on which I'd writ-ten the alphabet. "I'm going to learn all these little sons-o'-guns, all right! You'll see! Much obliged to you, Miss Sinclair! Bye now, Mrs. Sinclair!"

And off he ran down the beach. He moved as loose-limbed and carefree as a child. Mama raised her head and said, "Good gracious, he runs like an animal."

And in spite of myself, I smiled. I pictured myself running down the shore with him, but where we were off to together, I had not one single notion.

The next morning I accompanied Winnie to the little market, which was built on long stilts over the Roanoke Sound so that people traveling on small boats could dock and come up to fetch their supplies.

Winnie had been back and forth to the market and the post office in the hotel a few times already, fetching items that were desperately needed for our first couple of days at the beach, so she had met a few of the local "Bankers" already.

In a loud rant in the kitchen one morning, Winnie had expressed her exasperation with their stubborn ignorance and "evil eyes," and she told me she was looking forward to the start of the weekly packets of fresh vegetables and fruit from the plantation so she wouldn't have as many dealings with them.

Maybe it was because I'd been cooped up all day at the house, but I was curious about the folks who lived here permanently, having met Mr. Whimble. I guessed that they were all as simple as he was, with no schools or much industry to speak of out here.

I knew already that they were an independent sort of people, since they were notoriously pro-Union during the war. Daddy had complained, back when the war began, that many of the folks out here had more ties with New England, with all of their shipping concerns, than with the land-bound inner cities of North Carolina. He said that they were as good as Yankees.

Now Winnie and I walked down a little pier to the market, and a tanned, big-boned woman with a ragged old bonnet and patched brown homespun dress emerged from the back to greet us. Her dark, crinkled eyes looked me over, and I felt, suddenly, foolishly dressed, with my fine linen dress cascading unnaturally with crinolines over the warped wood. With a cheek full of chewing tobacco, she asked Winnie what we'd like from the market.

Winnie, likely with visions of her famous fried catfish and okra dinner in her head, examined the produce first, then asked what kind of fish was available. With expert hands that cradled and caressed the sweet potatoes and watermelon like newborn heads, she chose several fat catfish and a basketful of fresh vegetables and fruits.

As Winnie loaded our baskets onto the cart, the woman spoke to me. "So you from that fam'ly what built the new house on the ocean side? That piney house down yonder?" she asked, pointing a crooked brown finger southward, toward the ocean.

I smiled at her unexpected interest. "Yes, that's right. I'm Abigail Sin—"

"I can't for the life of me feature why all you folks built those houses so close to the ocean. It's the devil's own foolishness, we all agree. We'll soon see yer house a-floatin' with the next storm. Serve you right, it will." With that, she spat an arc of tobacco juice over her shoulder and retreated into the shack without a thank-you or a good-bye.

My body pulsed with indignation. I complained to Winnie as we walked to the hotel to fetch our mail. "Who does she think she is, speaking to me in such a manner? I doubt I've ever been spoken to so rudely." I was certainly accustomed to Mama's simmering anger, but not to outright rudeness.

"It just their way out here. They a peculiar bunch of folks, from what I can see," said Winnie, looking around to see if anyone was listening. "She never done learned her manners, living out here like she do. I reckon some folks see you and figure they got the short end of the stick."

She bit her lip then and averted her eyes from my face. "And too, she might feature you all to be wasteful kind of folks, just handing out perfectly fine dresses like you do."

"What are you talking about?" I asked.

"She the one I gave your dirty dress to. She gonna give it to her daughter. She 'bout your age, I reckon. So if you see that dress out yonder, wearing itself out on some poor old white gal, don't get all huffy over it, mind!"

My mouth dropped open. The terrible luck of my nice dress ending up in the hands of that woman! I started to complain, but Winnie smacked her hand over my mouth.

"You'll catch flies in that gaper, so close her on up," she scolded. I knew from experience that she couldn't be bothered by me anymore. "And Miz Abby, you got to thicken up that pale skin of yours if you want to live out here with these Banker folks. It ain't like living in the big house no more."

It seemed that I stewed over the repossessed dress for a long, long time before the withered old postman at the hotel finally handed over the Sinclair pile of letters. On top of the pile was a thick beige envelope addressed to me, Miss Abigail Sinclair, care of Mr. and Mrs. Nolan Sinclair, Nags Head, North Carolina. The letter was sealed with the Newman family seal, a cross with a medicinal herb in the middle of it.

On the cart ride back to the house I opened the envelope, my fingers stiff with anxiety. Hector Newman had written on two sheets of engraved white stationery, in bold, slightly illegible black cursive.

June 18, 1868

My dear Abigail,

I hope this letter finds you and your family settled and peaceful there at the ocean's edge.

The days are turning hot and humid here in Edenton, and I find myself thinking of you a great deal, envious of your ocean breezes and clean air. You may find that you have some new neighbors next year. I have been accompanying my father on his visits to his patients, many of whom have already contracted the yellow fever. At my father's insistence, they have heartily vowed to make a trip to the ocean next year to take the air.

Indeed, I would like to make a visit to the island soon, to see the sights. I will write a request to your father and mother. I have also inquired about lodging at the local hotel there on the island, and would be honored if you and your parents would accompany me to supper there one evening.

I will wait eagerly for your reply.

Most sincerely,
Hector Newman

I was flattered that Hector hadn't forgotten about me yet. I was sure that in my absence he would have found a bevy of other young Edenton girls to visit while on his summer hiatus. Perhaps that was still true. I really didn't *know* Hector at all, having only entertained his company three times in the early spring.

But he had stellar prospects. He currently attended the medical institute at Yale University, and his father was the revered Dr. Newman, our family physician since before I was born. People in Edenton were already talking about how purely wonderful it would be if Hector followed his father's career path.

'Course, Hector was uncommonly handsome. His face was so perfectly put together that I never was very sure what words were coming out of my mouth when we were conversing.

Sometimes, during fits of boredom, I'd imagine myself married to him, living in a stately home on Water Street with a garden overlooking the Albemarle Sound. I could play the role of doctor's wife very well, I thought.

"Save any lives today, my dear?" I'd lovingly ask him at supper.

"Oh, only a few," he'd say with a chuckle.

But it was embarrassing how Mama just fawned over Hector when he came to call on me, monopolizing the conversation with medical and ethical concerns and plying him with things that she had learned in the thick medical textbooks that she read as a kind of hobby.

I planned to show Mama the letter when I returned, and discuss Hector's visit with her, but she was upstairs napping again. And Hannah, with a mischievous glint in her eye, whispered to me that Mama had vomited her dinner in a mixing bowl before taking to her bed.

CHAPTER FOUR

Benjamin Whimble
June 27, 1868

[My father] told me . . . that mine was the middle state,
or what might be called the upper station of low life,
which he had found by long experience was the best state
in the world, the most suited to human happiness, not
exposed to the miseries and hardships, the labour and
sufferings of the mechanic part of mankind, and not
embarrassed with the pride, luxury, ambition, and envy
of the upper part of mankind.

—ROBINSON CRUSOE

PAP PULLED HIS HAT DOWN A BIT OVER HIS WATERING BLUE EYES, BUT I
could still see his saggy face. I knew someday, and probably sooner
than later, I would have a face like a loggerhead from working in the
sun's glare day after day, but it didn't bother me none. I liked to think

that Pap's face belonged to the sea, as much as the fish we pulled from it did.

We'd been out on the Pamlico Sound since the middle of the night, laying the nets for spot and croaker. But I had to meet up with Mister Sinclair for yet another fishing run later this morning, and the day wouldn't end anytime soon.

For such a gnarled coot of a man, Pap was a patient fisherman. He had a sixth sense for fish—what kind they were, where they might be, and what direction they were heading in.

Ever since I was a youngun, and Ma had passed, Pap's been learning me about fishing, and I'm not ashamed to say that I know all I know from him. Pretty much grew up on his work boat. I helped mend his nets and listened to his far-fetched fishing tales. Pap told me early on that fishing was a holy skill, that it said so in the Bible. I figure Jesus must look on Pap very kindly indeed.

It's like me and Pap got seawater for blood. If it's swimming in the water, we just know by instinct how to catch it. We not only catch any type of fish God made, but all nature of water creatures. Porpoise, turtles, oysters, crabs, eels, and sometimes whales, depending on if we need the money that bad to go off on the hunt. I will say that whaling is much easier when the beasts wash dead onto your beach.

But fishing on a June day like today is my favorite thing to do, being mere inches above the sound. It's like a passel of little miracles happening all day long, just for me.

The rest of the country can scurry around like rats, packing guns or politicking, but out here people are free to be simple. I like to think of mainland North Carolina as a great big brass band a-playing in a stuffed-up room, and the Outer Banks as one easy stroke on the fiddle, cutting right through the clean ocean air.

But it ain't often easy. Pap and me arise afore dawn and follow the sun all the way across the sky, most days. Oftentimes we just catch a few winks on the boat, an old sail for a blanket. We breakfast on seafood, we sup on seafood. And shitting over the side of the skiff in broad daylight isn't a circumstance.

As a way of living, it was all getting old to me.

Today I was sloppy pulling the nets up, and Pap was getting real cross with me. But try as I might to think on hauling, I kept wondering on Miss Abigail Sinclair. There was just some unruly quality to her, even though she was all shelled up in those fancy clothes. 'Course, she was easy on the eyes, no denying that.

Now, don't get me wrong, I have myself a gal, Eliza Dickens. She's a hard worker and a good cook, make me a fine wife. I've known her since we was 'bout yay high, no taller than my shinbone. She's got me thinking it might be a good idea to have a wife, set up house. So maybe early next year we'll tie the knot, once I get some learning. I figure if I'm a lettered man, there ain't nothing holding me back from a decent job.

See, a new lighthouse is set to get built down the Banks a ways, in Cape Hatteras. The whole Banks is in an uproar over its construction. Number one, they say it's to be the tallest brick light in the world. And number two, its building is expected to give Banker folks jobs left and right.

And it won't stop there. Word has it that the U.S. government wants to build lighthouse after lighthouse on the Banks. Plenty of jobs for able men, if you are so inclined to believe the talk. And there's not a soul on the Banks that don't want to get hired.

Sure, there's lifting and hauling jobs aplenty, but I like the notion of those finger-pointing jobs, myself. It's my bet that they're having a devil of a time finding men around here to scribble down the little whatnots, and mull over the bigger ideas, and that's where I hope to fit in.

I've heard tell these government jobs pay men regular good

money by every hour they work, and a steady job like that is mighty tempting, out here where we never know when our next catch of fish or flock of geese might show up. Just thinking on the money to be made in Hatteras by a bookish type of man, and with skills like mine to boot, makes me want to dive off this old boat and start swimming down there today. But I'm far too yellow-bellied to reveal my high-falutin plans to Pap just yet.

Still, I've been reciting the list of letters in my head over and over, sometimes backwards to frontwards even. My mind seems real natural at it, so far. I been wanting to learn reading and writing since I was a young feller, seeing the Banks visitors, and sometimes the Reb and Fed'ral soldiers a few years back during the occupation, reading their thick newspapers and carrying 'round books that looked like they told of the mysteries of the world. Made me feel a big old buoy-head, not even able to write my own name.

But native folks 'round these parts don't read or write much, so there was nary a soul to teach me. Pap told me to forget about schooling. But I don't want to haul pound nets and live in Pap's humble abode for the rest of my life. I sure don't want to trade kegs of fish and strings of bird for every last thing I lay my hands on in this world.

I see how bone-tired my pap gets nowadays, with a lifetime of labor riding his back. I try to haul extra hard to make up for his loose limbs. I look on him, his pouched-up red face and his white shaggy brows, and feel terrible sad for the thoughts in my head. I'd miss Pap greatly if I were to leave him. I'd miss the water, too, and this skiff. This skiff we called *Tessa*, after Ma, but no one would know that because we didn't know how to write the letters on her. And Pap was too proud to ask anyone to do it for him.

When Pap slumped over for a catnap on the way back to Nags Head, I pulled out the paper that Miss Abigail Sinclair had given me last week. The paper was getting all bent up and stained from my pulling it in and out of my pockets, and from tracing my fingers over the letters.

I recollected the way the pink tip of Miss Sinclair's tongue peeked out the corner of her mouth a bit as she wrote the letters on the paper, and my face reddened as if from a long day in the sun. I'd sure hate to have Mister Sinclair read my thoughts right about now. He's the breed of man you just don't want to disappoint, like a man o' God.

Mister Sinclair is the tallest, broadest man I've seen hereabouts, a rare giant of a man. Every man, woman, and child around stares after him like they seen a Jesus miracle walk by, all wide-eyed and pointing. His head is crowned with a mess of curly red hair, and his short beard is ruddy gold. The trimmed facial hair gives him such a dignified look that I have a mind to grow hair like his on my own chops.

I'm no bootlicker, but I've been studying him, his high-bred manners and such, ever since that day last autumn when I took him goose-hunting up yonder on the North Banks.

He's what they call a "gentleman" planter, come down a few generations. I know he's rolling in money since he always sports the finest fashions, even though all we do is fiddle around in the dirt and water and mess with bloodied fowl and fish. And anyone that's willing to pay good money for some other man to help him hunt and fish must have a pocket full of rocks.

Back in December I picked out some men hauling pine over to the ocean, and we all watched Mister Sinclair's cottage grow up bit by bit during the winter. We'd take to gathering at the ocean on our time off, to cook up some bluefish or trout on a fire and polish off some mountain dew while we looked on the unlikely sight of a house being built smack on the ocean sand.

It seemed of late to be the fashion for the rich men on the mainland. We all liked to speculate on what kind o' men'd like to do something like that—must have sponge for brains. Either that or they'd never seen the ocean wash clear across the island and meet up with the sound.

But when I met Mister Sinclair, he was so high 'n' mighty like, seemed to know more than even I did about his chances, that it didn't seem right to back-talk him. He said he planned on sending his family to the cottage in the summer, to take the air, like many mainland folks been doing for years now, just not on the ocean side. We Bankers, we all hunker down under the trees, and if you don't mind me saying, it's a much safer spot.

∞

Once we docked in Nags Head, I helped Pap salt and load our catch in crates and haul it to the hotel. The summer folk were almost on their knees begging for fresh fish, enough so that we were talking about bringing in Jacob Craft, a comrade of mine known widely for his ability to tell a good yarn while plucking a banjo. He was also hands down the best waterman around. He had about ten years on me, though, so I cut myself some slack.

Coming back from the hotel, I saw Mister Sinclair waiting on me near the pier. He was early and all slicked up, as usual, in spite of the heat.

"Something wrong, Mister Sinclair?"

"Something's come up. There's to be a change of plans today." He turned to look across the Roanoke Sound. "You familiar with that runaway-slave colony over on Roanoke Island?"

No one really called it a colony for "runaway slaves" 'round here. It was the Freedmen's Colony, a much nicer turn of phrase. But I just said, "Oh, to be sure. Not many left in the colony proper, but there's a number of folks that look to be staying on the island."

He slapped at a gallnipper on his neck with a big hand. "You got time to take me over there today? I'll make it worth your while."

"No fishing, then?"

"Plenty of fish to catch tomorrow. I need to see this place. It just can't wait."

He called the shots, as usual. But it did sound mighty peculiar to me. Not many folks cared to see the Freedmen's Colony these days.

I wasn't much bigger than a boy when the colony got started, but I recall watching a steady stream of Negroes hitching boat rides to the island during the war. They'd heard that the island was Union territory after the Battle of Roanoke Island, and they were hell bent to get to free land.

But before anyone knew it, Roanoke Island was overrun with nearly starved black folks with nothing to do and no food in sight. Man alive, was it pandemony. More folks on the island than there ever had been. Few thousand people, at one point. And it ain't very big—only eight miles long and two wide.

Next thing I heard, the Yankee government took over the island's unoccupied land—the land that belonged to the white Rebs, you know—to build the colony. The local white folks gritted their teeth and complained among each other, but went along with it even so. Trees got felled, then a handful of schoolhouses and churches got built, and houses with proper roads between. The colony even got a steam sawmill. Things were on the up-and-up for those folks.

The colony did all right for a few years, before the Reb soldiers came home to the island after the war and realized that Negroes had set up hundreds of homes on their land. That didn't go well a-tall. 'Course, the freedmen ended up with the little end of the horn, in the end. Got forced out one way or the other. But some stayed on, hoping things would turn around.

Still, it wasn't much to see, and I couldn't prophesy what business Mister Sinclair might have there.

Pap was done for the day, so I used *Tessa* to get us over to Roanoke Island, a couple miles west of Nags Head across the Roanoke Sound. With the skiff docked, we borrowed two horses and rode over to the remains of the Freedmen's Colony on the northwest side of the island.

It had been a while since I'd ventured over here, but I could tell this part of the island had seen better days. The trees that used to grow on the northern part of the island were almost all gone, cut down for firewood and freedmen houses and wartime buildings. Must have taken a lot of wood, for sand was all that was left.

In the village itself, three wide avenues—called Lincoln, Burnside, and Roanoke—cut through about twenty-six streets, but the lines marking the sides of the streets were less and less clear-cut. Everywhere were weeds and little trees already taller than a youngun, no one with the gumption to pull 'em up no more.

The square lots looked to have a bit less than an acre apiece. Good-sized, if you ask me. But the split-log houses on the lots were right sad. I could see the cracks between the logs just by standing in the street. They all had clay chimneys and little vegetable gardens, half of 'em covered in weeds and rabbits, nary a vegetable in sight.

We rode up and down the empty dirt streets. He asked me, "Where is everyone? Don't tell me they're working?"

"Oh, but they are. Trying, at least. Fishing or progging 'round, I reckon."

He snorted, looking down the street. "They got places of worship here?"

Seemed to me like he was looking for something particular, but he wouldn't say what it was. I pointed through the streets. "I know of one church. Over yonder a ways, in a grove of trees off Burnside."

We rode to the church, a small thing not much better than the log houses. But I liked the way it was situated among a few oak and pine trees. Mister Sinclair dismounted and walked 'round and 'round it, peeping in the windows and such.

After a good while of staring at the church from all different angles, we made to go back to the docks. Along the way I pointed out the falling-down schoolhouse, near the old Union headquarters. He shook his head sadly and said, "And folks like you—good, hardworking white folks—don't even have a schoolhouse. That, Benjamin, is a travesty. What is this country coming to?"

I guess I could see his point. I always pined for a schoolhouse, and would have built one myself if I could have found a teacher for it.

He guffawed at the building in front of us. "By God, that is one pathetic schoolhouse. It hardly looks to last another winter out here."

"Well, it don't matter to them. They all want to learn their letters, and you really can't blame 'em."

He squinted his eyes as he looked me over. "Ben, think on this. Do you want the darkies to learn their letters before our little white children do? Would you prefer to hand over the white man's land to former slaves? Just *give* them our hard-earned fields, our family's land? How about our homes, our horses, and our places of business?"

His long arms made big sweeps through the air as his voice rose. His face was red and slick with sweat. "Hell, let's just hand over our wives and children! Because they're as good as Negro fodder if we don't do something to stop them."

My face burned like I'd been slapped backhanded. This black hate was surely a side of Mister Sinclair I never thought to see, even though I knew he was a well-to-do planter man.

He kept on with it, too. "I'm not the only white man who's dismayed at the direction this country is heading in. We want what's ours to stay ours, and we're willing to do what's necessary to keep things the way they always have been."

"Who's 'we'?" I choked. A ropy knot had tied itself into my throat.

"Can't exactly tell you that," he said.

I looked off to the Croatan Sound, through the line of old barracks that lined the shore. The water shone so bright through the dark patches that I had to turn away. I closed my eyes for a second so I could think a bit more. It sounded like he was mixed up in one of those secret clans of men that were cropping up around the South. Bunch of sore losers, banded together in fear.

I swallowed a hunk of spit that had some trouble going down the pipe. "Well, if I get your meaning right, the freedmen on this island have riled you all in some way?"

"I guess I need to explain it all to you," he huffed, and shook his head. "After the war, the native white folks here needed our help. They wanted their land back, because the good-for-nothing runaways just wouldn't leave. Thought the land was theirs, fair and square. But it never was. *It never was, Ben.*" He leaned in so close to me I could see his red nosehairs. "The natives want the island to be like it used to be, without so many blue-blasted Negroes all over the place, taking what few jobs are out here and planting land meant for them, for their children. It's time for them all to go."

I fought down the urge to just ride away, leave him in the dust. Yet on he went, and with a smile on his face, too. "Our interest in this colony paid off. A real uppity darkie has come to our attention." He started snickering, then lowered his voice, even though not a soul was about. "Friends of mine have been looking out for this man for years now, and there he sat, in plain view. But here's the best part—from what I've gathered, all the runaways follow him around like he's made of chitlins and corn pone. If he goes, they all go. The so-called Freedmen's Colony will be done for good, and things will be turning in the right direction."

"But where will they go? What will they do?" I asked, my brain mired in a fog that wouldn't rise.

He snorted. "I don't give two handfuls of horse shit where they end up, as long as they're back on the state's plantations doing work that needs doing. This is a small island. A *family* island. It's about justice for North Carolina."

"And the man you're after? What of him?"

His eyes took in the little rows of houses through the dust from the horses' hooves. "We'll get *our* justice, too. It's been a long time coming now." He spit out a hunk of tobacky juice and stared at me with squinty eyes, not answering me. "If you tell anyone about this little talk, white folks included, I won't be pleased—and I don't have to tell you that my friends are not a group of men to disappoint. But if you help me out when I need your services this summer, and keep real quiet, I'll put in a word for you with Dexter Stetson. He's the lighthouse construction supervisor. Choosing his crew as we speak, no doubt."

I started to sweat bad, but not from the heat. I already knew that a crew was getting raised—word travels fast around here—but just the mention of his knowing Mister Stetson raised my interest. I had a gnawing feeling this was how things got done in the big world, knowing folks that mattered.

He watched me careful as he said, "I heard they need a crew to start building their own barracks and blacksmith shop, to get the site ready for work in the fall. And they'll need good local men to build the crane, and the lightering boats and wharf. I thought of you right away."

It was bad business, but the scenario sounded good to me, even so. Government paychecks steady in the mail. Two solid years of non-stop work, easy. They were laboring jobs, but still. I could work my way up to the better ones.

I gripped the reins so hard the leather almost cut my skin. "What sort of 'services' would you have me do, to get me such a job? I ain't a man-napper, if that's what you're after."

He wiped his brow with a crisp hankie, then looked down at it to see what he had mopped off. "I like you, Ben. I've seen the way you move around these islands. It's like you're made of sand and seawater instead of bones and blood. Never seen anything like it. You're a natural, son. Fact, you remind me of my brother, Jack. He was a born farmer. He was happy as long as he was out of doors and tending to the land. Not such a hardy soldier, though, as it turned out."

I nodded, sweat pouring down the small of my back. "Sorry to hear that."

He stroked his beard real slow. "I stick out like a sore thumb, especially around these parts. Can't just do what I want without folks taking too much notice. You, my boy, can help me. So just sit tight, 'til I determine what the course of action will be. It won't be long."

I stared off and couldn't make my mouth work. I hadn't given him a yea or nay.

He laughed. "I've never seen you think so hard before, Ben! Don't get yourself in a bother. It's not much, in the grand scheme."

"As long as I ain't breaking the law."

He kicked his horse happily and rode on. He looked so pleased with himself that a looker-on would think he'd just stumbled upon a buried treasure. It was a letdown to realize he wasn't as grand as I thought he was, not by a long sight. In fact, he was the worst kind of racist, and he wasn't afraid to admit it, either. What had the folks in the Freedmen's Colony ever done to *him*? He made it sound so personal.

But I couldn't see how I could get out from under him now. He had some kind of devil hold over me. And the worst part of it was, I still found myself wanting to do good for him. I couldn't make a lick of sense from the feeling.

⌀

I left Mister Sinclair on a bar stool after we got back to the hotel, a burn growing slowly on his cheeks, and dragged my dead legs over to the Sinclair cottage without washing up. I didn't want to be late and get the housekeep into a pucker.

But no one was there to answer the door, so I walked 'round back to the porch and there in the breeze sat Miss Abigail Sinclair, wearing a dress that spilled in all directions over her chair, and reading that same big book, as natural as you please. Made such a picture I almost forgot about her pap.

Did she even know how powerful strange it was for me to see such a fine young woman reading a book like that? I wished I could somehow crawl right inside her brain to see what all else she knew about, because it had to be a lot, by the way she carried herself all upright.

She jerked at my appearing so out of the blue like I did, and had to grab on to the book with both hands to keep it from flopping over to the porch. "Oh my stars, Mister Whimble, I didn't hear you walk up. The sand sure does muffle footsteps!" she said, her face flustered.

"Now, I told you to call me Ben, so unless you want me to send over my pap, you best cease and desist with the Mister Whimble. If my comrades heard you calling me that, they'd crack up 'til Christmas. I'd be Mister Whimble 'til I was pushing up daisies! They'd carve it on my headstone!"

She grinned a bit, showing her pearly whites, and seemed to relax her backbone some.

"All right . . . Ben." She paused and squinted at me, kind of like she would a beetle she was thinking on squashing with the heel of her nice boot. "How old are you? I'm sorry to say that I can hardly tell," she said.

"Well, I'm nineteen years of age, but I probably look seventy-nine, being out in the sun all day. It's common knowledge 'round here that fishermen start growing scales on their faces after a few hard years on the sea."

"You do look older than nineteen, I will say. But I don't see any scales." She laughed and called into the house, "Mama, Mister Whimble is here!"

She rolled her green eyes at me and said, "I mean, *Benjamin.* I'll get used to it."

But the house was quiet as a tomb. She said, "Mama isn't feeling well at all today. We might be on our own."

I shrugged. "Okay by me." I'd just as soon not have the woman listening in.

So we set to work with no one to eavesdrop except the gulls. Out loud I listed every single letter in order. Then I set to writing them all down on the slate, big ones and small ones. I only made one bitty mistake, much to Miss Sinclair's astonishment. Forgot to cross the little *t*. I said that wasn't a circumstance, but she said it was important to do so, or folks would think it was the little *l*.

Then she set to schooling me on the sounds of the letters, writing short words on her slate and pointing out their sounds to me with her clean, white fingers, and that's when I started to get confused.

Con-sonnets were all right. Having the same sounds word after word, you usually knew what to expect with them. But those vowels were tricky little sons-o'-guns, changing up their sounds to suit their places in a word. Or that silent *E*, the way she plops herself at the end of a word, like "Lookie here, I'm the letter *E*!" but she don't even make a sound. I'll be doggoned if that makes a bit of sense.

But I tried hard to learn all that she tried to teach about the sounds of letters, either by themselves or paired up with others, until finally she declared that I had learned more than she had expected me to in just one day.

She then wet the nib of her pen in ink and wrote down my whole name on another piece of her real nice paper. She told me to take it home and learn it and to come back tomorrow knowing how to write it by heart.

"But I don't own a writing instrument, Miss Sinclair. How am I to practice?"

She thought on this snag a moment, her rosy lips pursed up, then said, "You can take one of my pencils home, and some paper, too, for practice. Free of charge."

"Free of charge? That's a good one." I laughed.

She cut her eyes at me. "Well, paper isn't cheap these days. I just can't be handing it out whenever you have a need for some."

"My, my, aren't you the thrifty one. I never would have thought a lady wearing yards and yards of rich cloth would care about the price of paper!"

She looked down at her slippery green dress. "It's just that times are hard lately."

I rolled my eyes. "Oh, sure, it's a rough life for you. Let me fetch my fiddle. A big house on the beach don't look too hard to me."

She looked up at the porch roof over our heads and started to grin. "You should see our home in Edenton."

"She's a big one, huh? I wouldn't doubt it," I said. "What's she like, then?"

She said real soft, almost to her own self, "Oh, it's a lovely home. Old, and so grand. You should have seen it in its prime, before the war."

She seemed to see something far off over the ocean that I couldn't yet lay eyes on. "But the really special part is the land. It stretches on forever. The soil is so fertile, it can grow just about anything." Her smile faded just as fast as it came. "But that doesn't mean anything anymore, for planters like us." She gnawed on a thumbnail, then whispered, "I think we're going bankrupt."

I tried to whisper, too, then. "I didn't know things were that bad off for you all. Your pap . . . he never said a word about that. And to my eyes, you all look to be living in fine style."

She groaned and waved her hands about. "That's all anyone seems to care for. Appearances aren't everything, you know."

"Don't I know it! Well, if I know your daddy—and I think I do, now—he's not the type to just roll over for dead."

She sighed. "That's Daddy. He's used to getting what he wants."

She then pulled out that book that she thought I would take to, called *Robinson Crusoe*, written in the year 1719 no less, by a man with the name Daniel Defoe, and began reading aloud from chapter one.

And darned if that Mister Crusoe didn't hook me on his story from the get-go, talking about his need to take his own way in life in spite of his family trade and his father's wishes. I soaked up every last word, and thirsted for more after she closed the book for the day. The sound of her voice, mixed with all those big words, sure did agree with me.

What I took to be her younger brother and sister came scampering up the porch to see what we were up to. The little redheaded Sinclairs stared at me with three bright hazel eyes—the fourth one was covered by an eye patch.

"You're Mister Whimble, aren't you? My sister's told us about you," said the little gal, skinny as a twig, even with that dripping wet bathing uniform pulling on her. "She was right—you sure are dirty!"

Miss Sinclair's hands flew to her mouth, and she said, "Phhsssh, I said no such thing, Martha!"

"Why, yes, ma'am, I am. Mister Whimble at your service. But you can call me Ben. That's what my friends call me."

"I'm Miss Martha Anne Sinclair, I'm ten and a half years old, and I can read big books and write in cursive like Abigail, and this here is—"

The boy elbowed Martha out of the way. "I got a mouth. I can talk, too! I'm Master Charles Aaron Sinclair, and I'm six years old, and I can read, too, and I don't care to learn cursive writing!" he said real loud, sticking out his hand to shake with me.

"Say, I sure do like your eye patch."

He cackled and sliced the air a few times too many with an imaginary sword. "Do I scare you?"

"Oh, yeah. I wouldn't stand a chance if it came to a duel. Let's just be comrades."

He grinned, then lifted the eye patch to look at me. "Is it true you can't read nor write? I didn't believe Abby when she said that."

"It's true. There ain't no schools out here, nor teachers, neither. Can you all read and write?"

Their eyes about popped out of their heads. "Sure we can! Watch us!"

Martha started to read straight out of *Robinson Crusoe,* and Charlie began to write all over the slate with the chalk. What he wrote, I had no notion. But it sure was a sight, watching the two of them. The louder Martha read, the more Charlie squeaked the chalk.

I liked them already. I said, "Hey, now, I got a grand idea. How about you all come to the horse penning on Independence Day?

Bring the whole family, and your friends, too. It's a real fun time. The whole island goes. I'll be there, corralling the ponies."

The younguns clapped their hands and hollered, "Pony penning! Yee-haw!"

"That sounds like fun," said Miss Sinclair.

"Well, plan on it, why don't you. But I've got to skedaddle now. I'm taking my gal to a frolic tonight, and I got to wash up. Ain't that right, Martha?"

Martha laughed loud, and Charlie said, "Don't do it, Ben. Let's be dirty!"

I mussed up his red hair and looked to Miss Sinclair, feeling shy.

"I-I want to thank you," I stammered out. I wanted to say more to her, but after all that book learning, words of my own were hard to come by.

"You're welcome. And please, you can call me Abigail. Miss Sinclair is my mama!"

I wasn't used to hearing her laugh. It was a good bit louder than I thought it would be, her being such a lady and all. It really set me to wondering on what else she had stored up inside her.

CHAPTER FIVE

Abigail Sinclair
July 4, 1868

*Accordingly I went, and found [the goat] where I left
it; for, indeed, it could not get out, but almost starved
for want of food. I went and cut boughs of trees, and
branches of such shrubs as I could find, and threw it
over; and having fed it, I tied it as I did before, to lead
it away. But it was so tame with being hungry that I had
no need to have tied it, for it followed me like a dog; and
as I continually fed it, the creature became so loving, so
gentle, and so fond, that it became from that time one
of my domestics also, and would never leave afterwards.*

—ROBINSON CRUSOE

THE LARGE WHITE SCHOONER SLICED THROUGH THE LIQUID GREEN OF THE
Currituck Sound, its white sails yawning in the early-morning

breeze. I could see only water and trees, mostly pine and wax myrtle, curved from many years of ravaging winds. Here and there, water-birds circled figure eights in the gathering heat, looking for something to eat, or maybe just passing time.

The horse penning was to take place a few miles north on the Banks, in a sparsely populated fishing village in Currituck. Daddy, Charlie, Martha, and I awoke at first light to travel with Daddy's friend Mr. Viceroy on his fine boat, with the name *White Storm* painted in bold black cursive on her side.

Mama stayed back at the cottage, too ill to travel. Whatever ague she had caught out here, it sure was sapping her strength. I doubted very much if she would have the energy to get to the Independence Day party at the hotel later this evening.

But she wasn't the only one battling a bout of sickness today. I was trying, from my position on the bench near the bow, to concentrate on keeping my eyes steady on the horizon, advice from Mr. Viceroy, an experienced waterman. And it seemed to be keeping the boatsickness under control so far, although my head still seemed far too heavy for my neck.

Daddy said that Mr. Viceroy was a famous Conservative newspaper editor in eastern North Carolina. Everywhere he went, he walked quickly and purposefully, with a sideways tilt of his head, which for some reason made me want to turn my head and snicker.

Yet his sharp black beard, dark slanted eyebrows, and beady, watchful eyes gave him a satanic look, which usually served to quell the titters. I didn't think Daddy had known him long, but he had been traveling to Nags Head on *White Storm* since the summer began. The two seemed to be deep in conversation back at the helm, which made me wonder what a planter and a newspaperman had to talk about.

Martha suddenly sat down next to me. She grabbed my hand and slid a circle of twisted twine on my finger.

"Do you, Abigail Sinclair, take the most *handsome* Benjamin Whimble to be your lawfully wedded husband?" she squealed.

She had apparently taken a fancy to Benjamin. She talked about him all day and night. She especially liked to ask me questions about our tutoring sessions, and how he was getting along. Yesterday I caught her writing a letter to him. When I asked her what it said, she hid it behind her back and told me to mind my own business.

"Well, you might not want to use your fanciest cursive penmanship, since he can't yet read it."

Martha had gasped and looked down at her letter. Then she'd crumpled it up and started a new one, in giant print fit for a blind man.

I did wonder why she thought he was so handsome when you couldn't even see his facial features through all the dirt. I pulled the wedding twine off my finger and tossed it overboard. A hovering seagull swooped down to inspect the discarded object, then flew away with it in its beak.

Charlie started to march and chant. "Horses, horses, I want to see the horses!"

We were all looking forward to seeing the wild horses, even Daddy, who said that he was interested in buying one for us to use in Nags Head. Old Mungo still wasn't taking well to the sand. Whenever Justus tried to hitch the cart to him, he raised his lips and bared his long teeth. It might have looked to other folks like he was smiling, but Justus's shinbone knew differently.

I'd already seen horses and cows and hogs and sheep, too, roaming around free as they pleased all over Nags Head. Folks from the mainland let their stock run wild over here to graze on the common sea grasses and shrubs, and it seemed there were more animals than people out here.

The smaller stock liked to lounge underneath the houses that were set on pilings. If there were no latticework screens to keep them out, they'd lounge like fat and comfortable relatives until someone forced them out with a long stick.

$$\infty$$

The sun blazed hot in a cloudless blue sky when we finally rowed the yawl boat ashore. The fishing village of Duck appeared to be nothing more than a desolate strip of windswept sand and a couple of old shacks.

We were met by a mule-drawn cart, driven by a ratty-bearded, happy old man that Mr. Viceroy called Cyrus. Over the endless sand, he drove us to an empty pen that stretched along a narrow part of land along the Currituck Sound.

I stepped out of the cart onto the sand and immediately I could feel the sun's heat through the fine suede of my boots. I couldn't imagine Benjamin walking barefoot through such sucking hotness, all the days of his summers.

I looked around the village and saw that hundreds of noisy on-lookers already filled the area. Some wore their summer finery, like us, and some wore ragged homespun; a festive cacophony emerged. American flags flapped from the fence posts, and ladies at little tables were selling fireworks and red, white, and blue trinkets.

We sipped warm lemonade in tin cups, sold by a local woman in a dirty apron and a limp bonnet, while we talked with Cyrus about the tradition of horse pennings.

From what I could pull from his twangy lisping, the twice-a-year pennings involved the gathering of all the horses on an island. Riders would fan out early in the morning to find the herds and drive them steadily toward the pen.

Charlie was having a hard time with the concept. "But what do they aim to do to the horses in the pen? Surely they won't kill them?" he asked; he still recalled the nightmarish stories of soldiers and civilians alike killing their horses during the war so the enemy couldn't ride them.

The old man cackled, his toothless red gums shiny with spit. "Sakes alive, son! What kind of heathens you think we are out here? The owners just want the spring-born younguns to get their brand on 'em, so we know who's who."

He placed one worn boot on the fence post in front of him and leaned on his leg with a patchy elbow. "Folks like to use 'em for pulling carts and wagons. They're good workhorses, strong like you don't know, and easygoing, so they sell pretty good, 'specially with the lacking of good horses these days. A good lot of them'll sell today, you watch."

⁂

I heard the commotion before I saw it, like a distant rumble of thunder announcing a coming storm. The hollering of the riders and the snorting, whinnying stampede of horses, shuffling quickly through the sand, could be heard for several hundred yards down the island. Riders were scattered throughout the herd, wielding sticks. The crowd quieted, amazed by the sight of the horses all running in the same direction.

I found myself squinting into the sun, checking the faces of every rider to see if I could find Benjamin. But I was having trouble getting good looks at the men because they were turning this way and that on their horses and calling out to the volunteers who were helping narrow the column into the enclosure. And most of the riders wore wide-brimmed hats.

It wasn't until the very last rider came trotting up the beach that I saw him, driving a scruffy little red horse along in front of him. He was riding bareback on a wide Banker horse, and unlike any rider I've ever seen, he was barefoot, and digging his rough, sandy heels into the horse's sides for support.

"There's Benjamin, Abby!" squealed Martha. "Doesn't he look grand? Just like Sir Lancelot!"

I snorted. With a stick for a lance, a broad-brimmed hat for a visor, and shabby rags for armor, he certainly did not look like a knight. But men perched up on horses always seemed gallant, somehow.

We all waved hello to him and he gave us a big smile as he drove the red horse into the pen and shut the gate.

"Hey, Sinclairs! Bet you haven't seen the likes of this afore!" he hollered. The high rip of the sleeves on his shirt showed the muscles in his tanned arms, shining with sweat. I couldn't look away from those arms, hard as I tried to tell myself that arms were nothing interesting to stare at.

He jumped easily off his patchy brown and white horse and tied it with a frayed rope to the fence.

"Is that your horse, Benjamin? It sure is small!" said Charlie.

"Oh, sure, this here is Junie. He's a Banker horse, like all the rest of them here," said Benjamin, pointing to the horses walking exhausted around the pen. They kicked up a fine dust from the hot sand.

The horses looked like a different breed of animal, with their small stature, long hooves, and matted fur. But there was something else distinctive about them, too, something to do with their jerky movements and deep, watchful eyes that hinted at their wildness.

I could tell that the horse pen was as unnatural to them as a barn filled with oats and fresh water. A periodic brand on the hindquarters signified the horses' only contact with mankind.

Benjamin explained that the wild horses preferred to wander at will over the sandy bluffs, living out their existence on coarse sea grasses and salt-laced freshwater, found by digging holes in the sand with their long hooves.

I thought that Uncle Jack would have enjoyed these particular animals, even though, at heart, he preferred oversized, purebred stallions.

We all crowded near the fence as the horses in the pen were examined and counted by their owners. The youngest colts, hovering next to their mothers, were held down by strong men and branded with the quick touch of a hot poker. The branded colts whinnied loudly and ran off to another area of the pen to nurse their flesh. Charlie and Martha stood with their backs to the commotion and their hands over their ears, but all around me the locals were whistling their approval and jostling for space near the pen.

As horses and a handful of humans shifted around the enclosure, the red horse that Benjamin had driven down the beach came ambling along over to us. Her coat was a remarkable russet color threaded with gold. And she looked thickly strong, in spite of her squatty height.

"Abby, look here." Benjamin laughed. "I've seen this pony ever so often, wandering and foraging. She's real spirited for such a little gal—and she ain't got an owner. She's authentically wild. They say her daddy was a rough one we called Dragon's Breath. He was a huge ol' red stallion with a whole mess of mares in his flock."

As Benjamin handed me a small yellow apple, he whispered out of the earshot of Charlie and Martha, "I brung her over special for you. I just knew you'd like her, you both being redheaded and all."

I reached my hand through the fence and the little horse came right over on her short, knobby legs. She took the apple and munched slowly, as if meditating on her current predicament. We looked at each other, and neither of us blinked.

Benjamin hooted loudly. "Now, ain't that something. That pony's· usually right skittish."

Daddy sidled up to us. "How about this one, then? She'll give old Mungo a rest," he said.

"She might be too wild for you," warned a young local man who had been eavesdropping. "Even us Bankers wouldn't deem to put a saddle on that girl. She's feral as all get-out. Benny shoulda known better."

Benjamin interjected, "Oh, hush up, Henry. She'll be all right. She's just got personality is all. Ain't nothing wrong with that."

Henry spat some tobacco juice away from me. "I'd pick another, I was you. She won't do right."

I shook my head. "She'll do just fine."

Daddy had never met a horse that he couldn't break, so he ignored the man named Henry, too. He called out to a nearby rider and offered to pay him to halter and break the horse, to ready her for labor.

The crowd erupted in applause when the red horse—a local favorite—was taken by the rider. He held out his hand for her to snuff while he scratched his other hand over her ears and neck. He then slung a rough-looking saddle on her back and after a few more sweet treats and petting tried to jump on her back.

But she was wary of the maneuver. She'd probably seen this type of thing before, at a distance. She jostled away from his hold and the saddle slipped off her back. The crowd cheered loudly, and the rider just smiled. He took his time approaching her again, offering more sugar and scratching. He whispered into her ear, yet still she resisted.

I watched the rider try and try again, as the crowd got more and more rowdy, faces red and eyes straining.

"To the mud with her!" they all yelled.

The more the horse's feisty nature was displayed, the more I felt that I didn't want her after all. She obviously wasn't ready to give up the wild life, but I felt it was too late to tell Daddy to forget it. He was enjoying the spectacle, hooting with some of the other men and commenting on the horse's particularly female attributes.

Finally the rider led the horse into the thick sand of the sound. The horse walked around and around in the muck until she grew tired. When the rider jumped on her back she remained quiet, and the crowd sighed collectively with relief. With her head hanging down and a saddle on her back, she was ours for the taking. Everyone clapped like there was no tomorrow.

⚭

When the commotion died down, Benjamin wandered off to talk to some of the local folks, and I watched him from the corner of my eye, knowing full well that I shouldn't care what he was up to.

A couple of young men slapped him on the back with gusto, and the women smiled at him and offered him food and beverages.

I found myself wishing that he would come back to talk to us again. I guess I was used to having him all to myself on the porch. But he seemed happy to be where he was. He had taken up some horseshoes and was playing in a contest with a few other men. The clanging of the metal echoed periodically through the dusty air.

Charlie, Martha, and I sat on the back of the cart and spread out the picnic lunch Winnie had packed for us. The children had hardly eaten a mouthful when the old cart driver came over to ask them if they'd like to ride some of the ponies still corralled in the pen.

So with their chicken gathering flies, I watched Charlie and Martha ride as if their lives depended on it. They called out, "Buy this one, Daddy! This one! No, this one!" They wanted them all.

But Daddy and Mr. Viceroy were absorbed in quiet conversation with a couple of other men. As the dust swirled around their boots, they pressed themselves into a watchful circle, horselike.

I was busy gnawing on a drumstick when I heard Ben say, "This is her, boys. Abigail Sinclair."

I looked up to see two men about Ben's age gawking at me as if I'd grown a beard and mustache. I quickly choked down the chicken meat and wiped my hands on a linen napkin.

Ben directed a thumb left, then right. "This here is Harley Stickle and Jimmy Juniper, my best buddies. I told them just now about our learning hours on the porch of your cottage, and they didn't believe one word I said. So you think you can set them straight?"

I smiled and said, "It's true. I'm teaching him how to read and write."

Harley and Jimmy snickered. Harley said, "Pardon me, but what in tarnation are *you* doing setting on a porch with the likes of Benny Whimble? I just can't feature it. If it's boredom that's got you in its grips, I've got better cures than learning a fisherman every afternoon!"

Jimmy counted on his fingers. "You like fishing? We may not be better fisherman than Benny here, but we got better boats, for sure. We can take you—and some of your fine lady friends, of course— down to the New Inlet, or over to Roanoke Island, or how 'bout cart rides on the beach? Ladies like you sure do fancy a good cart ride down the shore of an afternoon. You like pork barbecues? You drink beer? Probably not . . ."

Ben hollered, "All right, that's enough out of you. I didn't know you were going to act so simple. You're humiliatin' me in front of Abby here. Get lost."

Harley and Jimmy looked shocked at Ben's dismissal. "Well, okay then. But listen, Abby, if you need something to do to occupy your-self when Benny's tiny brain dries up, just give us a hoot and we'll come running!"

Ben turned them in the opposite direction and pushed them away. They started laughing to themselves on their way back to the horse-hoe game.

"Sorry about that. I just thought it would be nice if you met some of my friends. They're good people, but sometimes they act denser than driftwood."

"That's all right. I enjoyed them. It's been a while since I've en-joyed such an easy conversation. My uncle and I used to horse around a lot, but I think I've forgotten how. Maybe I *will* go for a cart ride with them sometime."

"Well, I wouldn't give 'em too much encouragement, if I was you. They're not much different than stray dogs looking for the odd belly rub."

I giggled, thinking that they did have a sort of doglike affectation.

Ben's tone dampened suddenly. "Those men friends of your pap's?" He pointed to the group of men, still in conversation.

I shrugged. "I've never seen them before in my life."

He stopped and looked around before continuing. Concern edged his words. "They ain't locals. You have any idea what they're talking about?"

I laughed and took a sip of lemonade. "No, I couldn't imagine. Perhaps politics. The state's current political chaos is Daddy's fa-vorite topic of conversation."

He continued to watch the men. Then he spoke tenderly, saying, "You be careful 'round him, Abby, you hear?"

I looked away in confusion. Why would he warn me against my own daddy? "Benjamin, you need a rest from the sun, I think."

He reached over to scratch the red horse's neck. After some silence, he said, "I'm sorry. I sure don't like to mess around in other folks' business."

He fiddled around with the horse for a while, as if he wanted to say something else, but he never did.

As the event was drawing to a close, Ben offered to tie up the horse on *White Storm* so that we could take her back to the cottage with us, but it took a long time to get the job done. Even though she must have been exhausted, she whinnied and jerked around, and her muddy legs shook something awful, causing her long hooves to scrabble around on the slippery deck.

Benjamin kept stroking her and talking in a low, soothing voice, and when he looked to me it was with a twinge of regret in his eyes. "Reckon she'll be all right after a week or so."

I nodded. "It's probably the first time she's met with a boat. I'll take good care of her."

As we set sail back to Nags Head, Ben called out from the docks, "Hey, Abby, some of us are getting together at the ocean for the fireworks tonight—not too far from your cottage, matter o' fact. Why don't you all come out to see them? There's to be a barbecue and beer. Should be a real fun time, 'cause Snuffy Hobbs is hands down the best fireworks man alive."

I was sure that Daddy would not want to mingle with the locals on such a grand occasion as Independence Day. "We have plans to go to the hotel, for the fireworks party on the sound."

"Well, that's all right. The hotel fireworks won't be nearly as sparky, but you all have fun, hear?" He gave a mock salute as we drifted out into the Currituck Sound.

I could barely hear him as he hollered, "See you on Monday, Miss Defoe!"

The hotel was in full swing for its Independence Day party. The band squeaked out crowd favorites one after another, and the warm ball-room smelled powerfully of fried seafood, smoke, and liquor.

Exhausted from the long day, I stood in the doorway for the fresh air, watching the vacationers dance the "Balance All."

The circle of connected young men and women spun left and right around the ballroom. The dance was more of a country one, but Maddie Adams was enjoying herself even so. Her face was flushed pink from the exertion in the tight bones of her corset, and the tops of her breasts bobbled like two dead jellyfish.

I was giggling quietly to myself when I heard Daddy's voice be-hind me, carried through the night. "Buxton's likely listening to that bastard this very minute. I can't for the life of me feature giving ear to that man's inauguration speech. It's likely a stream of the most radical bullshit anyone's ever heard."

A voice that I didn't recognize said, "Do tell. An evening in Nags Head is time better spent, in my opinion. I'm sure we'll get the report from Buxton in due time."

I had read in a newspaper from home that the newly elected Re-publican governor of North Carolina, William Holden, was giving his inauguration speech in Raleigh today. Mr. Adams must have at-tended the ceremony for political purposes, but I guess he didn't think it all that politically necessary to bring his wife and daughter.

Two days before, Holden had ratified the Fourteenth Amendment, which gave citizen status and voting rights to blacks. Our newly elected senators, whom Daddy called a bunch of "scalawag" white men, Yankee carpetbaggers, and inexperienced Negroes, were set to take their seats in Congress.

Daddy seemed to take a bite of something, then said with a full mouth, "Buxton's a bootlicker, to be sure. But he'll be good for us in a couple years, once all this shecoonery shakes down." In a lower voice, he said, "He's got some ideas about those newfangled smoking cigarettes."

"If you can hold on to your land," mused the man, "you might be in business."

Cigar-ettes. *Little cigars?* An unexpected feeling of hope sparked in my chest.

With my heart pounding against my corset, I slowly turned to face Daddy, but it was hard to see anything in the darkness. I strained to keep listening to their conversation, but the owner of the hotel began to holler for everyone to walk out toward the pier for the coming fireworks.

The crowd roared with anticipation and began to stream for the soundside exits. Charlie and Martha led the crowd past me, hollering about sparklers. I had no choice but to walk along, and give up, at least for now, hearing more about the cigarettes.

Daddy was swaying a bit when I walked up to him through the sand. He still held a stubby glass from home. He held his elbow out to me for me to hold, but I think he wanted *me* to steady *him*. "Here she is, my daughter Abigail," he said. "Bought her a horse today, a little red Banker pony. Don't know which one's got more spirit, the horse or the girl."

The middle-aged man he was standing with briefly smiled and bowed, top hat in hand. "Mr. Hugh Bondfield, Abigail. Pleased to meet you."

"Mr. Bondfield is taking a gander at the Outer Banks this weekend," said Daddy quietly.

"A vacation like no other," said Mr. Bondfield, a peculiar smile on his face. "Just a dream come true."

The two men snickered, but then quieted when a loud popping and sizzling broke the night in two. We all gasped at the white sparks soaring through the sky, leaving trails of light that were still there when our eyes blinked.

At almost the same time we heard a boom, then faraway cheers, and I saw the sky over the ocean light up. Ben's party had started, too.

I grinned at the outright competition between the Bankers and the vacation folks, and everyone along the sound shores cheered madly. Then a group of liquored men started singing "The Star-Spangled Banner," and soon the entire mass of people was crowing along— even Daddy, who outright butchered over half the words to the song.

Charlie and Martha and dozens of other children just ran up and down the little sand hills, oblivious to everything but the sparklers that they whizzed through the night.

But sometime during the war of brother against brother, I'd started finding it much harder to get excited about Independence Day. And I thought it was curious how we all still believed it necessary to carry on the tradition of marking the birth of our mixed-up nation. In truth, I think most folks just enjoyed the fireworks and called it a day. Yet as the crowd sang the anthem over and over again, I found that there was still something stirring me. *". . . O say does that star-spangled banner yet wave . . ."*

Yes, in spite of it all, that stubborn flag still waves, I thought. *That has to count for something.*

Over and over, the sizzling colors lit up the dark glass of sky like shooting stars that arched and fell slowly down, melting into the black Roanoke Sound. Such dazzle, gone forever. And then I was filled with such a longing for life, like a fist punched through my chest.

Against my better judgment, I decided to tell Daddy that I was going back to Maddie's cottage for her private party. And Daddy, soused as a sailor on a spending spree, said good night to Mr. Bondfield and took the tired children on the cart back home. I then walked the wooden planks down to the ocean side, to see how Ben's evening had gone.

Some torches driven into the sand were still lit, and the smell of cooked pig lingered in the air. A few men and women sat on blankets, facing the moonlit ocean, and several others were standing around the embers of the cook fire, laughing along as a young man told a story. He was throwing his whole body into the telling, wringing his arms and back in imaginary net pulls.

I was glad of the darkness, for I suddenly felt like an intruder. I'd never paid such an informal social call, and I turned to go back the way I had come before anyone saw me. But there was Ben in front of me, rolling a big barrel of beer along the sand. I gasped, and my hand flew to my chest.

"Have you got a name for her yet?" he asked casually.

I was so disoriented, it took me a moment to figure out who he was talking about.

"No, not yet," I choked, my heart pounding. "I've never named a horse before. Usually my uncle did that—he had a real knack for it. But I can't seem to think of anything grand."

He sat down on the squat barrel and rocked back and forth. "I suppose you rich folks have your ways when it comes to naming animals. Have yourselves a big christening ceremony and whatnot. But around these parts we just come up with something simple, like Salty or Moonbeam, and that's that. Maybe you'd fancy naming her after a character in one of your books! I've taken a fancy to Robinson, myself!"

"You're making sport of me, Benjamin Whimble!"

He laughed good-naturedly. "Naw, Abby, I wouldn't reckon you'd do it any differently."

Just as I was about to ask about the fireworks, a young woman in a tattered homespun shirtwaist and skirt came striding up to us through the sand.

Ben said, "Hey now, Eliza? This here is Abigail Sinclair, my teacher. And Abby, this is Eliza Dickens. She's my girl."

"Evening, Eliza, how do you do?" I said evenly.

She snickered at me. " 'I do' just awful, Abigail. And how do *you* do, cutting up with my feller?"

Ben made a choking noise. "Aw, now, Eliza, whatever is puckering you, you don't need to take it out on Abigail here. You act nice, you hear?"

"Well, it looks to me like she came out here 'specially to see you, Benjamin Whimble, and I just want her to know that you're spoken for. I'm not blind, like my ol' granny. I can see why she's here tonight."

"She already knew I had a gal, I told her from the get-go! Eliza, you're beside yourself tonight! I'm cutting you off."

Her rough face looked gutted in the light of the fire. "Playing teacher is one thing, but coming out here to parade yourself around like the queen of Nags Head, looking for my feller, just won't do. You keep to your teaching, whatever that may be, and that's that." She stalked back over to the quiet group of young men and women. I heard one of them give a low whistle.

"I do apologize about her. She has a temper on her sometimes, 'specially when she's had a couple drafts of beer." His voice dropped to a whisper. "And you don't have to worry none, Abby. I know you'd never have nothing to do with the likes of me."

Mortification set in, suddenly. "Of course I wouldn't! That would be . . . wrong."

We had somehow crossed the line of friendship, and I wanted to go back, safe behind the teacher-student line again.

My eyes took in his old button-down shirt, its sleeves long ago dismembered from the body. His cutoff trousers with the strings dancing along the edges were as frayed as Winnie's dust rags.

"I think you should know that I'm being seriously courted by Hector Newman. He's a doctor's son from Edenton, attends a prestigious medical college in the Northeast. He's coming to visit me next weekend, as a matter of fact! And he's very handsome!" I rambled loudly. I felt several sets of eyes turned toward us in the darkness, the fish-haul story not nearly as captivating as our conversation. "Make sure you tell Eliza that I'm only interested in teaching you how to read and write, nothing more!"

And I walked quickly down the beach toward the cottage, hoping the darkness would swallow me up in one gulp. Mercy, I wasn't thinking clearly tonight. The long day in the sun and the horse and the fireworks had mixed me up somehow.

Benjamin was a friend, a student. I shouldn't have let my anxieties propel me into this unfamiliar terrain.

I groaned, thinking of myself, a young unmarried woman, sitting alone with a young unmarried man, on the porch of an isolated house in Nags Head. It was highly unusual, from anybody's perspective.

And it was hard to believe my own parents had encouraged me in it. The noble excuse of education went only so far in explaining the social stumbling. Folks were likely discussing the issue this very minute, curled up in their beds.

But as strange as the situation was, I enjoyed teaching. It made me feel useful, and good.

Even so, I was teaching someone in particular. I was teaching Ben. And there it was, an understanding like light trailing after a firecracker. I was glad that it was *me* teaching *him*.

July 5, 1868

Dear Hector,

Thank you most kindly for your previous letter. I enjoy receiving correspondence here, for it gives me a chance to ride to the docks during the day, to see for myself the Nags Head resort life.

The hotel is bustling from morning until night every day, so I'm afraid that you won't get much sleep during your stay. I hear the crashing of the pins at the ten-pin alley at the hotel directly after breakfast. And hundreds of people carry on at the beach from morning until evening. All I ever hear is how "healthy" the ocean water is. Even women take the water, covered from neck to ankles in the ugliest bathing costumes you've ever seen.

But in spite of that, everything is so much slower here. We don't do much except set on the porch and watch vacationers stroll by. It's a beautiful island, and the ocean is really something to see.

I am pleased that you will be meeting us for dinner on the evening of July 10. My parents are excited to show you around a bit, and I, too, look forward to seeing you.

Most sincerely,
Abigail Sinclair

The morning arrived hot and overcast, and I was plagued by such an awful feeling of humiliation that I wrote a letter to Hector in my best penmanship, sealed it with wax, and instructed Hannah to walk it to the hotel for immediate sending. I wanted to do something that felt normal today, and writing a letter to a beau felt like something I should be doing.

But Ben was as good-natured as ever, and every thought of Hector evaporated into the thick air. All grins and dirt, he was carrying a long, clinking shell contraption of some kind, which he unfurled and held out at arm's length.

He stood erectly and said, as if giving a practiced speech, "I just wanted to tell you that I'm sorry about my girl acting up yesterday night. She's been surly like that since infancy. Takes a while for her to warm up. So, to make amends, I made this here wind chime. You all can dangle it from the porch roof in the wind and it'll bring the most pleasing ocean sound to your ears."

The chime was an old basket turned upside down, with long strings of shells attached to its edges. My heart squeezed as I thought how long it must have taken him to collect all those shells, each a different shade, size, and kind, and to thread and knot the string through the shells one by one.

In spite of its rough quality, it was hands down the most beautiful present I have ever received. "Apology accepted. I like it very much," I said, fingering the shells gently. "But you don't have to apologize for her. It was my fault, for coming down there."

He looked down at his dirty feet and spoke so softly I could hardly hear him over the noise of the beach. "I'm glad you did. Come down there."

I smiled, not daring to look directly at him. "I shouldn't have. I lied to my daddy about where I would be. And I took you all by surprise. It's not like me to act so . . . devil-may-care."

"How *do* you act, then?" he asked, a little smile playing on his lips.

That was a good question. When I was a young girl, I pretty much ran wild. But the older I got, the more rigid I became. Life pinched me so tightly now. Yet here in Nags Head, I couldn't deny that I was loosening. In truth, I could feel my whole family unspooling.

"I'm not sure anymore," I said.

Ben gazed at me curiously, as if he were looking at something etched on my forehead. I forced my eyes to the curling waves.

I asked tentatively, "Say, is Eliza still angry?"

He snorted. "She's always angry. She takes after her mama's sour nature."

I wondered what Ben saw in her, if she was always so unpleasant. "She can't like the thought of you coming out here. Sitting with me . . ." I said.

"Ain't that the truth. She's jealous as a she-cat. But the heart of the matter is, she don't like the idea of me learning. She wants me to stay ignorant forever."

"You'd think she'd want you to learn, for the opportunities it could bring. If you were to marry, she'd benefit, too."

He nodded sadly. "She don't see it that way a-tall. She's happy doing what she's doing. Don't want nothing to change. She wants everything out here to stay the same."

Even I knew that nothing on such a slender land of sand and wind could possibly stay the same.

Before he left the session, Ben hung the chime from the roof overhang with a hammer and a hook that he had brought along. The chime stirred a little in the light breeze, its long extensions of shells barely touching one another as they swayed.

That evening Daddy said his farewells for the week and departed on the packet schooner back to Edenton. It being Sunday, the hotel wasn't open for meals, so Winnie prepared a scrumptious fried

chicken and sweet potato dinner. We ate on the porch, now our preferred dining room.

Mama didn't eat much of the fine fare, though. And when the tired
and whining Charlie and Martha were shepherded to bed by Hannah,
Mama started to cry. I didn't think I'd ever seen her cry a single tear.
The pitiful sobbing sounded as if it were coming from some foreign
animal, lurking wounded under the cottage.

I hurried over to her chair. "Mama, what on Earth is the matter?
Don't cry, please," I soothed, searching for a handkerchief in my reticule.

Her pale face was mottled with pink splotches, and her robin's egg
blue eyes were bloodshot and puffy. She couldn't look at me, and
even tried to shake off my awkward caresses.

"Haven't you figured it out yet?" She dabbed at her cheeks with
my handkerchief.

"No, Mama. Figured out what? Are you ill?"

She laughed heartily at the question, a harsh sound after her display of sadness. "You could say that, I suppose. Yes, I'm ill, Abigail.
I'm ill with child. I'm to be a mother again."

I don't know why I didn't figure it out earlier, except for the fact
that it was believed by everyone that Mama couldn't get pregnant
again, after a near fatal complication following Charlie's birth six
years ago.

"Have you confirmed this with Doc Newman yet? Are you very
sure?"

"I think I know my own symptoms. If you recall, I am somewhat
of an expert on the matter."

If I had the count correct, Mama had been pregnant nine times before. She had given birth to five babies, but only Charlie, Martha, and
I had survived past infancy. Little Ned and Lucy, both born between
me and Martha, had died within two months of their births.

Four of Mama's pregnancies had resulted in frightening early and midterm miscarriages. Mama suffered pitifully following two of the miscarriages, and after the birth of Charlie, she stayed in bed for nearly two years recovering from searing abdominal pain and debilitating weakness. Doc Newman believed flat-out that Mama would never become pregnant again, due to the trauma her insides had endured during her childbearing years. And for six years, he had been right.

I forced myself to smile. "Why are you sad, Mama? It's a miracle that you've conceived again!"

She turned to me with blank eyes. "Oh, it's quite a miracle, divinely ordered. God wants me dead, and I'm afraid He'll get his wish this time. I can't endure another pregnancy, and I certainly can't endure another birth. This baby will kill me."

"You don't know that, Mama. You're strong. You could pull through it like you did with all the other pregnancies. And then you'll have another little child!"

Mama's face appeared to age ten years before my eyes. Moisture dampened her vocal cords, making them creak like tired wagon wheels. "I don't want another child, don't you understand that? I never wanted children. I wish to God that I had been born a man."

"But you have a family! We aren't so bad, are we?" I grabbed for her cold hand. My voice squeaked when I said, "You do love us, don't you?"

She sighed deeply. "But I never wanted you, Abigail. Nor Charlie, Martha, Ned, or Lucy. Not really. God is punishing me for my lack of motherly love."

And she dropped my hand, got up from the chair, and walked back into the house. The screen door slammed shut behind her, its harsh bang like a blow to my back.

CHAPTER SIX

Abigail Sinclair
July 10, 1868

One day about noon, going towards my boat, I was ex-
ceedingly surprised with the print of a man's naked foot
on the shore, which was very plain to be seen in the sand.

—ROBINSON CRUSOE

THE CARVED WALNUT MIRROR THAT HUNG ON THE RAW WOOD OF THE BED-
room threw off so much light from the nearby windows that it hurt
my eyes to look into it.

But I could guess what I looked like. I imagined that my red hair
glowed and my freckles popped appealingly next to the sage silk of
my dress, just like Mama and the dressmaker had planned.

Mama had stayed in her bedroom for the entire day, but a supper
with Hector was not to be missed. With Winnie's help, Mama was
washed and dressed before Hannah had even tied my corset.

When I finally made my way out to the porch in my ballooning skirts, Mama's pale face creased itself into a starched smile, and Daddy whistled.

Mama declared, "Hector won't be able to resist you. As long as you don't start running down the boardwalk, a marriage proposal is inevitable."

Her midsection was tightly corseted. Mama was thinner than ever now.

The little red horse pulled us through the sand with just about as much difficulty as Mungo had, but I knew it wasn't the unfamiliarity of the sand that vexed her. Justus had been hitching the cart to her every day for practice, but she still hadn't taken to it. With a sense of dread, I watched her hindquarters stretch and her neck strain all the way to the hotel.

Hector, with not a wrinkle in his black dress suit, stood when he saw us enter the dining room. He strutted over to Daddy to offer a white-gloved hand, then bowed to Mama and me, hat in hand, and held our chairs for us to sit down.

It had been several months since I'd seen him, but I hadn't forgotten how nice he was to look on. His eyes were his best attribute—deeply brown and bordered by thick dark eyebrows and long eyelashes. His nose was imposing yet finely sloped, and his jawbone was strong and chiseled. His black hair wasn't too long, nor too short, but thick and well coiffed. It was parted cleanly down the middle.

But tonight I noticed that there was a feminine quality about his lips. They were too pink, too full, for his masculine face. I couldn't stop looking at them.

Daddy joked, "I can't believe I'm dining with a man who goes to a Yankee college! What's it like up there, all coal dust and immigrants?"

Hector smiled. "It's an excellent medical school. But home will always be North Carolina."

"Good to hear it," said Daddy, settling himself into his chair.

Over her glass of sugar-laden lemonade, Mama said, "Tell us how you've been spending your summer hiatus, Hector."

I could see that she had applied the tiniest bit of powder and rouge to cover her pale, yellow complexion.

"It has been entirely restful. I'm rather embarrassed to admit that I've been sleeping so late into the mornings that I've found I've long missed breakfast and quite nearly come upon the midday meal!" he said with a flourish. He sat stiffly upright, a one-dimensional board propped in a chair. "I must admit, though, that I have a hard time tearing myself away from Daddy's library. I do so enjoy the field of medicine. I'm still looking for ideas for my medical thesis. It's due at the end of the term next January, and I can't wait to get started on it."

"Going to follow in your old man's footsteps, then?" Daddy asked.

"He has indicated to me that he would like me to continue in the family business, so to speak, so that he can have a rest in his old age. Although I don't think he's willing to cease the practice of medicine anytime soon."

"Oh, I should hope not," Mama interjected, her eyes round. "I would hate to see Dr. Newman retire. You never know when you're going to need a skilled doctor, and they are so rare around these parts."

I already knew that Mama, thinking of the baby growing inside her, was anxious to procure the services of Doc Newman, who had attended all of her previous births and miscarriages.

"Why, Mrs. Sinclair, you look the absolute picture of health, a rare eagle of a woman perched firmly in the prime of her life. Such a woman should not be requiring many medical services, of that I am sure!"

Mama blushed at the compliment, and Hector looked over at me in the ensuing silence with a self-satisfied smile. He brushed a stiff-cuffed hand over his hair and winked at me, just barely. But I could only stare at his perfect orderliness, my mind suddenly picturing the marked crease between Ben's freshly washed hands and his still-grimy forearms.

Daddy picked up his whiskey and took a long drink. I wondered if he knew of Mama's condition, and whether he'd be pleased. One more mouth to feed, one more body to clothe.

Mama said, "If your father does have to retire, perhaps you would consider taking us on in his place. I *have* known you since you were a small boy, you know, when you came around with your father on his calls." She paused to smile coquettishly at him. "But I do think it would be much more convenient to have a doctor already *in the family*."

I breathed in sharply, causing my glass to almost slip out of my hands. If Hector had the slightest inclination of proposing marriage to me one day, she had probably just sent him running directly for the sand hills.

Yet Hector just smiled and nodded his head, as if she had just commented on the pleasantly warm weather Nags Head was experiencing. He then filled the rest of the meal with elaborations of his days at Yale, his father's medical endeavors, and his own successes.

It occurred to me then that as a doctor's wife I would be in for a lifetime of Hector's trials and tribulations. I would be expected to sit quietly and smile for the rest of my days, while Hector boasted and carried on. I had never realized just how much he liked himself.

Yet it was newly obvious to me, especially after spending so much time around the Bankers, that his many accomplishments were of the indoor variety. His skin was the color of milk, and his arms and legs were lanky from lack of labor.

I also noticed that he ate like my sister, Martha, daintily holding the fork and knife with his pinkie finger jutting out and carving up his soft crab with small, careful movements, perhaps the way he had been taught in an etiquette class for boys. He chewed a mouthful of crab meat and potatoes about twenty times before swallowing it all down. And he even sipped his watered-down whiskey like a kitten, taking several tiny sips at one time.

When it was time to order dessert, Hector declined, explaining that he was restricting his intake of sugar for health reasons. Of course, Mama also turned down dessert (she had turned a bit green during dinner), but Daddy and I took great pleasure in ordering the most decadent item on the hotel's menu—Kill Devil Cake, a dark-chocolate fudge cake with sugared blackberries on top. I couldn't help taking slow, luxurious bites.

Perhaps all the self-enforced forswearing caused Hector to ask me to dance in a quick, blunt fashion, hardly waiting for me to put down my fork after my last bite. He rose stiffly from his chair and took my outstretched hand in limp, gloved fingers. We made our way to the crowded saloon, where the band played a waltz.

As we circled the room, I blurted, "What do you do for amusement, Hector? It can't be all books and studying, can it?"

He smiled patronizingly. "I'm afraid it can. They just don't hand out medical degrees, you know."

I blushed, and stammered, "I-I know that. It's just that since I've been living out here, I've seen many men swimming in the ocean, and fishing with a rod and reel . . . I wondered what it was that *you* enjoyed doing, in your free time."

Hector's hand stiffened in mine as he forced a smile. "Women have the silliest notions about doctors. They have no idea of the work involved to become one! Medicine really occupies my every waking minute. I don't have time for much else."

I was silent as we navigated the room. The vision that I had of the two of us sharing intimacies at a supper table as husband and wife haunted my thoughts like a fading spirit.

He finally offered, "I like to read the newspaper every so often—at breakfast?"

I nodded politely.

He tried on a joking attitude. "So, what have *you* been doing to pass the time here, Abigail? I have no notion of the kinds of daily activities a young lady might find herself doing in a cottage by the sea. I know of several acquaintances of mine from Edenton who are currently summering here. Perhaps you've had the opportunity to socialize with them?" He named a few members of Edenton society, including Maddie Adams.

I spoke carefully. "I've already had the pleasure of visiting Madeleine Adams's cottage, and it is quite charming in the moonlight. Very cozy, surrounded by trees with excellent views. And I'm tutoring a local man down here, at my parents' suggestion. I'm teaching him to read and write."

Hector stopped dancing in mid-pivot and drew me to a deserted corner of the saloon with a grip that was much more forceful than I could have imagined him capable of. Several of our fellow waltzers looked our way and started whispering to one another.

"Perhaps I didn't hear you correctly. You say your parents arranged for you to tutor a *man*? Indeed, they said nothing of this at supper! Nor you, in your recent letter! What kind of a man?"

I felt quite queasy all of a sudden. The cake seemed to be expanding inside my stomach.

"He's my father's guide this summer. He is about your age, and a fisherman by trade, among other things . . ." I trailed off. It was difficult to describe what Benjamin did for a living without listing several different occupations.

Hector gazed at me with a pinched-up look on his fine features. "This is highly unusual!"

"Yes, you'd think so, but let me assure you that he is lacking in all manner of culture. He is completely uneducated, and he smells of dead fish, and he is so dirty you can't—" I stopped and looked out a nearby window. I felt like I was betraying good-natured Benjamin by discussing his personal hygiene with a man who had received every kind of advantage in life.

"His name is Benjamin Whimble, and he has lived here all his life—the only child of a fisherman. My parents believe him to be harmless, and you must know how my mother feels about education."

Hector collected himself, patting his slicked-back hair carefully and breathing in deeply. "I see, I see. It's nothing, to be sure. Good for you, teaching one of this island's indigents. I hear there are many out here, poor souls ignorant of the benefits of medicine and trained medical treatment. Indeed, something must be done, and a spot of education is the place to start."

He stopped to give a practiced half bow to one of the ladies, who had flirtatiously called over to him. "I'd like to meet this Benjamin Whimble, to see what a real Banker is like. Perhaps our paths will cross this summer, since we seem to have something in common now," he said pointedly.

We continued to waltz after that, but stiffly. His determined, bony arm held me tightly around my lower back, and I found I was holding my breath as we spun around.

When it was time to leave, he awkwardly escorted me out to the cart through the piles of sand surrounding the hotel. He picked his way through, one foot at a time, lifting his legs high as if marching in a cavalry and shaking his shoes with each step to get the sand out.

He jerked my arm down with him as he stumbled, then muttered about never having seen a place with such large quantities of suffering sand. I figured that Hector was more cut out for the fine northern streets of New Haven, Connecticut.

He finally let go of my arm and said to Daddy, "I've had such a superior time out here that I think I'll stay on at the hotel for a bit, see the sights. Perhaps I'll see about making some progress on the sad state of medicine on the island. Might be a good concept for my thesis, actually."

He looked at me then, and I glimpsed something like hope in his eyes and a familiarity in his bearing. Even in my cool silk dress, I grew itchy.

Mama, still a bit green, cried, "We'll have to have you out to the cottage soon for supper!"

"How I'd love to see the house. People have been talking about it all over Edenton," Hector said, looking me in the eye. "I hope to be seeing quite a lot of it this summer."

Riding back on the cart, Mama gushed on and on about what a wonderful husband he would make for me, and how lucky I was to have received such a popular suitor, who had traveled all the way to Nags Head just to visit me.

She said that I had bewitched him so completely that he had decided to stay on the island indefinitely, most likely to venture a marriage proposal by the end of the summer season. Remembering his iron grip, I felt certain of the possibility.

And yet I found myself consumed with thoughts of Benjamin Whimble and how naturally he moved through the world. He walked—even through the largest of sand piles—with a virile self-assurance, in spite of the fact that he was dressed in tatters and he stunk like a dead fish baking in the sun.

He carved out an existence on this rough island with his own physicality, eating what he caught or hunted, riding a horse that had grown up on the sandy land, and fishing from a boat that he constructed himself with materials he had found washed on the shore.

He was charming, in a way that I had known only once before.

In that moment, I was sure that I never wanted to see Hector again, much less marry the man. But I was afraid to show Mama and Daddy even an inkling of my disdain. I would have to carry on with the courting.

CHAPTER SEVEN

Abigail Sinclair
July 13, 1868

In a little time I began to speak to him, and teach him to
speak to me. And first, I made him know that his name
should be Friday, which was the day I saved his life. I
called him so for the memory of the time. I likewise
taught him to say Master, and then let him know that
was to be my name.

—ROBINSON CRUSOE

THE CASTLE WAS AS TALL AS CHARLIE, ALMOST. OVER THE COURSE OF THE
morning, our hours of work had transformed it from half a pail full
of poorly congealed wet sand to an impressive structure, complete
with a moat full of seawater and shells for windows, that soon caught
the eye of every beachcomber out.

Hotel folks who had strolled south down the beach stopped to gaze at it and chat with Charlie, who had really done most of the work.

I kneeled in the damp sand to finish carving some stonework, with one eye on the upstairs windows. Mama would skin me alive if she caught me messing in the sand. Then she'd holler at me for not wearing a bonnet, especially in the midday sun.

I leaned back on my elbows and closed my eyes. The sun whitewashed my eyelids so that when I opened my eyes again, Winnie's image was blurred, doubled in number.

She growled, "Master Charlie, you give me back that pot right now. That's the best pot we got out here, and I don't want you sandin' it up."

"But I need it, Winnie. Look at the big circles it makes!" Charlie cried.

Winnie sighed resignedly as she surveyed the bleak landscape. "I just can't escape the sand. The beach is the devil's work, you ask me. Just a tiny grain o' sand can wreak a whole bunch o' havoc. It's my bet that hell itself is covered every inch in sand."

Sweat trickled down my back as I gazed up the beach at the women in their bathing costumes, splashing in the surf on this humid day. Slapping a fly away from my cheek, I said to Winnie, "I think I'd like one of those bathing costumes after all."

She eyed me with amusement. "Oh, would you now? If I remember correct, you swore you'd never be caught dead in one of those getups."

"Well, I've changed my mind is all. It's hot out here. I should be able to get myself wet."

She cackled. "I ain't sure your mama want you wearing one of those things. She say it all right for the children, but you . . . I wouldn't count on it, Miz Abigail. Those women out yonder don't know no better."

She grabbed my face then and looked me over. She clicked her tongue and said, "And where your bonnet at? You know your skin gonna burn like dry kindlin' on the fire! What your mama gonna say?"

"Am I burning?" I asked, patting my face, all of a sudden worried about having red skin for Ben. He would be here soon for his lessons.

"You ain't peachy, that's for sure. Best get on inside."

Winnie was right. When I went to my bedroom and saw my face in the mirror, I almost screamed. It was the color of a lobster and about a hundred new freckles had appeared all over it. I scrubbed myself hard, hoping the freckles would come right off, and repinned my hair just in time to hear Ben's footsteps on the porch outside my window.

His arms strained with what I thought might possibly be an enormous dead snapping turtle. He laid it down with a little thud.

He saw me in the window and said, "Uh-oh. Did someone forget her bonnet today?"

"Never you mind, Benjamin Whimble. I was helping with the sand castle over there and clean forgot about it."

He laughed. "Forgot about it? I thought ladies like you wore bonnets morning, noon, and night."

"The sun just felt so warm on my face. I couldn't help myself."

He took a couple of steps closer to me and peered critically at my face. "Woohoo, look at those freckles! Must be thousands of them."

I put my hands over my face. "Look away, now."

"Aw, I like them. They're like glazing on a pie."

I peeked through my fingers at him and saw that he was gazing at me fondly. "Well, are you going to tell me what that thing is?" I asked.

He looked to the shell with a burst of satisfaction. "Oh, right. I was fishing with my pap when I caught sight of this here cooter, making her way up a little stream. She was about the stubbornest one I've ever seen. But just look at the size of her!

"I dove on in after her and swam I don't know how far under the water to catch her. Should have kept her myself, she was so heavy to carry. But I thought Winnie might know how to cook cooter stew, so I brought her on over."

I leaned my head out the window to look at it. Its shell was a shiny olive brown, but I supposed its dead body was still curled up inside somewhere. "How do you know it's a female?"

He laughed. "Stubborn, you know."

"Ho, ho. Well, is she dead?"

"Oh yeah, I killed her and bled her for you." He made a slicing motion across his neck.

I wrinkled my nose, thinking about Ben dismembering the turtle's head, her blood draining. He was so nonchalant about killing sometimes.

I grabbed some teaching supplies and walked out through the cottage to the porch.

"We don't eat whatever you call them—'cooters'—in Edenton. I doubt Winnie knows how to make the stew, either, but I'll ask her." I grinned. "First a wind chime, now a turtle. What's next, Moby Dick?"

He scratched at his messy hair. "That's a whale, right?"

I smiled. "A white one."

He looked down at his naked feet on the dry wood of the porch. "Well, don't count on that. Don't think I ever seen a white whale, anyhow. But I always say, it would be a shame to arrive at the pearly gates not having enjoyed what God put on the Earth for us. Cooters included."

I just nodded, thinking on the untold numbers of things I hadn't done in my boxed-in seventeen years of life. Ideas of all I'd been missing out on multiplied like scurrying field mice in my mind.

∞

After the lesson, I pulled *Robinson Crusoe* from the pile of things on the table. I spanned the pages with my thumb, the paper stirring up the air as it fanned from cover to cover. We had already read through three quarters of the book, I was amazed to see, as I removed the little leather bookmark.

This was my favorite part of the lesson, and sometimes I snuck glances at Ben while I was reading aloud, to see the rapturous expression on his face. At times my eyes would accidentally meet with his startling blue ones, and I'd hurriedly look back at the page. But sometimes Ben would be staring out to sea, lost in the story. I wondered what everything on the island looked like in Ben's imagination, and if it looked the way it looked in mine.

From watching him under my eyelids the past few weeks I had learned that he paid the strictest attention to the parts of the book that bored me to death with their details, such as the building of Crusoe's cave house or the descriptions of his tools.

Ben would nod and shout vigorously in approval at his craftsmanship, and outright marvel at Crusoe's persistence in hunting and fishing. Then he would regale me with his own stories and techniques. I think he was proud that his very own occupations were written about in this book of literature.

In today's reading Crusoe was finally about to have contact with another human being, after twenty-five years on the island with only himself, the goats, and his parrot Pol for company. A footprint had been found in the sand, and Crusoe was afraid for his life. Ben's fingers drummed loudly on the table, and his right leg jiggled up and down as I read.

I sailed through the part about Crusoe saving Friday's life from the savages, and the bit about making Friday his slave, until Ben interjected irritably, "I don't get why Crusoe wants Friday to be his own personal slave. You'd think he'd be pleased enough with the company. Couldn't Crusoe and Friday just be friends?"

My answer came too quickly for me. "It's repayment for saving the man's life. You can see that Friday doesn't mind. He *wants* to help Crusoe."

Ben snuffed through his nose. "Have you ever been saved by someone? Did it turn you into a dog, your savior into your master?"

"I've never found myself in such a situation, thank God."

"Well, 'course you haven't. You have your book learning, and it's mighty fine and all that. But I know about other things, about fishing, hunting, boat-building, and yes, since I have to do all these things on the water, I know about saving lives, when I have to.

"And if there's one thing I'm certain of, it's that men don't go following around the one that saved them like a slave for the rest of their natural-born lives. Might invite 'em to supper or give 'em a haul of fish for their thankfulness, but slaving, no ma'am."

"Maybe that was the custom in the early 1700s, when Defoe wrote the novel. Myself, I always try to take into account the historical framework surrounding a book. It's part of the critical interpretation." My didactic tone landed too heavy on the pine porch, even to me.

"You mean the part of history back when white folks decided that enslaving the blacks was a dandy idea? Seems to me Crusoe is a racist, plain and simple."

A thick tar bubbled and stirred inside me. *Crusoe, a racist?* "No, I don't see it that way at all."

"You know, I find I don't have as much in common with Crusoe as

I thought I did," he said petulantly, crossing his arms across his chest. "Friday. What kind of a knucklehead name is that, anyway?"

Ben's words caught me off guard, as if an adorable, playful puppy had suddenly growled and bitten my finger with its needle-sharp teeth. I had no idea he felt this strongly about anything, except maybe fish.

He pointed agitatedly to the book, in which I was still marking the page with a forgotten index finger. "And 'course, the man's black. What if he had been a white man? I bet it would have ended up an entirely different kind of book."

"I don't think so," I said stubbornly.

He looked at me with narrowed eyes, as if suddenly seeing me in a bright light. "But I guess you and your family were slave owners, and not too long ago at that. I bet your pap wishes he still had his slave shacks filled to the roofs."

My sunburn suddenly felt cool on my cheeks. "Pardon me, *Mr. Whimble,* but you are being rude. We have done nothing but help you! You will apologize for your criticism of my daddy, or I'll have you fired from your guide job!"

I accidentally kicked Ben's shin under the table when I uncrossed my legs, but I couldn't apologize.

His face created a crookedly evil grimace I'd never seen him make before. "Now, you don't have to go and tattle to your daddy. We're just talking here, you know, having one of your 'critical inter-pa-tations.' I might as well ask you, though, where it is *you* stand on the issue of black and white, being a planter's daughter your whole life. What's it like having folks serve you all day, every day?"

The sickening sludge inside me was sloshing around, hot and thick. I couldn't tell him that I thought it was a comfortable life, a happy life, while it had lasted.

I said quietly, "I suppose not many folks on the Banks owned slaves before the war."

There were no plantations, no extensive fields of tobacco, rice, or cotton for the Bankers. Slavery had likely never taken hold on the islands, with nothing to grow except vegetables, nothing to sell except fish and feral horses.

"Guess you could say we're our own slaves out here on the Banks. We each do our own work. It's just our way."

His self-righteousness irked me. I said, "And I suppose you all get along like pie out here. One big happy family of white and black."

"There's good and bad of both colors. But I have lots of Negro friends, sure. I'd trust them with my life."

"*We* care for our Negroes. They're like our family members. We all get along fine. We know where the other stands. And we are helping them to have better lives. We have made Christians of them, and take them to church with us."

He rolled his eyes. "Better lives? Christians? You don't actually believe that manure, do you? Somebody fed you that stuff, and you ate it up and licked the plate clean. You're not fooling anyone with all that do-good talk."

My rage lowered my voice to a hiss. "My uncle Jack died fighting for the South. He was the best man I have ever known. And our Negroes loved him. They saw his goodness."

I could hardly discuss my dear uncle with this disgusting fisherman who didn't know me at all.

"I'm sorry about your uncle, I truly am, but he died in vain, fighting to keep black folks in bondage. Owning other people just ain't right."

I shook my head. "I love Winnie like my own mother! She didn't leave us after the war, because she cares for our family. Can't you see that? We have given her a home, with a bed, and good food. You can't call that wrong."

"Are you that simple? You don't even know the hardships she's had to endure at the hands of your family. As for the woman's bed, I've seen her sleeping in a hammock on your porch! I don't see any of *you* sleeping out of doors. You should ask her sometime how she really feels about you folks!"

He was an insufferably ignorant buffoon. I couldn't even look at him anymore. "How dare you judge me, my family? What do you know about anything, Benjamin Whimble? Fishing? Hunting? Anyone can do those things, and probably better than you can!" An angry tear squirted from my eye and ran for its life down my cheek. "You don't fool me. You're an expert at killing, not some benevolent nature saint, like you want me to think. You take the lives of ducks and geese looking for a place to rest, a bite to eat. You ambush those beautiful waterbirds for their feathers! For ladies' hats! And you lay down nets at the exact spots fish come to lay their eggs. You chase down turtles for stew! So be careful who you judge, Benjamin. We all take advantage when we can. You're no better than anyone else."

He looked at me, his face a mask of gray revulsion. "I reckoned you to be a different kind of gal, Miss Sinclair. But you ain't nothing special after all."

He stood up and walked quickly down the porch steps, taking out a little piece of paper from a trouser pocket and throwing it down in the sand.

"Don't bother coming back here, Benjamin. You're not welcome!" I hollered, even though he had already disappeared around the corner of the cottage.

I stood up slowly on trembling legs, my head throbbing in shock. Ben's scrap of paper skittered over the sand like a gull feather. I stumbled down the porch steps and chased after it. It was a torn piece of old envelope, folded in half. My name was written on the outside: *"Deer Abee."*

I opened it to see Ben's childlike lettering over every inch of the paper. He had tried to write in smaller letters than he normally did, so that he could fit everything he wanted to say on the little paper.

"Heer iȝ the res apee fer cootr stu."

He went on and on, describing in minute detail how to make a stew from the turtle's meat. At the bottom of the paper, he wrote, *"keep the shel fer a stu bole."*

He thought he was so smart. Didn't he realize that Winnie couldn't even read a recipe card?

Keep the shell for a bowl, he wrote. How lovely. I could just imagine proper company taking notice of it on our dining room table back home.

As I crumpled the note in my hand, I hiccupped laughter through a stream of tears. I looked over at the turtle shell sitting innocently on the porch, the headless body curled inside somewhere.

Winnie walked up beside me and placed her big warm hand on my miserable head. "Don't you worry none, Miz Abby. This messed-up world ain't nothing to do with you."

I turned to look at her with my sore eyes. She had somehow been listening to our every word. "Were you spying on us? For Mama? Even you don't trust me to act a lady?"

She shook her head. "Your mama don't know nothing about me setting at the window, so don't you be saying nothing about it, mind?"

"But why?"

She looked at me with the mischievous eyes of a child and recited the alphabet, right there on the beach. Then she bent over and, with her forefinger, scrawled her name in the sand.

I realized then that Ben hadn't been the only person I was teaching.

She must have been standing right by the porch window during the lessons, memorizing and reciting along with Ben.

But the thought of Winnie, sneaking around in the name of learning, pulled me down with a bucket of sadness. She was trapped in her dark skin even though the slaves had been free for three years now.

Mercy! All around me people were yearning for just the smallest amount of education. Twenty-six letters, that was all. They all lined up in my mind now, a row of orderly sticks and curls. Five vowels, twenty-one consonants. Endless combinations, and the basis of all education.

In Winnie's handsome face I saw myself, a baby in her rocking black arms. The seed of racism grew inside me even then, an infant in the arms of a slave. It was as common and as simple as the alphabet, the origin of all of my future learning. Since then, it had penetrated and poisoned each and every part of my mind. I doubted I could even think without it.

I grabbed Winnie's hand and held it so tightly I thought I'd break the bones in both of our hands.

CHAPTER EIGHT

Abigail Sinclair
July 18, 1868

*But I wronged the poor honest creature very much, for
which I was very sorry afterwards. However, as my jeal-
ousy increased, and held me some weeks, I was a little
more circumspect, and not so familiar and kind to him
as before; in which I was certainly in the wrong, too, the
honest grateful creature having no thought about it, but
what consisted with the best principles, both as a reli-
gious Christian and as a grateful friend, as appeared
afterwards to my full satisfaction.*

—ROBINSON CRUSOE

I DIDN'T EXPECT BEN, EVEN THOUGH I SAT MYSELF IN A ROCKER ON THE
porch every afternoon, watching the shell chime dangle in the breeze.
I squinted at the male beachcombers as they strolled up and down the

shore, but they didn't have to get very close for me to pick out their unnatural gaits and virginal skin.

I wanted to reread *Robinson Crusoe*, to try to see the book with fresh eyes, to figure out what went wrong that day and try to make things right again. I opened it up to where we'd left off and read a couple of sentences, but I was distracted by some grains of sand that had lodged themselves along the spine of the book, and the pages that had warped a bit in the humid air. I closed the book without swiping the sand away. And now it stared at me from the porch table, its innocuous brown cover disguising its questionable contents.

As the afternoons dragged by, my spirits deflated so markedly that Winnie hurried to procure some cloth and a pattern from New Bern. The package had arrived midweek, and she was still busily sewing my bathing costume. Whether Mama had given her approval for it or not remained a mystery. Except for Winnie, no one had laid eyes on her for days. We just heard her hollering for lemonade and toast.

Winnie kept holding the ugly gray thing up for me to see, hoping to cheer me. It looked like a dress with bloomers. I couldn't imagine it taking on water very well. And now that Ben had disappeared from my days, I found I didn't really want to splash in the surf anymore. I felt idle and useless.

To make myself feel better, I had insisted that Winnie cook the cooter stew.

I dragged her out to the porch to show her the shell. "I ain't even trying to feature how to clean that thing," she had said, her hands planted on her hips.

"Well, at least it's missing its head," I said. "One less appendage to worry about."

She clicked her tongue. "Lord have mercy."

Together, we read the recipe that Ben had written. Then she

sighed, picked the turtle up from its resting spot on the porch, and carried it away to the kitchen house. A few minutes later I could hear her hollering for Hannah to come help her pry the bottom shell off.

With dollops of cream and a shot of brandy in each of the bowls, the warm stew was savory, and the turtle meat was so delicate that it seemed to melt on my tongue. I could taste the clear blue sound water, the mysterious plants and animals that had sifted through the turtle's blood. It made me think of Ben, and the things he knew about the Banks, the things he cherished.

I felt closer to him with each bite. I ate until I was more than full, and I was a bit happier than when I'd started.

Ben finally returned to the cottage when Daddy arrived for the weekend. Saturday morning I heard his voice outside, on the western side of the cottage, talking with Daddy about the day's fishing plan. Just hearing his good-natured drawl for those brief minutes made me want to cry out his name through an open window like a lunatic.

But I just sat on my bed, staring at *Moby-Dick*. As the day wore on, I got the worst headache I've ever had. Winnie said it was from squinting at a book in the sun, but I knew very well that I hadn't read an entire page in days.

⟋⟍

Dreams of water coursed through my turbulent sleep that night. Rain and ocean waves pooled and puddled all over the hazy images. In one dream, Ben and I sat on the porch, but his face was wet and his clothes dripped. He looked skeptically toward the clouded sky and said, "We're in for some weather, I reckon. Best batten your shutters."

But when I looked at the sky, I saw only sun shining, absolutely no hint of bad weather at all. Nothing was for certain here in Nags Head, and I found this oddly comforting. I said confidently, "You never know, Ben. Some things are too unpredictable to know for sure."

Distant thunder shook the air, and the waves crashed with determination. He looked me straight in the eye and said, "Oh, some things there's no mistaking. Sometimes a man just knows things."

I wanted to strangle him for his stubbornness. "From where I sit, it's sunny. Just look at that sky and you'll see!" I pointed and pointed at the endless blue.

He turned around to look, and when he did, the light around us was almost yellow. Dark clouds were marching in earnest down the shoreline. The waves were rocky crags, blown by the northeast wind.

I felt horribly embarrassed. "You were right, Ben. It looks like a storm is coming."

He nodded and smiled at me, with affection in his eyes. I wanted to tell him that I missed him, really missed him something awful, but my mouth wasn't working right. The dream dissolved before I could find the right words.

⟬⟭

I felt I had just fallen asleep when I heard Winnie's nimble footsteps cross the floorboards of my bedroom. Before I could even wonder what she was up to, she banged the shutters closed and shut the bedroom windows.

She muttered to my closed eyelids, "Be a miracle if I can cook up a hot breakfast today, with that storm a-ragin'."

"Storm? What storm?" I mumbled.

She scoffed. " 'What storm,' she say." Then I heard the rain scouring the roof upstairs. And the ocean roared too closely, the wind whistled too high. I hastily dressed and walked into the parlor, where Charlie and Martha and even Mama perched on the edges of their chairs.

With the shutters closed and the storm water plopping monotonously into a little tub in the sitting room, the house mourned the change in weather. Winnie and Hannah darted to and fro, taking up the rugs and filling crevices around the windows with small rags.

The wind raged against the screen door, which lacked a proper latch. It squeaked open, and then banged erratically every few seconds or so, making us all lurch.

Mama's face was green, but there was life in her eyes. She likely still wished to be in bed, instead of sitting with us in this sad state of affairs. But during the night the water had leaked through the shingles on the roof and soaked her bed linens, so she hadn't had much of a choice. The linens wouldn't be dry for a long while.

In silence, we fiddled with our cold oatmeal and stale bread. Winnie's efforts to keep the cook fire going were soundly unsuccessful.

Mama slammed her hand down on the table, causing bowls and glasses to jump. "Curse your daddy for building this house on the beach! Where is he, now that we need him? Left us just in time, and didn't even stay for church!"

She got up from the table, white-faced and shaking, and began pacing the length of the rattling house.

Then Charlie wailed, "I want my daddy! Daddy, Daddy, help us!"

And Justus, who was hovering nearby, hollered, "Mark my words, this pine-wood house gonna be our coffin! Oh Lordy!"

Hannah taunted, "Justus, hush up, you scaring the children."

Then Martha started crying, "I don't like this! I want to go home!"

And Winnie went to rock her in her arms.

Nobody ate much after that, not that we had much appetite to begin with. I got up and cracked open the door to the eastern porch and, feeling confrontational, stepped out into the powerful wind.

I'd never seen the ocean so angry. As far as I could see, the water snarled, its teeth sharp-peaked white caps.

Blotchy-faced Charlie and Martha soon peeked out the door after me, their eyes wide, and I gathered them closely to me. After days of existing peacefully with the land, sweetly lapping the shore like a cow licking salt, the ocean was fighting the earth in a fierce battle for territory.

Sea spray filmed my face and wet my hair, and my sleeves soon clung uncomfortably to my arms.

Charlie suddenly pointed out to the sea, scaring me nearly to death with his yelling. "Look, Abby! I think that ship is in trouble! Over there, see?"

I looked through the driving rain and dark clouds to see a ship turned brokenly on its side, caught on an outer bar far out in the ocean. Its mast leaned almost completely sideways, like a bird mired in the dirt with a broken wing. Water washed relentlessly over the hull.

My stomach clenched in panic as I tried to figure out what I should do. Perhaps we had a whistle or something, maybe some pots and pans to bang!

But before I had time to run back to the kitchen I saw six men in puffy dark jackets come bolting down the beach, pulling a boat outfitted with oars. Without hesitation they dragged the boat quickly into the water, their legs pushing insistently through the raging surf. Once they got it out a ways, they jumped into it, facing seaward. Their strokes cut through the waves, but they made slow headway in the dips and crests marching their way.

I watched them in a trance as the boat bobbed wildly on the waves, until the gray sheet of rain and swirling mist swallowed them up.

Several people—hotel guests and locals alike—were also making their way to the beach to take in the scene. They stood on the wet sand, their Sunday clothes covered in blankets. Eventually Mama, Winnie, and Hannah came out to the porch as well, attracted by the unfolding story of the sailors and the brave men who were trying to save them.

It seemed we stood on the porch for hours before we could see anything that indicated life. And then a terrifying sight—two oars from the rowboat came washing violently ashore. Everyone pointed to them, exclaiming loudly over the bad omen, but no one went to fetch them. They just stuck in the wet sand as the waves washed over them.

Finally I saw the lifeboat, rocking helplessly. Five men were inside, one of whom appeared to be a slumping sailor from the wreck. A few of the men on the beach ran out into the thrashing water to try to grab the boat as it slowly drew toward shore.

I scampered down the steps with one of our wool blankets, out into the pelting rain and wind. Charlie and Martha cried after me to come back, but I had seen something far out in the white-capped sea—something moving and splashing. I hollered out to the crowd of people up the beach and pointed with an outstretched arm to the speck of movement.

But no one could hear me above the commotion; they were busy tending to the weary men who had come ashore on the boat.

I watched helplessly as the awkward splashing slowly grew closer. I could see that it was one of the local men, wearing the telltale life vest, and he was dragging a man along with him as he swam one-armed through the water. As they neared the shore, the waves pushed them both out to the beach, tired of the game.

I ran over to them as fast as I could in a wet dress, my damp hair tangled down my back. The man with the vest was lying facedown in the sand, totally exhausted. His back labored up and down as he sucked the air into his lungs, coughing and spitting.

But the other man, who was lying faceup, stared at the rain clouds, his eyes like marbles. There was no sign of life in his pallid face. I screamed to the crowd of people for help and tried to drag him to a safer spot up the beach, but he was too heavy for me.

At last some of the men came running down the beach to us. One of them—a black man with a vest over his flapping rags—pulled the sailor by the arms away from the surf and started pumping on his chest. I watched him in awe, never having seen a black man try to save a white man's life before.

The man who had tried to rescue the sailor from the wreck was moaning a bit, and struggling to push himself into a sitting position. Pebbles of sand stuck to his forehead, and his blond hair was plastered to his skull. Yet his blue eyes shone through the gray light.

I hardly recognized him, without the usual grime all over him. He was as slickly clean as a shell in the sand, and so handsome, in his bravery, that I had to remind myself to breathe.

Ben smiled faintly to see me standing over him, but he was still breathing hard through his mouth and couldn't speak. I walked around the back of him and hooked my arms under his and helped him to his feet. I unfolded the blanket I had brought and wrapped it around his shivering body. We stood close while I clasped the blanket at his neck. We looked at each other, but his eyes were hard to read, in the chaos.

"I shouldn't even be here," I said. "I'm useless."

He shook his head slowly. Then he rasped, "You carried a blanket." He swayed on his feet like a drunk, his hair streaming ocean water down the rough wool.

Then Ben looked to the man working over the petrified body of the sailor. Ben's white face was so filled with sadness that I started to cry. Hot tears mixed with the rain on my face, but I didn't make a sound.

The man must have tried to work the water out of the sailor's lungs for a quarter of an hour, until Ben stepped over and stopped the tired arms from pushing.

"Jacob, it's all day with him. Best cease and desist."

The crowd had gathered around us now, watching the persistent efforts. The Banker women clicked their tongues and whispered prayers into the wind and finally walked away, slowly, back to their homes on the sound side.

Eliza Dickens came running toward the beach, screaming Ben's name in the whipping wind. She stopped to question a few of the retreating women, then came tearing down the sand to us, strands of wet hair lashing her panicked face.

I said quickly, "Come tomorrow, Ben. We can finish the book."

Ben's eyes closed, as if he had half a mind to sleep on his feet. The book was likely the last thing on his mind now.

Eliza didn't even look at me as she ran past. With a little owl screech, she ran right up to Ben and hugged him desperately, kissed his blue, trembling lips and heavy eyelids with rapid little pecks.

I turned my head and made for the cottage, where I could see my family, tiny blurs on the porch. As I stumbled up the shore, I heard Eliza scold, "I told you not to try to save no more folks from the sea, now, didn't I? You nearly drowned the last time, you recall that?"

I remembered the time Daddy had referred to Ben as "a local hero." Now that unlikely description made sense. Ben and his black friend Jacob were two of the handful of people here who cared enough to risk their lives to save those poor souls drowning in the ocean, yet he never said a word about that to me.

No wonder Robinson Crusoe upset him so much. It wasn't about power over another, out here. It was about respect for the island, a simple love of mankind. *Just doing what was right.* The realization hit me like the force of the wind.

A few folks, mostly hotel guests, stayed nearby, lingering in death's aftermath like surviving soldiers, happy to be alive but wondering what else was in store for them.

Later in the evening, after saying a prayer for the sailor who had succumbed to death so close to our own cottage, we ate a somber, and still cold, meal.

Then I volunteered to check on the horses, since Justus, who normally tended to the animals, seemed to have other plans for himself. He was superstitious about storms, apparently. He had been cowering in a corner of the kitchen all day, his arms wrapped tightly about his long legs, flatly refusing to move a muscle until the wind stopped whistling.

While everyone readied themselves for an early night, I pulled the hood of a walking cape over my head and strode through the soggy sand to the small wooden stable.

The night seemed bruised and tender, recovering from the storm's beating. The air felt fleshy against my skin, darkly alive.

Mungo and Clementine the cow were restless, knocking back and forth in their stalls. Their hides were damp, and their food was almost gone. I fed and watered them and crooned to them until they relaxed their necks and snorted peacefully.

Then I walked down to check on the Banker pony. She stood quite still and looked at me calmly over the top of her gate. She didn't look disturbed in the least. She must have weathered similar storms in her wild life on the Outer Banks.

But something was definitely bothering her. She hadn't eaten any of the oats that had been put in the stall. In fact, she hadn't eaten much of the food that Justus had given her since we'd purchased her over two weeks ago. As I examined her in the darkness, I could see her ribs swimming beneath her nappy red coat.

I hugged her neck to my face and whispered, "You're as finicky as Mama. The other horses like oats just fine."

She brushed her nose firmly into my cold hand, sniffing the remnants of the meal I had just eaten. I tied a rope around her stout neck and reached around to push the door open. Then we both stepped out into the night.

She strode through the wet sand and soon found what I knew she was wanting—a hearty growth of soggy saltmeadow hay. She feasted as if she had been dying for food. I knew then that it would be hard for her to break the habit of this hay. She would always yearn for it, no matter what was put in her stall.

The horse finally got her fill of the salty hay, so she turned to go back north. But as we neared the stable, I untied the rope around her neck.

"Run along, girl." I smacked her hindquarters firmly.

She snuffed at my hands one more time and then left me. I watched her meander up the beach until I couldn't see her anymore. The darkness swallowed her up, but I knew she was out there somewhere, feeling her way back home amid the shredded strands.

Scraping the sand off my boots at the cottage, I realized that I had never given her a name.

The next day I spent deep in my reading, trying hard not to think about Ben, and whether he would come for his lesson. The supplies were in their places on the table, the pages of *Robinson Crusoe* occasionally ruffling in the ocean breeze. Even Winnie kept poking her head out the window, pretending to be looking at the waves, still rough from the storm.

But the afternoon came and went without him. I was on the verge of hysterical tears, trying to read through the same page of *Moby-Dick* that I had been stuck on for hours, when an insistent rap on the western screen door startled me.

Hannah answered the door, and a few seconds later came to find me on the porch, her eyes dancing. "There a young man here to see you, Miz Abigail. Says he's Jacob. He say he got a message for you from Mr. Benjamin."

I jumped off the rocking chair and tried not to outright run around the porch to the other side of the cottage. And there stood the man who had tried to save the sailor's life the day before. He was Ben's good friend, I knew. He was looking up at the house and running his hand over the wooden porch rails.

When he saw me he took his hand off the rails, briefly flashing a rough ivory palm. He didn't smile.

"Ben sent me to tell you he won't be coming to get his learning today." He donned his cap and turned to leave.

My stomach in a knot, I blurted, "Wait. Please, Jacob. Did he give a reason for his absence? Did he seem . . . angry?"

"He nursing a bad cough, sound like he gonna bring up a bird's nest. But no, he ain't angry. Just dead tired is all."

"Do you think he'll come back?"

"I do. He say he like it here." He paused for a few seconds, trying to hide a wry smile by looking at his feet. "Even though the house is mighty unlikely."

Encouraged by his frankness, I moved a couple steps closer to him. "Ben said our house was strange?"

He snorted a bit. "Well, it ain't the most natural sight in the world."

As I looked at him shuffling under me, I became conscious of my higher ground. I walked down the steps to stand next to him, eye to eye. And I felt like it was the first time that I had really looked at a black man.

I could see that Jacob's skin was very black, from his time in the sun. His features melded well together, and taking in his face was as refreshing as gazing out the open window of my cottage bedroom for the first time. There was nothing in the way of unsullied appreciation.

"What do *you* think of it?" I asked.

He looked at the house in front of him and shrugged. "I used to think it the devil's house, when I first sees it. Gave me the heebie-jeebies. But I reckon I'm getting used to it. Folks can get used to just about any sight, they sees it long enough."

I scanned the flat terrain, dotted here and there with locals still scouring the beach for remnants of the shipwreck. Earlier in the day a barrel of wine and several drowned chickens had washed ashore. "Everyone must think we're simple-minded. And maybe we are. I'm not sure anymore, myself."

He laughed, showing spaces between his teeth. "This here house has been the talk this summer, no doubt. I try to weave it into most every yarn I tell. Most everybody took bets on when the ocean would take her."

For some reason I pictured that rude woman at the market keeping track of the Bankers' bets, cackling hopefully about the house's demise.

"Oh my Lord! That's terrible! I hope you all lost money after yesterday's storm. The cottage weathered it well, I think."

He snorted. "Don't mean a circumstance to us, one bitty storm like that was. We'll think what we're gonna think. We'll wait for September, October to come 'round, and then we'll think on it some more."

I nodded. Bankers knew more than we did about many things, I thought. "Tell Ben that he can come back here any time he wants to. Tell him that I'll be waiting."

He looked me in the eye for just a second and then wagged his head slightly up and down. He strolled a few paces, then turned around and came back.

"Ben may look strong and talk the talk and all. But he's soft under that browned-up skin o' his. He's a simple man. He's not cut out for all"—he stopped and surveyed the cottage one last time—"this here."

Then he walked off for good, his legs moving so fast he was almost running. I had the feeling that he couldn't get away from the cottage fast enough.

Hannah appeared at the screen door with a broom in her hands. "He seem like a real nice man, that Jacob. Ooooh, and strong, too. Those arms, just like sweet hams! What he like, Miz Abigail?"

I tried to focus on Jacob for lovesick Hannah, but I could see only Ben's face in my mind. I rubbed my hands over my arms gently and said so softly I could hardly hear myself, "I like him very much."

CHAPTER NINE

Benjamin Whimble
July 22, 1868

How infinitely good that Providence is which has pro-
vided, in its government of mankind, such narrow
bounds to his sight and knowledge of things; and
though he walks in the midst of so many thousand dan-
gers, the sight of which, if discovered to him, would
distract his mind and sink his spirits, he is kept serene
and calm by having the events of things hid from his
eyes, and knowing nothing of the dangers which sur-
round him!

—ROBINSON CRUSOE

I WAS FRYING UP SOME FLATBREAD AND EGGS OVER THE COOK FIRE WHEN
Pap came out of the crooked outhouse, still half asleep. Pap's black

Labrador, Duffy, followed along, sniffing 'round the fire for some forgotten tidbits.

I gave Pap a tin cup of well water and a plate of food and sat down on the ground with him to breakfast.

The light through the thick stands of pine and oak trees was mostly silver shadows. It was so early, the sun hadn't even poked over the horizon yet.

After a few bites of the hot food, I attempted the talk that I had been dreading for days. "Pap, I got some news. You might think on it as bad news, but try to look on it as something good for us, bring us regular money."

He couldn't look me in the eye. He shook his fork in the air. "You going to work that construction site in Hatteras, I reckon," he muttered.

I nodded, then blurted in a rush, "Yessir, I aim to venture down there come September, see how it goes. 'Course, it might be a big ol' waste of time, and I'll likely mosey on back again. But then again it might be a real good thing. I could make enough for you to retire, rest yourself for a change. And until then, I got Jacob all set to come over and help you out. You won't even miss me."

He blew out a whistle of air and shook his head. I got up, my heart scrabbling like a crab in a pot, and walked over to the bucket to wash my plate and skillet.

"So you gonna leave your old man, just like that. What you think I can do on my own, son?"

And here I thought he'd be proud of me, getting a paying job like that, even though I didn't get it on my own accord. With one letter, Mister Sinclair had somehow fixed it all, like he said he would. He told me Mister Stetson had agreed to take me on as a crew worker without so much as a face-to-face. I'd be pouring sweat for a good long while to come, but still, I was right dumbfounded at Mister Sinclair's letter-penning skills.

'Course, Pap would never know all that business, if I could help it. He'd likely kill Mister Sinclair with his bare hands for messing with his livelihood.

"Listen, Pap, we both know you can't fish forever. You get tireder by the day—heck, by the *hour*. I got a job that can support us both. You can finally rest, lay abed! Sounds good enough to me!"

"I thought I raised you up better 'n that, you ungrateful boy. But I see I failed you in your sense of fam'ly. Your ma must be wreaking some kind of pandemony in heaven, to hear you talk so to me."

Duffy heard his agitation and came to lie down next to him. Pap sat rubbing her ears and muttering under his breath, "First he starts learning his letters . . . hobnobbing with town folk, thinking better of himself . . . Now he's gonna leave his old pap, Duff."

He brought his head up quick and said right loud, "Well, here it is—if I can't fish, I'll die. How's that? I'll lay around this old shack some poor sample of a man, and die dreaming of the water, his own flesh and blood having left him for a godless gov'ment job, no less. Just like every other young man out here, thinks he's gonna make something of himself. What they don't know. Suck out their souls, more like it."

Duffy barked at me, two short, angry yips. "Pap, I have to do this, for both of us. Now, you'll be fine. Jacob's a good man, and a hard worker. I don't want you to kill yourself off over this."

I looked to our house, a one-room cabin made of lopsided pieces of broken wood, washed ashore from some hapless ship. The roof—if you could rightly call it that—leaked in about a hundred places when the littlest drop of rain came. We slumbered on pieces of old ticking stuffed with seaweed, and owned just a few burnt-up pots and pans, left over from Ma's long days of working over a cook fire.

It was hard to admit, since we worked so damned hard every day, but we barely scraped by, never knowing what the winds of fortune were going to bring. It was a tough life, and I wanted something better. And not even my pap was going to keep me from trying to raise myself up.

"Pap, I aim to start this coming autumn."

It just about killed me how quiet Pap was on the boat. I kept trying to make conversation about this and that, but he'd have none of it. Just sat slouched over, smoking on his pipe, and made me stake all the nets, even though my arms still felt like stewed dumplings in sauce. The sun came out awful hot, too, so that the back of my neck burned fierce and my whole body turned to runny clabber by the afternoon.

To make the time pass, I thought on Abby, and how I was to see her again, after that bad turn of events the other day. How Jacob had told me what Abby had said yesterday, that she'd "be waiting on me." I made him repeat what she had said, word for exact word, 'til his eyes rolled back in his head. I featured those words written in gold writing on a piece of Abby's nice paper, they sounded so good to me.

I had been kicking myself for letting my temper get the best of me that day we argued, and it gave me no end of grief during my fitful recuperation on my flimsy pallet. Her flinty green eyes and red hair came a-blowing into my dreams full of tall waves and drowning folks reaching for the sky.

It wasn't like me to get so angry, 'specially not at a lady like Abby.

There was just something about her that got my blood pumping. I wanted to make her sit up and think. I wanted her to know that she was pure iron underneath that puffed-up outer layer of hers.

She didn't see it yet. To me, she always looked like she wanted to say more than she ended up saying. Like the truth of her was still inside her, bursting to get out. I just knew she was something special, a pearl in a oyster.

And when I finally got to her cottage later in the day, I saw her there at our learning spot on the porch, all alone and "waiting on me," I reckoned. And I have to say, it felt real good to be back at that strange house again.

"I thought you'd given up on me," she said.

Feeling giddy as a forgiven dog with his tail thumping low and his ears back, I fairly ran up the steps. "Well, I still got some learning to do, ain't that right?"

"Everybody does," she said, a little smile on her mouth.

Before she could say anything else, I said, "Look, Abby, I had a notion of you that wasn't right. But I hardly gave you a chance to explain yourself, and that wasn't nice of me. 'Specially after all you done for me."

Her eyes danced in the sunlight. "You *were* quick to judge me. The fact that my family owned slaves must have been bothering you for some time, from the sound of it."

"I just wanted to know you better is all," I said. "You haven't been too forthcoming about yourself, and here I am, spilling my guts to you all the time. It ain't fair."

"I'm not in the habit of discussing those kinds of things. You just . . . took me by surprise."

"I'd think a smart gal like you would want to mull over such notions as racism."

She took a deep breath and started fiddling with her thumbs. "My uncle died fighting for the South. He was a good man, Ben. I can't just disregard everything he died for." She dropped her voice to a whisper. "I can't seem to let him go."

I looked at her, sitting there with her lower lip wiggling up and down, and I wanted to hug her tight to my body and never let go. She was struggling mightily against some unseen demons in her breast.

"He called me Little Red Reb because I was such a dutiful defender of the cause," she said. "I liked that he thought of me in that way. I wanted him to be proud of me."

I bit my cheeks with my back teeth so I wouldn't grin at the nickname. If she was the little one, then her daddy just had to be Big Red Reb.

She rubbed the cover of *Robinson Crusoe* and said softly, "I would have sent him this very book, but he died before I could do a thing to help ease his pain. I had so many books he might have liked, and now they're just collecting dust . . ."

With that, I figured she was set to cry, but she surprised me, for her eyes looked almost happy. She said, "When we first met, I felt superior to you. Me, with my clean clothes and big, important books. I thought those things meant something." She pounded on the book cover with a little fist and said, "But I'm the ignorant one here. All my education, all those books, didn't teach me to think with plain common sense. To question the things around me."

"It ain't your fault, Abby. It's what you were born to."

"I know that. But I still think the same way I always have. I don't know why, but my mind doesn't want to think differently. I *like* feeling superior! The other day, with Jacob, I tried to see past the color of his skin, to carry on as if it didn't matter. But it was still there, his blackness."

I laughed. "He'll always be a Negro. Can't change that."

She slammed her hand over her heart. "It's *me* that I'm afraid I can't change. You were right to be hard on me. And I won't begrudge you if you don't want anything to do with me anymore."

"Aw, you can't get rid of me that easy, Reb. Sounds to me like some shifting's gonna take place up there in your brain, so that folks sit on a more even place, all together like."

Abby sighed and rubbed her forehead with a shaky hand.

"Oh, come on now. Take a look at me, sitting here every afternoon, displaying my ignorance day after day in the company of a pretty gal. You've got to know anything's possible if you just want to work at it."

She reached across the table then and grabbed my wrist real hard. It was the first time that I had actually felt her. Just like I had thought, her skin was soft as a butterfly wing. But her bones underneath were hard as nails. My whole arm burned up to the shoulder socket. She just lit me up.

But I couldn't even enjoy the feeling on account I heard someone cough real loud, right close to the window. It gave me pause, wondering if someone was spying on us. Abby must have worried, too, for she let go of my wrist right quick. I started to wonder if I had dreamed the whole thing up.

We sat for a while, shy like, watching a long line of pelicans flap down the shore. After a bit she said, "I let the horse go. I couldn't feature her pulling our cart around the very land she used to roam free. It just wasn't right."

I chuckled at her newfound pluckiness. And I felt such goodness, like the pop of a backbone, thinking on that red pony wandering the beaches free again. I never should have offered her up to begin with. "Your daddy know you did that?"

"No, not yet." She grinned. Then she pulled out her slate, but after all that talking there wasn't much time left for the lesson. Soon enough, though, we got to *Robinson Crusoe*.

Maybe it was just me, but I felt she read the words with a new fire in her voice. She read right loud, too. She was rooting for Friday, I could tell.

⟨∞⟩

Eliza lived close by Pap and me, out in the scrubby wooded flats just a touch south of the Nags Head Hotel, with her mama, her two young brothers, and her old granny. Their diggings was near to as small as ours, but had a real fine view of the sound through an opening in the trees.

Taking the view, I waited on a rotten step for Eliza to freshen up after work at the fishery, where she spent her days mending the seine nets. She was real good with needle and thread—her granny having taught her back when her eyes were good—and was now making regular pay doing what she was good at. I was right proud of her.

But I was starting to sweat with nerves, thinking on what I was about to do to the woman I'd thought to marry someday. I tried to black out the memories I had of Eliza as a youngun, full of grit, with her dark eyes and brown body, running the sand hills and swinging on the treetop grapevines with me.

She always took to playing with the boys, having no desire at all for more feminine accomplishments. We were so alike, looking at Eliza was like looking in a mirror. We guzzled moonshine, snuffed tobacky, swam naked in the ocean, ran away to Roanoke Island and hid in the marshland—we did all that with each other. Now a grown woman, she shot, rode, fished, and managed the boats as good as any strong-armed Banker man.

But as good a woman as she is, she never made me want to look inside her brain, to see all the things that she knew piled up like freshly cut firewood. She never made me want to reach inside her and pull out a long-lost treasure, swipe the sand off it, and hold it up to the sun to admire its quality.

And her touch never burned down to my bones, the way Abby's touch did today.

Soon I heard the screen door slam and her old boots clomping. I smelled her particular scent of woodsmoke and chicken fixings. But when I turned to see her, she was wearing a real fine dress I'd never laid eyes on before. And her brown hair was pinned up on top her head in a circular fashion. I just stared at her, my mouth agape.

She guffawed. "My, my, I never seen a man so dumbfounded for words. What d'you think, Mister Whimble? You like me in it?"

She twirled 'round two whole times so I could see the full display of the white dress. It hung a little in back, where a gal like Abby might have worn something or other underneath, but otherwise it fit her just fine.

"I think it might make a real fine wedding dress . . ." she hinted, a twinkle in her eye.

I had trouble convincing my mouth to spurt out its words. "Wedding dress? Oh, well, I don't know . . . Where did you come by it? Did you make it yourself? I could believe that, with your fingers." Eliza spun her own cloth and made her own clothes, long as I could remember.

"Some housekeep gave it to Mama at the market a while back, said there was no need for it anymore in her lady's house. Mama—who's not much for handouts from townsfolk, you know—looked it over and declared it to be almost brand-new and made right well, so she agreed to take it off her hands. The dress being as fine as it is, I think she was looking ahead to the day of our nuptials, too. Whenever *that* may be!" She kicked me in the left hind cheek with the toe of her boot, and not so gentle, neither. "But I don't care for it that much—it don't even have pockets. There's nowhere to put anything. And I'm bound to get it dirty in a split second."

I knew my face was a block of stone about then. The dress looked all wrong on her, like she was playacting in the theater. Can't say why, but it made me angry, seeing Eliza trying on a dress that didn't suit her.

I mumbled, "Ain't it bad luck for the groom to see the bride in her wedding garb before the wedding?"

"Pshaw—I don't believe in that foolishness, and with our good fortune lately, who need worry about silly tales like that?"

Oh Lord, I couldn't even look at her pinned-up hair. My guts filled with guilt, and the damned gallnippers started biting on my ankles.

"Something wrong, Ben? You look poorly, all a sudden . . . You still tuckered from that ocean swim?" She sat down on the step with me, caring nothing for her white dress on this moldy wood. She ran her rough hand over my cheek.

The half moon rode low in the sky tonight, filling the spaces between the pine trees with cool light. The marsh frogs sang their night songs. I reached over for her hand, started stroking its work-tough skin.

I took a big breath. "Eliza, I got bad news for us. I hate hurting you, you know I care much for you and have for a long while, since we were younguns."

I tried to keep her hand in mine, but she pulled it right away.

Her eyes were so dark now. Little black stones. "You're leaving me, ain't you."

I nodded, head hung down in shame. This was the second time

today that I had let down someone I loved. "I can't lie to you. I never have been able to. For some time now I have felt strong feelings for someone else. It's mighty strange, given that I still care for you. But I don't want to lead you into thinking about marriage with me, knowing that I can't enter into it with a truthful heart. Which is what you deserve."

She let out such a terrible screech it nearly popped my eyeballs outta their holes. "It's that Abigail, ain't it? I knew this was going to happen, I did! She had her claws into you from the get-go! I saw how she looked at you, come running down there on July Fourth to find you, and all the while knowing you were with me! I declare, she's a no-good, calculating, slick little witch! And with her leaving at the end of the summer, too! She's not worth it, Ben! Don't pine over someone that don't deserve your affection!"

I saw Abby in my mind as she appeared that day of the shipwreck, with her long hair water-logged like red seaweed all 'round her white face, with pride for me written all over it. I felt then that I'd won some sort of carnival prize, even though a man's life was gone.

"I can see how you'd think unkindly of her, but she ain't like that. To tell you the honest truth, I ain't sure if she'd ever have me. But I can't find out, knowing I'd be dodging behind your back."

"You can't *find* out, and expect me to be waiting on you when it all goes to shit," she hollered. "I ain't that kinda woman, Ben! You can't treat me so, and expect me to swaller it down and ask for more!"

The cicadas in the trees seemed to ratchet up their music all of a sudden. The pine needles on her porch smelled musty and dark.

"Well, I know that, Eliza. I want you to have a good life with a man that can love you, I do. I thought it would be me. It's awful for you to hear, but there it is."

"What do you s'pose is gonna happen when you declare your

affections for little miss fancy skirts? You think she's gonna throw her books in the air and swoon with happiness? She'll probably laugh you right offa that porch, featuring herself with a poor fisherman. She won't ever love you like I do, Ben."

It was true, Abby might not ever take to me in that way, but I didn't care none. I had to go whole hog.

Eliza's face was peaked in the moonlight. "And here I thought that wearing this dress would make you see me the way you see her. I wanted to look nice for a change, thought that would make the difference with you." Tears ran all over her thin brown face.

"And you look pretty as a picture, believe me. But it ain't her dry goods, Eliza."

She cut her dark eyes at me. "Maybe it's what's underneath those fine clothes you're hungering for. Maybe you'll get a taste of the top crust and find it a little too tough. Then what'll you do? Come find ol' Eliza, sample her wares?"

"No, it ain't like that, either. It's mighty hard for me to explain. She just has some quality that's . . . worth wondering on." I couldn't say it all to her, the way Abby and I just went together, and helped each other along, like two oars moving a boat.

"Is it 'cause she can *read*? That ain't no circumstance! I could learn my letters, if I *wanted* to. Problem is, I don't want to! I like who I am, unlike you, who can't stand himself and who's reaching for things he can't have!"

She was having herself a conniption fit, with her hands stuck flat over her watering eyes, and I was sore afraid that Mama Dickens was gonna pop out to see what the matter was. She'd prob'ly lash me there on the spot. So I thought to take my leave, slink away like a scolded dog that's shat in the house. Eliza's sadness was too awful to witness.

I searched and struggled for the proper good-bye. "I still want to know you, Eliza. When we get over this rough patch, I mean. You're my best friend. Oh Lord . . . I'm sorry to botch us up like this . . ." I trailed off.

She looked out to the slapping sound and whispered my name over and over. Nearly set me to crying myself. I had to leave her then.

CHAPTER TEN

Benjamin Whimble
July 23, 1868

I descended a little on the side of that delicious vale,
surveying it with a secret kind of pleasure (though
mixed with my other afflicting thoughts)—to think that
this was all my own, that I was king and lord of all this
country indefeasibly, and had a right of possession; and
if I could convey it, I might have it in inheritance, as
completely as any lord of a manor in England.

—ROBINSON CRUSOE

NAGS HEAD WOODS IS, IN MY HUMBLE OPINION, WHAT HEAVEN MUST LOOK
like, except it's here on Earth for us to enjoy. You have never seen
such a forest, 'specially one situated between big sand dunes like it is.
The woods grow up real thick in the dunes' shadows, out of the sea
spray and wind.

When you're inside the woods, you'd never guess the spot was midway between the Roanoke Sound and the Atlantic Ocean, it's that much like a true forest. There's near to about five miles or so of pine trees, and oak and hickories, too. Beeches, red maples, dogwoods, hollies bigger 'n those on the mainland. It's unusual they grown so tall out here on the island, and I sure do respect their rebellious natures.

Everyone who's anyone goes to the freshwater ponds in the woods to fish and carry on, since they're only about three miles or so from the Nags Head Hotel. Folks take horse and cart through a winding sand trail along the sound to get there.

The Fresh Ponds are so wide and deep you'd think you were in the mountains, and today we were heading for Great Pond, the biggest one of them all.

At times during the summer there were more fishing rods than fish in the water. The fishing ain't like it used to be, that's for certain. Pap's told me some legends of yore about catching all kinds and sizes of fish in the ponds, but I've never seen such glory there, myself.

Feeling all out of sorts, I tagged along this morning with my buddies Harley and Jimmy on Jimmy's daddy's ol' buggy. Even Jacob agreed to come along for a bit of a holiday.

We fished for a couple hours in the quiet early morning, afore the vacationers came along to scare the few fish away. It was just the fish and us, breathing the cool forest air. Harley decided he was fit to be famished, so we got off the dory to fry up some of the perch we caught. While the fish and doings of bacon and onion was sizzling up nice, I told the boys about breaking it off with Eliza.

"That mean she's free to go out with me, then?" Jimmy jibed. "All the good women on this island are spoken for."

"No, that ain't what that means. You keep your stinking catfish whiskers offa her if you know what's good for you," I said.

Jacob said, "Why'd you do it, Ben? You ain't hankering for that Abigail, are you?"

Harley called, " 'Course he is! Pretty piece like that. Wouldn't you? I see you're a Negro and all, but still. She could make you happy. You could have some nice yellow-skin babies, with freckles galore."

I popped some corn bread into my mouth and said, "Listen, don't go wagging your tongues all over the island now. But there *is* something 'bout a smart schoolmarm that sets the heart afire."

They punched each other in the arms as I turned the fish over in the pan. "I couldn't go behind Liza's back. And you know, I *surely* couldn't get caught cheating on Mama Dickens!"

They all guffawed at that one. Eliza's mama's bad temper was legend 'round the Banks. She ran off her husband, old Jonas Dickens, over ten years ago. Folks used to hear her screeching and hitting him with the frying pan way past the middle of the night, some nights. I thought he was a decent man, but Mama Dickens always said he was a good-for-nothing sack of potatoes, couldn't even clean fish proper. Last I heard, he took up with a roughshod clam-digger gal over on the mainland somewhere. Eliza hasn't seen him since, so I guess he *was* a bad catch, at that.

Jacob said, shaking his head back and forth, "Abigail must have learned you those letters of the alphybet real good."

"That she did, Jacob. That she did."

But instead of looking happy for me, Jacob looked right sad. I never knew he favored Eliza that much.

After that we ate our food in the peace of the cool woods. Then the boys started working at their musical instruments. Me lacking any sort of musical ear, I dove on in the pond for a swim. I splashed 'em after a while, bored all by my lonesome, so they quit their plucking and blowing and jumped in, too.

We were dunking each other and having a frolic when a cart chock-full of dressed-up ladies and gents came rolling into the woods, pulling a boat behind them. We all poked each other under the water and spoke low about how dense it was to dress up like that for a day of fishing and visiting. We just could never understand those folks from the mainland towns and their mixed-up ideas of fun.

Seemed like they couldn't do a thing without their driver, neither. He was helping them get off the cart and watering the bays and un-hitching the boat into the water's edge and fitting hooks, lines, and poles, while they were all cavorting around in their finery.

Having seen this spectacle many a time before, I swam over to Harley to dunk him again. Just as I was holding his head under the water and starting to feel like I was getting him good, I heard Jimmy say to Jacob, "I gotta say, those town gals sure do put our sweethearts to shame. That redhead one is a pure delight. Come to think, she looks like I've seen her afore."

Jacob looked over at the group and groaned. He plucked Jimmy hard on the head with thumb and forefinger and said, "Jimmy, that ain't just *any* redhead."

I let go of Harley's head like greased lightning, and up he came, sputtering at me. But I had caught sight of Abby's sweet face amid the trees and finery and his hollering wasn't a circumstance. She was talking right much with a young dandy about my age, with a nice suit of clothes and a thick head of hair. Abby was as pretty as ever in a puffy yellow dress and fancy hat. It sure was different to see her out-side in the world, away from our porch.

I called out, "Hey now, Abby! Didn't make you out for a fishing gal!"

The group of folks jumped when they heard me holler at them, and Abby gave a slow little wave at me with a gloved hand, then turned back to the feller.

My boys all looked at me stupefied, and then Jimmy whispered, "Looks like she got herself a beau, in any case. Now you don't have to make an ass of yourself."

Harley said, "Reckon you best make it up with Eliza now. You, loverboy, are all washed up."

They started snickering and falling all over themselves at the pickle I was in, so I got kinda defensive. "She likes me, boys. Just you watch this."

The group of folks was fixing to get in the boat with their rods and tackle and basket o' goodies, so I sauntered over to show off my skills. And blasted if they didn't turn to me slowly like I was some kind of varmint, something to be afeared of. Made me want to look over my shoulder to see what was lurking behind me, but I knew it was just me. As I walked, I snuck a glance down at my brown toes with the black lines of dirt beneath the torn nails and finally saw what folks like Abby saw: a poor, dirty Banker.

But I was still myself, in my own Nags Head Woods, so I just stuck my chest out and said, "If any of you needs any help at all with your fishing skills, Benjamin Whimble here, at your service."

They all just eyed my wet clothes, not saying a word. I felt mighty half-witted, standing there mumbling and dripping while they was all dry and nice. Why had I come over here in the first place?

"Fact is, I'm Abby's daddy's guide this summer, ain't that right, Abby?" Good God, I sounded as bumble-brained as I looked.

All her friends looked over at her, disbelieving that we could even know each other. I had caught the yellow-haired gal's attention, for certain. She looked at me real curious.

Abby fidgeted with her white gloves afore she said, real quiet like, "Yes, that's right. Benjamin knows the Outer Banks like the back of his hand. In fact, he's usually out fishing this time of day."

She gazed off a second, then said, "Benjamin Whimble, I'd like you to meet Hector Newman. His daddy is our family's doctor back home. And this is Madeleine Adams and Alice Monroe, and Red Taylor and George Wakefield, friends of mine from Edenton."

So that Hector Newman was her beau, then, all the way from the Yankee school. I'm no judge of men's outer looks, but I knew a slick catch when I saw one. I tried to keep from staring at the man.

I saluted them all and said, "How do, folks. And those ruffians over yonder in the water are Harley Stickle, Jimmy Juniper, and Jacob Craft. Don't pay them no mind at all if they start acting like they ain't got any sense. They don't know better."

The boys all waved their arms and grinned like cats in the sunshine, but Abby's group just muttered "How do you do" and then pulled foot, eager to be away. Even their driver eyed me suspicious.

Her beau stuck out a stiff, clean hand for me to shake. "Good to put a face to a name. I've heard a bit about you from Abigail. And I thank you for your offer of assistance, Benjamin, but I think we can manage. It *is* just fishing, after all."

With that, the fellers all set about helping the ladies into the boat. Never in my life have my fishing skills been so underhandedly slandered. I wanted to say, "I reckon we caught about all there was to catch this morning," but I didn't have the heart. I walked back to my boys with my sorry head hanging down.

"That went well, I reckon," joked Jimmy. "You're right, Ben, she likes you right well. Have you set a date for the wedding?"

"She's usually a spot more friendly than that, I will say," I said sadly. They wanted to laugh at me something awful, but thought better of it.

So we walked away from the pond and their pretend fishing party and lay down in the sun-dappled shade of the old trees, an unspoken agreement for a nap made between us. I rested my head on a duff of old leaves and breathed in the smell that I had loved my whole life. It was the smell of both rotten death and green growing life, and always reminded me how grand it is to be alive, even in this hard-luck world.

I thought on Abby and that feller Hector for a good while, and wondered what she saw in him. Maybe she liked her men clean and kept up, and in that case, I was up the creek without a paddle. I doubted my toenails could *ever* get clean.

After a while I slept and drooled in the cool forest, lulled in and out of dreams by a woodpecker's song. I dreamed of stormy ocean waters crashing on a perfect sunny beach, and Abby standing not on the sand but sitting atop the red horse in the middle of that rough ocean, as calm as you please.

In the midst of the dream, I had such a fierce longing to touch her warm face—real gentle like—with both my hands and just look at her for as long as I wanted. No books, no paper, no words a-tall to keep me from staring at her.

When I awoke from the mixed-up slumber, the sun was high in the sky and shining straight down through the branches. I sat up and the boys looked at each other with twinkles in their eyes. They took up their instruments—Harley on the banjo, Jacob on the fiddle, and Jimmy on the harmonica—and struck up a song they'd been working at.

Harley sang real soft:

> *"O here she comes, that gal o' mine*
> *Smilin' in her gown so fine*
> *She don't know she's in my dreams*
> *My stench makes her so sad it seems*
> *I've a notion to kiss her lips*
> *And lay my hands upon her hips*
> *Ooooh, I love my redhead beauty*
> *She's way too good for me*

I love my redhead beauty
The things she teaches me!
If I convince her I'm the one—and learn my letters every one
Then we will live forevermore—inside her house by ocean's
  door!
I love my redhead beauty
But she's way too good for me!"

I smiled polite and nodded my head, then said real peart, "If you ever play that song outside of these woods, I'll find you where you sleep and bash your brains to kingdom come with your music makers." They all whooped and hollered, knowing they had just gotten me good.

And I grinned along. The song did have a good beat.

About midday I smelled fish frying and figured Abby's folks were having themselves a picnic feast. I heard them all squealing and carrying on, so I was right surprised when Hector came picking his way real careful through the leaves and pine needles over to where we were sitting, trying to mend one of my old fishing nets. I couldn't ask Eliza to do it for me no more.

He bent over at the middle to speak to us like wayward younguns. "Abigail tells me you're a rather excellent guide, having had such success with her father this summer. I suppose you know how revered Nolan Sinclair is in Edenton for his hunting skills, so it means something to have a recommendation from him."

Oh, didn't I know it, all too well.

"Our little group expressed some desire to see the surrounding woods and the 'secret' sand dunes, so we thought it a good idea to bring the expert along. How about it, Benjamin? Care to show us around?"

"I can do that, sure. But those ladies don't look to be up for a nature hike in those clothes."

"Oh, well, right you are. We were *hoping* to travel in the cart." 'Course he was. Old Hector looked never to have walked a good furlough in his life.

I bade my comrades farewell, and as I was walking back with Hector, I heard them play the refrain from their new song. I had to stifle a snicker when Hector made comment on the boys' musical skills.

The ladies had already climbed atop the cart, tiny umbrellas at the ready. I couldn't get a read on Abby's shaded face, which neither smiled nor frowned. She had grown a stranger to me, away from the porch.

There wasn't room on the cart for me, so they all said, so I walked alongside, sometimes parting the thick growth of trees so the cart could make it through the path. I tried pointing out unusual sights, such as green orchids and the woolly beach heather, things you don't normally see in these parts of the country.

But the yellow-haired gal—Maddie Adams—groaned, "I declare, I've never been so bored in my life. I sure do hope you got something better than flowers and sticks up that ratty ol' sleeve, Benjamin!" She batted her eyes like she'd got some sand in them.

"Okay, Miss Madeleine. I can see you're a gal to be reckoned with. If flowers and sticks aren't your thing, maybe freaks of nature would grab your interest."

She looked me right through. "Oh, yes, I positively adore freaks of nature," she drawled.

We reached the point on the edge of the sound where the trees met up directly with a big sand dune called Run Hill. My favorite thing to do, when I had the time, was to climb the dune and sit at the top.

In the particular spot I'm speaking of, most of the trees are half buried in sand. See, the sand—so soft you'd never think ill of it—is slowly choking the trees as it marches slowly southwest toward the sound, little by little each year. The naked limbs reach out of the white sand piles like the arms of buried-alive corpses.

When I was no bigger'n a boy, those trees used to scare the daylights outta me. I'd have dreams of getting eaten by giant mounds of sand. The sand monsters had big dry holes for mouths, and they chomped after me as I ran. They'd eat me, and then I'd be a tree, buried alive. I'd reach down and my legs would feel just like bark, and my fingers felt like pine needles. I'd wake up gulping for air.

But I don't mind the sand trees now. Nature takes and nature gives. Even the trees that are cold as wagon tires, they're all part of the rarity, which includes a picture of the sound just behind the forest, and actual freshwater ponds that have bled into the skirts of the dunes. There's deer and fox and raccoons and freshwater fish, all on this tiny sandbar in the sea.

Abby was mesmerized by the sight and made to get out of the cart, so Hector scrambled 'round, trying to give his assistance.

Maddie said, "Oh, mercy, I forgot how much Abby loves to ramble around in nature. I suppose I'll accompany her this time, since sand drifts *are* so very interesting to look at. If Benjamin will be so kind as to help a lady off this godforsaken cart?" She reached her gloved hand out for me to help her.

The other folks looked cross, but I could see Maddie, being the biggest toad in the puddle, held sway over their attentions. They made a big deal about getting off the cart, and they soon cursed a blue streak when their fine shoes sunk almost knee-deep into the sand.

Maddie sat down on the edge of the cart, wiggled her feet at me, and said, "Now I can see why Mister Benjamin here doesn't wear shoes! Mine are so full of sand I can't stand it. But I can hardly bend over in these skirts to get them off. A little help?"

I stood there gawking at her, wondering if she actually aimed for me to help her off with her shoes. I wouldn't have the first concept of it, having never owned a pair in my life, 'specially not the ladies' kind. Thankfully, the feller Red nearly tripped himself trying to help her with the buttons.

Meanwhile, Abby was halfway up the dune, shoes and all, and holding her yellow skirts up high. Hector was trying to keep up with her but was having a devil of a time, huffing and puffing and sinking with his efforts. He stopped midway to get a hankie out to wipe his face, but Abby just kept climbing, hell-fired for the summit. The rest of the group just guffawed.

Maddie said, "Now, I always knew that Abigail Sinclair was cut out of a different kind of cloth than the rest of us. She's not as soft and delicate as some of us here."

With that declaration of feminine charms, she pulled a little tickler from the depths of her skirts and unscrewed it. "Anyone care to make this sorry adventure a bit more appealing? I'm not about to scale that dune in this dress Daddy brought me from New York."

All her friends took a little swig, then passed the tickler back to Maddie. She in turn passed it to me. "I'll bet you know how to handle your whiskey, am I right? Strong men usually do." She put her hand on my upper arm and gave a little squeeze, then tittered like a songbird, showing the dimples in her round cheeks.

I reckoned Maddie wasn't used to being told no, so I took a little swig of the old orchard, and it burned like the dickens going down. I took one more for good measure, then took off up the hill in search of Abby and Hector.

They had both made it to the top of Run Hill and were trying to catch their breath. Abby's bonnet hung down her back, and her hair was coming loose from her climb. And I didn't think I'd ever seen a splotchier face than Hector's. I had a notion to worry about him, but the feeling passed right quick.

I couldn't think about much anyhow, this high in the air. We stood there looking off to the Albemarle Sound, and at the very tops of the forest trees bunched along a freshwater pond below.

It was a warm, clear day, the best kinda day to enjoy such a view. Even though it was a good ten, fifteen degrees hotter out here than in the cool of the woods, the breeze blew strong. Abby's dress whipped backwards like a yellow flag.

It was peaceful here, like an empty church, and it seemed like we were the only folks on earth. I sorely wished skinny ol' Hector would vanish with the wind. I wanted to push him down the dune and watch his nice suit gather sand as he rolled on down to the pond below. And something told me Hector felt the same way about me. He stood so close to Abby that they shared the same shadow on the sand behind them.

She looked at a nearby pine tree that was buried to mid-trunk in the sand.

"I can't figure if this tree is alive or dead," she said.

The tree was a longtime favorite of mine. The dead branches had started falling off into the deep ploughs of sand, but the tree held on to a few sticks at the top that still had their green needles. Even the deader-looking branches had managed to keep some pinecones on them, dangling like ear fobs on a dead woman's lobe.

To add to her sickly look, brown vines, left over from better times, still wrapped themselves 'round the branches. The brittle vines most surely were dead, but they couldn't kick the habit of hanging on. I doubted they'd ever let go, their lust for strong branches forever in their veins.

"She's alive, but just barely," I said. "She's been struggling for years now. But I like to think she's biding her time. You know, taking shallow breaths, saving her water, staving off death 'til the sand finally moves southward and frees her. Trees are smart like that. It takes something to kill one."

Hector scoffed. "Trees don't think. If they did, they would have found some legs and run from this sand dune long ago. They're plants."

"I surely didn't mean to say trees think with *brains*. I meant they think with their hearts. There's a big difference."

He just shook his head. "Banker logic, I believe," he muttered to Abby.

But she said, "I think there's something to it. Sometimes I like trees better than I do people."

She started struggling through the sand, looking at all the dead trees and picking up pinecones and leaves. It was so quiet I could almost hear the trees gasping for help, like fallen soldiers lying in the ashes. Where she walked, the sand spread down the smooth dune like slow-moving river water. It was just like her, to walk where nobody had ever set foot before.

Abby turned to me and said, "It's a real struggle for life out here, isn't it?" Her green eyes were exploding with light up here so close to the afternoon sun.

I puffed out my chest and said, "It ain't easy, that's for certain. But that's what makes living here so special. It's what makes this place you're standing in so special. It takes a heap of toil and trouble to make something so beautiful."

Abby finally smiled at me then, a great big smile that caused her whole freckled face to shift upward. "Ben, the philosopher," she said.

And just like that, I was on top of the world, even if it was made out of sand.

With the sun sinking into the west over Roanoke Island, we made our way back down the hill to the other folks, who were getting right corned.

Maddie hollered out, "So, Benjamin, was that Negro with y'all a runaway slave before the war? I heard from my daddy that these islands were just swarming with no-good runaways and criminals once upon a time."

Her friends looked on like a pack of jackals. "You mean Jacob? Naw, he was born free, down in Ocracoke. He's got family there still."

"And do tell, do you keep him around to wait on y'all? Or are you actually friends with him?" She seemed serious, but with someone like Maddie, you could never rightly tell.

"Sure, Jacob is one of my best friends. He's a real jack o' trades, that one. He's a pilot and boat builder, and he can fish most folks out of the water. You should get him to tell you some of his yarns—they're famous 'round here."

Maddie snorted the air through her little nose. "If only we could understand his African gibberish."

Red piped up. "We don't usually speak with niggers, unless it's to tell them where the work is."

I stopped dead in my tracks and clenched my jaws. I hadn't heard that word in many years, and I wished to God it had been snuffed out along with slaving.

Then, out of the blue, Abby said, "Stop it, you all." And there was something in her schoolmarm manner that bade the cussed fools to shut up. "During that storm we had a few days ago, Jacob tried to resuscitate a drowned man, a man Benjamin here had pulled to land all on his own through the stormy sea. I saw it all right before my eyes. Jacob is a good man, a hero."

They all stared at Abby with dead eyes. They were trying to make sense of her little speech, but I could tell they were having a devil of a time. I doubted they'd ever heard a planter's girl step up for a Negro before.

Then Abby looked over at me with proud eyes. And with that one look, I knew that she had been acting so off-put because of the present company she was keeping. She was ashamed of them, but couldn't say so.

I thought the whole thing was done with, but Maddie declared, "Getting pulled from the sea by Benjamin might be a real treat, but getting resuscitated by a Negro—you've got to be joking! I'd rather die!"

I snorted. "I doubt the sailor would have cared what color the man trying to save him was."

Then Red said, "Seems to me like he died because a Negro was working him over! Should have been a white man doing that kind of work."

I hollered, "Now, you can't talk that way out here, folks. It ain't like on the mainland. And it shouldn't be like that there, either. What the hell is wrong with you Edenton folks?"

At that, I turned to leave them, even though it didn't feel right to leave Abby there on her own.

Maddie whined, "Awww, Benjamin, come back, now. Lordy, we didn't know you were such a nigger lover!"

I squirmed all over and walked on fast, ahead of the bumping cart on the pathway, 'til their liquored snickerings faded away. There was no telling what those uppity folks put the blacks through back in Edenton. I doubted they were freer now than they were before the war ended.

I shook my head in disgust. Out here, Jacob was as free as any man, with work to do and money to be made. Not too long ago we were out on the ocean fishing for blues, and he said to me, "I'm one lucky man, to be born and bred on the Outer Banks. On this here boat, on this here water, I'm free to do as I please."

And I had to agree with him. During the war, I had seen many runaways smuggled to Union territory on the boats of black watermen just like Jacob. With nothing but cotton sacks pulled tight over their only possessions, they'd hide in cotton bales or trunks on the boats. Then they'd hide out in the swamps 'til things died down, a whole town of runaways living on the lam.

That's how bad they wanted their freedom. And the Banks was a better place than most for them.

But now I saw what Abby was up against, with friends like those folks. They were likely all in the same club as her pap. I thought she was real brave to try to go against the tide like she was. But the more I thought on it, I was afraid for her, too. That tide was mighty high, maybe too high to get over on her own.

CHAPTER ELEVEN

Benjamin Whimble
July 25, 1868

... but it occurred to my thoughts, what call, what occasion, much less what necessity, I was in to go and dip my hands in blood, to attack people who had neither done nor intended me any wrong—who as to me were innocent ...

—ROBINSON CRUSOE

SATURDAY MORNING WAS GROWING MERCIFUL HOT WHEN I MET UP WITH Mister Sinclair on the docks. He didn't even want to fish today, and I had planned a nice outing on the ocean, hoping to catch a breeze, as well as some sea bass.

The change in plans made the hairs stand up on the scruff of my neck. This threatened to become a custom.

He pulled on my elbow. "Come on. Let's get a drink at the hotel. It's too damned hot out here."

I'd never actually set foot inside the hotel. It was a place for rich vacation folks, mostly. Folks exactly like Mister Sinclair. Even me and Pap conducted our fishery trade around back.

"I don't think I'm dressed proper for that. Don't I need shoes?" I asked, hoping to waylay the man.

But he just snickered. "Not if you're with me."

On the way, he curled his arm around my shoulders, weighing me down even more. He said softly, "Ben, you heard of a man called Elijah Africa?"

I nodded, a lump growing in my gizzard. His red beard looked like red ants feasting in the sunlight. "I heard of him, sure. He's the preacher of a church on Roanoke Island. Every Sunday the church is packed to overflow, every colored man, woman, and child coming to hear his sermoning. Some say on a good day you can hear his voice clear across the Roanoke Sound."

With a name like Elijah Africa, I thought even white folks might want to see what he was all about. But I just knew Mister Sinclair wasn't all perked up about the man's sermoning.

Mister Sinclair talked real quiet now, as we walked through the hotel, a-bustle with folks getting ready for their outings. "He's the one we're looking for. This preacher—Elijah Africa—is not who he says he is. He's a bad man, Ben. The worst of the worst. We think he's a runaway slave called Elijah Bondfield. But we've got to make sure before we take him."

"What do you think he did?" I choked out.

"Back in fifty-nine, he killed his master and mistress with a hatchet. He's been on the run ever since."

My eyes bulged. "Lord almighty! And you think a killer like that has turned preacher?"

His put his finger to his lips to shush me, even though the hotel tavern was empty so early in the morning. "You can see why folks want him caught. We'll take him down, then the rest of the darkies that follow him will go down with him. I'd say Jesus himself handed him to us, it's so perfect."

I wasn't so sure Jesus would involve himself in all that muck, but I kept that to myself. Mister Sinclair walked over to Jeb Mitson, the hotel desk man, and gestured with him for a bit. Then he came back with a grin on his face. Soon after that, Jeb came running over with two glasses of whiskey, straight up.

Mister Sinclair took a big drink, then waited for Jeb to skedaddle. "None of us knows what he looks like, except the dead man's oldest son. Trouble now is, we've gotten so many different descriptions of the reverend that we can't be too sure he's the one we want.

"People say he's as tall as me, the biggest Negro they've ever seen. Then others say it's just his girth that sets him apart. Then others say it's his manner of presenting himself, real uppity. It's made us wonder a bit.

" 'Course, my comrades want to string him up first and check for identification later. The reverend is trouble any which way you cut it. But Hugh—he's the Bondfields' oldest son—really wants to keep him alive, if you catch my meaning. And you can't blame him. He's been dreaming about his revenge for years."

The whiskey tasted like poison in this warm room. I said, "What did the man look like then?"

"Hugh remembers him to be real tall. 'Course, he was just a boy back then. But he did recall Elijah's holier-than-thou demeanor. Apparently he was always trying to learn." He looked at me like he was about to give up the secret of a magic trick. "The only thing he remembered for sure that could set him apart was the brand of the letter *B* on Elijah's right shoulder blade. Hugh's daddy branded all of his slaves, for just such an occasion as this." He glanced around and whispered, "You think you could set eyes on that brand for me?"

I rasped, "How in tarnation you expect me to do that? I ain't in the habit of laying eyes on half-naked men! Why don't you get one of your own people to look on him?"

"Look, I told you I need a local man, someone to blend in and move around like he knows what the hell he's doing. We don't want to scare him off. It took us this long to find the bastard, and we damn sure aren't going to let him loose again."

He held his glass back and shot down the rest of the whiskey. His breath, when he whispered at me, smelled of stale onions, tooth rot, and alcohol, the nauseatingest scent I ever sniffed. "The men involved in this are upstanding leaders—state politicians and attorneys-at-law and such. They can't be sneaking around some little island, peering at Negroes. You understand? We can't be implicated in this." He smiled a wicked devil kind of smile at me. "I've been helpful to you this summer, haven't I, Ben?"

I nodded. "I appreciate it all, Mister Sinclair. Don't want you thinking I don't. But . . ."

He turned his face away from me then. "Are you shirking your responsibilities to me, Ben? Because if you are, I can take away everything I've given you, like that." He clapped loud, making me jump. "My friend needs me, and I need *you*."

He snapped his long fingers at Jeb and ordered another round.

I said under my breath, "What are you going to do with him if you find out he's the one?"

"That's something you don't need to know. We'll take care of our own business. We don't like to involve the authorities, usually. They're too soft these days to do hardworking white folks justice."

That didn't sound good at all. The whiskey simmered in my stomach and my damp shirt was all sticky on my back. I mumbled, "I still ain't got the foggiest notion of how to sneak a peek at his backside, Mister Sinclair."

He laughed. "You're a clever boy. Just figure it out, will you?"

He leaned back on the stool, stretching his long back. "I'll be staying at the cottage, you know. Crops are growing up now, and I aim to enjoy myself for a couple of weeks. Come find me when it's done. And listen, don't let on to him what you're doing, and be quick about it. Justice is waiting on you."

Justice, he said. I truly wondered how I had gotten into this fix. This was some low-down, tricky kind of work, only fit for the world's scummiest scofflaws to carry through. It made me mad, thinking Mister Sinclair wanted *me* to do it. *He must think I'm desperate.*

But I reckon I was, at that. I wanted that Hatteras job like I'd never wanted anything before. And I wanted to keep seeing Abby, and learning how to read and write. Didn't know what I'd do if I couldn't meet up with her on the porch anymore. I figured if I did what he wanted, the debt would be paid and I'd never have to worry about this mess again.

And too, Elijah Africa was right respected around these parts. He might not be the man Mister Sinclair wanted after all. From what I'd heard, those kind of men had been known to make mistakes in their pursuit of "justice."

I said my farewells and slipped off the stool and out the door. 'Round the back of the hotel I hurled up the whiskey into a patch of sea oats. It smelled undigested, pure liquor, and I featured that little patch of green choking on it and dying a quick, painless death by the end of the day.

⬯

Sleep was not easy coming that night. Pap was blowing air out his mouth every other second—sounded like a snake hissing at me.

He'd like to slumber the days away if he could, life was stringing him out so.

But me, I just rolled around on my pallet, wracking my brain for a way to help Mister Sinclair. The man meant business, that much was clear. Taking my leisure just wasn't an option. But how to get sight of a naked Negro was a new and different kind of dilemma for me, and my brain just wouldn't latch on to an idea. The only thing I could figure to do was to peep at him through his cabin window.

But I didn't have the slightest idea of his daily habits. I reckoned I'd have to watch him for a good while. Watch him without him knowing I was watching him. It was the only way I could think of doing it.

So without catching a wink, I went over to the island before Pap even awoke, so I wouldn't have to tell him lies about where I was off to.

I took the old dory boat and rowed around to the western side of the island. I docked at an old Union pier and set to walking toward the colony, not really knowing what-all I was scheming to do.

It was Sunday morning, a sunny day with birds singing and water slapping. But I had no appreciation of the beauty, like I usually did. I felt sick all through my guts, to tell the truth. I felt like a puppet, and the evil spirit of Mister Sinclair was working the strings. I wouldn't wish the feeling on my worst enemy.

I soon found myself at the Sheltering Oaks Baptist Church. With a big sigh, I crouched myself in a stand of thick oak and holly trees, where I had a view of the comings and goings. Didn't know what else to do but wait 'til the service started.

Wasn't the first time I'd done such a thing, watching animals go about their lives from a secret spot. Just like hunting, really. And I was damn good at hunting.

I recalled the first time I took Mister Sinclair duck hunting in Currituck, back in November. He had surprised me with his skill, near about killed as many birds as I did on my best days. He fired his gun over and over, steady and quick, and I saw the splashes of the canvasbacks hitting the water. He recharged again and again, black smoke lingering around him. He just wouldn't stop 'til he was sure they were all dead.

He was so pleased then that he booked my services for the summer. Now that first hunting adventure seemed like some kind of fate for us. I wish I'd never met the man, but then I wouldn't have met Abby. And that is what Abby would call "ironic."

'Round nine o'clock a whole bunch of black folks came 'round to the front of the church. Squinting through the twisted branches, I counted about a hundred of them. They were a mighty scraggled lot. Unshaven, raggedy old clothes, bare feet, skinny limbs everywhere you looked. Only a couple of the women folk had bandannas and bonnets, and the rest were bareheaded, their snarled hair blowing free.

But they all seemed in right happy spirits. Laughing and talking and singing made their way to my ears, and the folks weren't even in the church yet.

Then I saw the preacher stroll up, hands full of papers and Bibles. Even from my spot, I could see he was right tall and strong-armed and as dark as a ripe blackberry.

He greeted the folks kindly, patted the children on the heads and gave them some sweetmeats from his coat pocket. They all followed him into the church like they were pups following the scent of cooked meat.

When I heard his voice boom out his sermon through the church windows, I had a hell of a time featuring him to be the killer Mister Sinclair said he was. That voice was like God himself. The man was meant to be a preacher—no one else could have sounded as right as he did.

After the sermon, he led a chant in his low, deep voice, and the Negroes answered him in the same tone. It wasn't really singing so much as shouting and, every once in a while, moaning. I heard them stamping their feet and clapping their hands in time to the song. It was miles apart from any church song *I'd* ever heard.

Just when I thought they were done, and moving on to some other kind of worship, they'd start up again, in a new and different tone of voice, sometimes sad, sometimes happy.

And I thought it to be true, what I'd heard about hearing those voices clear across the Roanoke Sound. Jesus Christ could hear them, clear up in heaven. I reckoned that was the point of it all.

Listening to the noise, I forgot my problems for a minute or two. The birds in the trees above me took off on account of the jollification. And then I was up in the warm blue sky, looking down at myself, my poor body sitting in a tight spot. I had pity for that body and for what he felt he had to do to get ahead in this world.

∞

When the service was over, I watched the folks stream out of the church and spread out down the island. The preacher took his time moving on, though. He talked to folks for a good long while before he made his way toward the colony proper, younguns and mamas in tow.

I followed along in their dust, slowly and with my cap down over my eyes. They soon met up with Lincoln Avenue and meandered down the lane for a while. No one took any notice of me, just like Mister Sinclair had reckoned. Finally I saw the reverend go up to a house about midway down and walk in and close the door. Folks called their good-byes to him as they continued on down the lane. I'd found his house, I figured.

It was a tidy-looking cabin, and his garden was one of the few that was free of weeds. I caught sight of some real nice tomato plants. I thought of the preacher building that house with wood he split himself, and I tried to block out the hopeful feeling he must have had as he hung the doors on their hinges.

I looked around for a good spot to watch him from. All along the back of his plot were some scrubby yaupon bushes and red cedar trees, the ones that weren't fit to fall under the ax. Could hardly see the sound through the hedge, it was so heavy. Preacher probably left it all there to protect his yard from overwash. It all looked like a pretty good hideout to me.

I backtracked a bit up the lane, then walked down the slope of sand along the sound and snuck into the brush from the back. I burrowed into the thick part of the bushes quick, the fallen leaves pricking my knees and palms as I crawled. Scared a couple of meadowlarks out, their tweetings fussy and trespassed against.

And there I sat, cross-legged as a Indian, peering out of yaupon bushes like I didn't have a lick of sense about me. Felt like I was in a fever dream. Couldn't even think straight, my whole head pounding like a drum. What was I going to do, catch him running buck naked around his backyard?

I couldn't even move a hair in this little space, branches on top of me like they were. I caught myself breathing too quick and tried to slow it down. Everything was moving too fast for me. I wasn't used to all this rushing 'round, trying to make other men's wishes come true.

I had my own wishes that needed coming true. But I didn't see anyone lining up waiting to help me out. Lord, the only one that *had* helped me out was Mister Sinclair himself. And that thought turned over and over on itself in my mixed-up brain, like a fatty piece of bacon in a sizzling-hot pan.

Half an hour went by, and I still could see folks out walking 'round the streets like regular people, happy on a Sunday, and here I was, stuck in a bush.

I saw a woman carrying a pot of something down the lane, and she walked right on up to the preacher's front door. I heard him talking to her kindly on the other side of the cabin, and I heard her answering him with a big, shiny voice. She went on and on—sounded like she wanted to do more than cook him his meals. Then I heard the door close again. Must be nice to have women bring you your meals all cooked up. Must be one of the perks of being a preacher man out here.

I watched her meander back down the lane again, her rump bumping slow from side to side. Soon I caught the scent of cooked pork through the windows, and it made my own belly start growling like a dog. But I didn't have a thing to eat or drink. *What I wouldn't do for a bowl of boiled oats and butter right about now,* I thought. *Even some well water would do.* It was hot as blazes, even under all those bushes.

I tried not to think about those things for a while. I tried not to think about anything at all. Sitting there by my lonesome was not helping matters, though. I began to think on good ol' Robinson Crusoe, and his twenty-odd years of alone time.

Would anyone even miss me if I went away that long? Would Abby miss me if I got shipwrecked on some wee bitty island? We hadn't known each other long, it was true. But I already felt as close to her as I'd ever felt to anyone, or anything. I wondered what she thought about me, if she ever did.

And yet, if she could see me sitting here in this bush, spying on a preacher man, she'd be shocked into hating me. After all we'd talked over, she'd gather up those skirts and books and papers and strut back into that cottage, never to be seen again. I don't think I could bear it if she ever found out about this.

Another hour, and still no sign of the preacher. I figured he lived there by himself, no sign of offspring, and women visiting with food. His yard in back was clean, no junk littering his land, unlike ours. Just the outhouse and a little shed and a few stumps. Even had some blue hydrangea bushes planted next to the house.

Pap and I had a big shed, a stable for Junie, boats and boat parts scattered all over, and nets and poles and old tools and a big garden with all manner of vegetables and herbs and whatnot. Trees big and small grew willy-nilly over it all, and dropped their own mess of pinecones and leaves and needles and deadness in the mix.

I wondered what the differences in the yards meant, what they told or didn't tell about the folks that owned them. Sometimes things that are too neat and orderly set my teeth on edge. A big mess is a sign of life, to me.

After a while the flies and gallnippers found me, like they knew I couldn't move a muscle, somehow. They swarmed off the marshes and took to biting me all over, so I spent my time slapping at 'em and cursing as quiet as I could. I made it into a game, seeing if I could swat the buggers before they stung me. I won the game thirty-six times before I stopped counting.

I heard Elijah moving about in the house, pushing back a chair or scraping a plate, cleaning up his pork dinner. But he never saw fit to come outside. Part of me wished he wouldn't ever show his face, and this awful thing would just be done with, but the other part of me wanted to go in there and rip off his undershirt, lay eyes on his back once and for all, and skedaddle out the front door. But Mister Sinclair wouldn't take to that at all. Had to be done expert.

I fingered the glossy yaupon leaves in front of me. I'd never really sat and looked at one before. Bankers made tea from these leaves, and so did the Indians before us, but uppity folks from the mainland like other kinds of teas better. Pap and I still made it right regular, because it perked us up in the mornings. And too, it's said to have medicine qualities. I could've used some right then, for certain.

But my stomach had long ago given up on me and had quit its churning. I was empty as a bell. The Croatan Sound lapped the shore so gentle, and the gulls were crying so soft. Soon the lack of shut-eye lay heavy on me, so I curled up best I could and fell asleep, but with one ear pricked to the house.

I felt to be sleeping on *Tessa*, by my cranked-up posture. But I didn't feel the water under me, swaying me with a lullaby. Just the hard earth, a slab of unfeeling soil. I tried to see it with some emotion like love, as Abby did. A giver of food, a drinker of sun and water. And it helped me to relax some.

I imagined Abby's arms around me, and her kissing my neck with those rosy lips, and I soon got hard, thinking on such an unlikely occurrence. So I went back to thinking of the land with a little more dislike, and the hardness went away.

Every once in a while I heard the comings and goings of creatures in the scrub brush, tiny feet scrabbling on sandy leaves. Felt their eyes take in my shape, wonder if I was friend or foe. I dreamed that I was one of them, gnawing flesh off bones with sharp little teeth and claw hands and scurrying through hedges, looking for trouble.

When my body saw fit to arise, dusk had arrived, silvery-blue. Soon it was night, stars and moon showing themselves through the bush leaves. With the change in light, I could see the reverend had lit a lamp. An orange glow now shone out the two back windows.

I wiggled back out the bushes and stood up, my joints cracking like

Pap's. It felt so good to stretch I almost cried out. I pissed a few yards away into the sand, then I tippy-toed up to the back window, my heart hammering hard. I looked over the ledge to see what I could see, hoping to God there was a naked man in there somewhere.

And then I had to rub my eyes to make sure I wasn't seeing double. For there were books, books, and more books. Books of all shapes and sizes and colors were all over the room, stacked to the ceiling in some places. He likely couldn't walk 'round the room without stepping on a book.

The man had gathered a library in his own little house, and who would have known? Wearing a full set of clothes, the preacher himself sat at a table reading by a conch-shell oil lamp.

Now, I knew enough to know that books alone surely don't make a man. But this number of books, I had to wonder. A nauseated feeling washed over me, so that I almost bent double. Mister Sinclair had said Elijah liked his learning, and now, here was proof of that particularity. Learning was every which way you looked.

I stood outside the back window for a time, just watching him read. Every few minutes he'd stand up and look around in the piles for another book. Then he'd sit down again. He read late into the night, but I kept my knees locked and my eyes steady on his back, wishing I could see through the cloth of his white shirt.

Eventually he quit his reading and doused the lamp. I heard the rope bed creak as he sat down to take his boots off. Then, with a sigh, he laid back. In a minute he was snoring, the memories of what he'd just read likely swimming through his brain like flotsam.

I cursed to myself and stumbled back to the bushes quiet as I could on my tired legs. I crawled in again, ignoring the smart scratch one of the branches gave my forehead when it snapped back into place. I curled up on the sandy earth and put my hands over my eyes.

I laid like that for I don't know how long. But I still couldn't black out the unlikely picture of all those books from my sight. The ground under me seemed to spin a little, with my eyes closed like that. I started to feel sick all over. No food or drink, no place to stretch out. But was it all that, the missing of those simple comforts?

Not hardly. I couldn't feature what I was doing there anymore, spying on a black preacher with a habit of reading. I had sunk to the bottom, for sure. And just when I thought I was raising myself up a little.

The darkness pushed on me, the bushes around me with branches like claws. The sound water smashed the shore too close near me, and the gull cries and bullfrogs and crickets sounded harsh and full of hate.

I started to sob like a youngun that's just gotten the switch. A strangled sob, trying for silence over the hard stab inside. Tears slopped down wet as an oar splash, all over my neck.

Why was it so hard to get ahead in this world, is what I wanted to know. I had hurt my pap bad, I knew. I thought of his sagging face as I cried, as if I'd killed him myself. I couldn't stop thinking on the two of us, all different ages and sizes, together on *Tessa*. Fishing, talking, sleeping the years away.

Just being there on the boat, on the water, after Ma died had helped us both get over it. We didn't even *want* to go back home. I remembered Ma, with her vegetable garden, her scavenging habit. If she wasn't at home she was out on the beach, looking for washed-up treasures. Now she was just a brown-face blur in my mind, and up and down the shores she'd held my hand in hers, blue-veined and short-nailed. I could hardly remember her face, but I did recall that.

I'd gone and ruined those memories of simple times with my sky-high hopes, and they used to bring me a good measure of peace.

And now *this* shecoonery, some other men's business, not mine. I couldn't help thinking how I would feel if something bad happened to this man, this man I was spying on. This man I was hunting like a prize buck. If I knew Mister Sinclair, the man would be hanging from the nearest tree in a matter of days.

Did he deserve the punishment that would surely come his way? I reckoned it was punishment enough just being a hunted runaway in a white man's world. Justice was a squirrelly concept these days. Just when you thought you'd trapped it good, it snuck out a hole you never knew was there.

But next to all that was the dislike I felt for my own self. I'd always felt friendly with myself. I always knew I was trying my best. I'd cut myself some slack if the going got hard. But tonight my actions disappointed me, and the reasons for my behavior were far-fetched indeed.

I couldn't make myself walk away, though. I just could not leave that bush. I was weaker than I ever thought I was. My eyes saw not one thing, not even the branches in front of them. It was all dark.

The morning came around, after a long night of back spasms. My head swooned with lack of sustenance.

But the sky was yellow as a daisy, and already warm. The birds peeped in the trees like nothing unlikely was going on, just another day to sing their songs to. The sound clapped happy onto the sand just as it always did. It all made me feel even worse, if that was possible.

Just as I was getting ready to crawl out and do my business, I heard the back door bang and saw the preacher make his way toward the back of the yard. He had a red flannel and a towel with him, and a mess kit for shaving perched atop the bundle. *Could it be?* Looked like he was set to bathe!

I stopped my breathing quick and bade my body not to make a sound, for he was nearing right close to my hiding spot. But he passed on by through a little bare spot in the foliage, heading directly to the sound.

The shore was a few hundred yards from where I sat, so that early-rising neighbors or passers-by couldn't see a man bathing. I myself couldn't see him, so I had to crawl out from the bushes and maneuver myself across the land on my belly to get a better view. Anyone could see me, crouched in the open like I was. I was so scared, feeling like a baby turtle scurrying across the sand to the sea before it got gobbled up by the gulls.

But before I could even suck in my breath, the preacher pulled off the thin shirt he had on. And there was the scar. I saw it plain as day, like the preacher was putting on a show for me. I knew it was the capital letter *B,* and it was as long as my hand, formed into a raised silver scar on coal-black skin.

The mark looked old, like it had been there for years. But it had healed perfect, the lines of the branding iron fashioned just so. It must have hurt like the dickens, going on.

The preacher peeled off the rest of his clothes and put them in a pile in the sand, flashing buttocks and hamstrings slick as porpoise skin. This would have bothered me, on another kind of day, looking on a naked man.

But today I couldn't notice anything except that *B.* I couldn't take my eyes from it. Some slave owner had insisted on its appearance, just had to see his own initial marking what he thought to be his property. It made the letter *B* appear the devil's letter, as good as a

pitchfork or snake in conveying evil intent. *B* used to be a sweet letter, to me. *Baby, butter, bluefish,* even *Benjamin.* Such good, simple
words.

I wondered what the preacher must think when he saw that letter
mixed up in other words. *Bible* words. Words that are supposed to be
good. I wondered if it gave him pause in his sermoning.

The naked preacher took a few steps into the shallow water, gripping his flannel. But the beauty of the morning grabbed his attention
so that he stopped and stared around him. The sound stretched out in
all directions, and every inch of it glittered in the new sun.

He stood there knee-deep in the swishing water a good long while.
I wondered if maybe he was recalling the gunboats and dead soldiers
that littered the water just a few years prior. Or maybe he was remembering the hundreds of boats full of runaways, making their
way to the island in the darkness of night. Maybe he had been on one,
with hope in his heart for better days ahead. Or maybe he was just ap-
preciating the beauty of it all, and was thanking God for sparing him
this long.

I saw him hold out his arms, as if dancing with an invisible partner.
And then I heard his prayer, just a set of mumblings from where I
crouched. I heard him call out "Amen." And that's when he broke my
heart.

He set to washing himself with the flannel, a few strokes under his
arms and a swipe at his groin, while I crawled back into the bushes for
the last time. I heard him strop his razor, heard the water splash and
drip. I reckoned there was nothing like bathing in the cool Croatan
Sound in the early-morning light to set a happy mood for the duration of the day. I just hoped he'd stored a lifetime of such happy
moods in his heart, to ready himself for what lay ahead of him.

After he shaved, he dressed again and began to walk back up the yard. He was about halfway up when he stopped in his tracks and looked straight to the bushes where I sat. He must have heard me, but I can't say how he did. He looked and looked, and I stopped breathing. He was close—too close even for blinking. I stared, and saw that he was a good-looking man. His skin was smooth across his high forehead and wide cheekbones, and he had full, even lips, like the kind carved on some statue of old.

I saw him smile, but if it was to me in the bushes or to himself, I couldn't say. He walked back into the house, humming a tune to himself. I sat there a long while in my cold sweat, 'til I was sure he wasn't going to come after me with a hatchet.

Back at home that afternoon, I cooked up the most fish I'd ever put in one skillet, mixed in some cut-up onion and celery and salt and pepper, and ate every single bite before I could feel how full I was. Washed it all down with a whole bucket full of well water, too.

I belched like a drunk and stretched out on my old pallet, never knowing it could feel so soft before last night. It was curious to me, but my entire mind had gone blank. Just empty of all thoughts, good and bad both. I rested like that for a while, savoring the feel of stuff in my belly and breathing the familiar air of my cabin.

Then I got up and took off my shirt and britches and went back outside, out behind the shed, and filled the bucket with more water. I found a old rag—a shirt sleeve in a previous life—and dipped it in the bucket. Then I lathered up a chunk of cracked soap in it and scrubbed it all over myself, 'specially my fingers and toes. I rubbed so hard my skin turned raw as a sunburn, as I tried not to think about a red flannel splashing sound water over a scar in the shape of the letter *B*.

I looked into a old rusty mirror that hung from a nail in the shed, hardly recognizing myself, the faraway look in my eyes. I combed back my wet yellow hair and put on a old cotton shirt Eliza had mended a couple years back that was now the best one I had.

Near my feet was a bucket of yaupon leaves, already crushed and ready for sweating in the hogshead. I looked askance at the bucket, for I didn't think I'd ever be able to drink that tea again.

Then I climbed atop Junie and made for the cottage to meet up with Mister Sinclair, to give him the good news.

CHAPTER TWELVE

Abigail Sinclair
August 2, 1868

It was now that I began sensibly to feel how much more happy this life I now led was, with all its miserable circumstances, than the wicked, cursed, abominable life I led all the past part of my days. And now I changed both my sorrows and my joys: my very desires altered, my affections changed their gusts, and my delights were perfectly new from what they were at my first coming, or indeed for the two years past.

—ROBINSON CRUSOE

I COULDN'T GET USED TO SUNDAY WORSHIP AT THE HOTEL. WE DINED there so often, it just didn't seem right to call on God there as well.

I looked around at all the men and women, singing and reciting their very hearts out in their Sunday best, and wondered if I was the only one whose stomach was having a difficult time distinguishing between suppertime and worship time.

But my fellow worshippers were in their own hell. Most of them appeared more than a bit pickled from the previous night's celebrations at the hotel. It was a good thing that most of the revelers had only to drift their way from a hotel room to the dining parlor on Sunday morning, or else I doubted they would ever make it to church. Even at the cottage, we often heard the band's music until the early hours of the morning.

The tables in the dining room had been removed, and the room was lined with chairs that faced a podium. It was a long way from the grandiosely old St. Paul's, back home. Out here, we couldn't even find a proper reverend. The wool-haired Reverend Weatherly was shipped all the way from Elizabeth City each and every Sunday to give us our sermons.

But the effort was lost on me today. Episcopalianism was the furthest thing from my mind. I was still on the porch of the cottage, not in this makeshift house of God. New Testament passages had become the words of *Robinson Crusoe*, and hymns resounded with Ben's easy, musical twang.

During the sermon I thought of Run Hill, that haunted half-dead tree, and how Ben had looked when he stood at the top of the dune, looking down. As if everything below us was his kingdom, hard-earned and well-loved.

I had never seen such adoration before, in anyone. This island was *his* religion. I wanted to see through his eyes, not just pages from a book, but everything out here that there was to see.

I tried desperately to un-think Ben by helping Winnie in the kitchen that afternoon, much to her consternation.

"Miz Abby, I don't need you in here, a-stepping on my toes when

I'm trying to get the supper made. Don't you got something to read?"

"I just want to help you is all. What can I do?" I asked, trying to stir a big pot of stewed vegetables, scallops, and mussels on the stove.

She snatched the wooden spoon out of my hand. "If your mama saw you in here getting all mussed with Hector a-coming, she huff and puff so hard she start a hurricane to blowing! So scoot!" She shooed me out of the humid kitchen, pushing me on my back until I was in the dining room.

I decided I could at least help lay the table. She couldn't object to that, since Hannah was still out with Charlie and Martha, supervising their clam dig on the sound. And Winnie was frazzled nowadays, spending most of her free time waiting on Mama, who lay up in her bed all day, every day. She hadn't even gone to Sunday worship with us.

I was just taking the plates out of the china hutch when I heard a knock on the screen door of the western porch.

I saw through the screen that it was Ben, and I was so happy to see him that my face flared from my chest to my forehead. We didn't usually see each other on Sundays, and I had seen him every day this week. He had been unusually quiet and dedicated, too, as if he were in some kind of competition with himself.

"Sorry to bother you, Abby," he said, his voice shallow.

"Please, come on in," I said, holding the screen door open for him.

Winnie hollered out from the kitchen, "Only if his feet is clean! I just done mopped every last sand grain from the floor, and you know I can't stand grit under my shoes when I'm walking on a Sunday."

Winnie strove for perfectly clean floors on Sundays, even at the beach, where it was next to impossible. In Edenton, we referred to them as her "Sunday floors."

We both looked down at Ben's filthy feet, which were absolutely caked in sand. With heavy eyes, he said, "I'll walk 'round to the back. It ain't no trouble, Abby."

I walked with him along the porch to the ocean side. Hardly anyone was out strolling this afternoon, it was so hot. I didn't think I'd be able to sit outside with Ben for long, but I didn't want him to go, either.

To my surprise, Winnie elbowed her way out of the screen door with two glasses of sweet tea. "You always look to be spittin' cotton," she said to Ben.

He smiled at her. "Thank you kindly, Winnie." He drank the whole thing down in one rippling gulp and handed the glass back to her before she could go back inside.

But she didn't budge. For several long minutes, she just looked at the two of us sitting there, all alone. Finally she clicked her tongue, muttered something to herself, and banged her way back into the house.

I snickered, but Ben just gazed at the sea, gently curling into crescents against the shore. "Is something wrong?"

He stabbed his fingers through his crisp hair. "Oh, it's been such a hot day is all. And it being Sunday today, you know. I just don't care for Sundays anymore. And now it feels like God is punishing me with the heat."

He stopped himself then, and glanced at me as he fidgeted in his seat. "Your pap and me were out fishing off Roanoke Island, and we didn't catch a thing. Your pap's so downhearted, he plopped directly on a stool in the tavern and won't be moved."

I smiled ruefully. "I can just picture it."

He said, "About the only thing halfway interesting was seeing your Madeleine and a few of those other folks sailing across the sound, heading to Roanoke Island for a day trip. She blew me a kiss."

"That's Maddie for you. She told me she goes to the island some- times, to get away from her parents. No telling what she does over there all day, unchaperoned."

He nodded. "Lots of visitors to the Banks like to go there, it's such a pretty spot of land, and all alone like. It used to have a calming ef- fect on me, but I guess I've grown tired of it."

I cocked my head at him. "Why would you grow tired of it?"

"Oh, just gotten used to it, really. Beauty gets humdrum, you see it enough."

"That doesn't sound like you at all," I scolded. "What in the world is bothering you lately? You haven't been yourself all week."

He shook his head and said nothing.

I prodded, "It sounds like you've spent a lot of time on the island."

"I know it as well as I know Nags Head. It ain't very big."

I smoothed my skirts with sweaty palms. I murmured, "I'd love to see the Lost Colony fort."

"Ain't much to see, tell you the truth. Just a few old outlines," he said. But then his face brightened up suddenly. "I could take you there, if you can get away sometime. You'd like it, I reckon. Full of history, more things to pack away in your brain."

I said as calmly as I could, "I'll see if I can get away. Tomorrow morning, maybe."

My mind immediately conjured plausible excuses. I could tell Mama that some of the Edenton folks were going, too, maybe even Hector Newman. She would be pleased enough to let me go alone, most likely. And I doubted she would ever find out the truth.

He said shyly, "You got time to teach me today? I don't want to wreak havoc on your Sunday . . ."

"Winnie would be more than happy to get me out of the cottage. And I like teaching you."

He narrowed his blue eyes at me. "You do?"

"I think we're doing pretty well, don't you?"

"I reckon we've *both* come a long way. Remember I couldn't even spell my own name?"

"And remember when I thought Robinson Crusoe a respectable gentleman?"

As I walked into the bedroom to search for the teaching supplies, Winnie met me at the door. She scolded, "What you doing with that boy, Miz Abby? Your mama sure don't want no hussy for a daughter. And it ain't his day to get his learning—it's the Lord's day."

She knew as well as I did that Mama was so caught up in her own misery that she hardly cared about anything anymore, except marrying me off.

I grabbed some pieces of chalk that had rolled under Martha's bed. "He's down in his spirits, Winnie. He's crying out for education today, Sunday or no Sunday. Who am I to turn him down?"

"You sure it's the *education* he crying out for? He after right more than that."

I stopped collecting the supplies and stared at her. "You think he fancies me?"

She cackled. "Miz Abby, if you have to ask me that, you are simpler than a Banker."

I grinned really big on the inside, then looked at her out of the corner of my eye. "You're welcome to join us out there today."

"No ma'am, no thank you. I've got a meal to cook and about a hundred other things to tend to 'fore suppertime."

Then she grabbed for my arm, nearly causing me to spill all the supplies I had clutched to my chest.

She whispered, "Don't be getting that poor boy's hopes up, now. You got to think on Mr. Hector. Think on your mama 'n' daddy."

I bristled. "*You* think on Hector and Mama and Daddy. They hurt my head, the lot of them."

I heard her mumble, as I walked away, "I'll marry Mr. Hector. And you can be *my* housemaid."

I laughed as I walked back out to the porch and sat myself next to Ben at the table, instead of sitting across from him at an angle as I usually did. I sat so close to him our thighs were almost touching. I could feel his bare skin's heat clear through my layers of clothing.

And instead of disgusting me, his sweat smelled earthy and primal. His dirty clothes looked humble. His bare feet even reminded me of Jesus.

He didn't seem to notice the change, though. He was as natural and as eager to learn as he always was. But my voice was high and watery as I read aloud from *Robinson Crusoe*.

I ran my fingers under the lines in the book, very slowly, so that he could read along with me. As our eyes moved together over the pages, I experienced such an unusual feeling of intimacy. I felt him, without even touching him.

He was attempting to say a few of the words with me. I had written a long list of regularly occurring words on a piece of paper for him to take home—words such as *goat, sand, ship, shoot, Friday,* and *island*. He had learned them all, and had even started adding words of his own to the list while we read.

As we worked, the sun shifted lazily to the west, shining its gold through the windows from inside the house. It was blindingly bright, so that we had to shade our eyes to see the book. After a while, though, when the sun had moved a degree farther west, I saw the outline of Winnie's lean body standing quietly near the open window. She had stopped to listen to us after all.

With the light behind her, her white head scarf glowed like a dove in the dark house.

∞

I never did get a chance to lay the dining room table. Charlie and Martha had returned from the clam dig with muck in their fingernails and sunburn on their fair faces. They were also grumpy from exhaustion, and Hannah had eagerly taken over where I'd left off, glad to be done with them.

Ben and I sat on the porch reading and writing until Winnie poked her head out the window, sending with it the scent of her hot seafood stew.

"Mr. Hector and your daddy riding over now. Better call it a day," she said sternly, furrowing her brow at Ben. It was Hector's sixth supper here.

Ben looked at me with a lopsided grin and said, "Don't want to keep Hector waiting, now. Reckon he's a punctual one, with a pocketwatch and whatnot."

I handed him *Robinson Crusoe*. "See if you can string together some sentences tonight."

He stared at me, then rubbed his rough hand over the cover, as a zealot would caress a Bible. He nodded his head and smiled. "See you tomorrow, Abby. Thanks for the Sunday lesson." Then he whispered, "Hotel docks, seven o'clock in the morning. Won't be busy yet, so don't be late."

I hurried inside to my bedroom to change my dress and wash my face, to try to ease the effects of the hot afternoon on my appearance. As I gulped down a glass of warm water from the pitcher, I could hear Mama upstairs, walking slowly around the room, getting ready for supper. The only person she dressed for nowadays was Hector.

I heard Daddy and Hector clomp up the steps of the porch and scrub the sand off their shoes on the scraper. Daddy looked like hell warmed over, his beard and curly red hair uncombed and his clothing rumpled, but Hector was creaseless, as usual.

He presented me with a large bouquet of perky orange lilies that he had carried with him. "These are all the way from Mother's garden in Edenton. Cut just today and sent on the packet! A taste of home just for you, Abigail."

I knew that his mama had a fancy English garden, renowned in Edenton for its prizewinning blooms. Whenever we rode by the Eden Street house in our buggy, I always saw four or five servants tending it. I wondered what Hector would think if I told him that I preferred to do all the dirty work of gardening myself.

But I just smiled politely and said, "They're beautiful. Please tell your mama that I adore them. They held up awfully well on the trip over here."

I handed them to Hannah, who arranged them in a vase and set it on the table as a centerpiece. The petals flickered like flames in the light of the setting sun.

We all seated ourselves at the dining room table. After Daddy's quick blessing, Winnie and Hannah began to serve the food.

Mama looked as if she was about to retch into her lap. "What is that stench? Is it seafood, Winnifred?"

Winnie didn't look at Mama when she said, "Mister Sinclair asked for it."

Mama looked to Daddy, who simply said, "You can't deny us our seafood while we're out here, Ingrid."

Winnie quickly said, "But I cooked extra biscuits for you, Miz Sinclair. Take as many as you please."

Mama took a deep breath and smiled at Hector. She then reached for the basket and took several of Winnie's buttery biscuits. She created a little tower of them on her plate, like a child would.

"I love seafood stew, myself. Tastes so fresh out here," exclaimed Hector.

Hector, particularly animated, occupied much of the table talk. He told us about his ongoing medical experiences with the Bankers, whom he said were highly superstitious and unusually resistant to any kind of medical assistance, even in the most dire of circumstances.

"They still use herbs, and scoff at any kind of medicinal remedy. One little girl gave a full vial of my specially prepared cough medicine to her pet goat—perfectly healthy, I might add—then came and asked for more." He laughed, shaking his head. "Living apart from the mainland has allowed them to live like savages. Something must be done to get them acclimated to modern medicine."

Daddy nodded along with Hector's opinions, but he hadn't spoken much at all, except to berate Charlie for dribbling stew on the tablecloth while he ate. He ate rapidly, spoon to bowl to mouth until the bowl was clean, and his whiskey glass had been empty for some time.

I asked him, "How was Roanoke Island today, Daddy?"

His spoon clattered in the bowl. "How did *you* know I was on the island?"

I recalled Ben's distressed demeanor today and suddenly had the feeling I shouldn't have brought up Roanoke Island after all. But it was too late now.

I said carefully, "Benjamin mentioned your recent interest in the island. He said you've been exploring over there."

"He told you that?" Daddy asked suspiciously, his voice loud with alcohol. "What else did he say?"

Something was obviously wrong. I tried to keep my voice casual. "He came over today for some tutoring, and he mentioned your interest in Roanoke Island in conversation. That's all."

Daddy just grunted and said, "Jesus Christ almighty. I need another drink." He pounded his glass on the table for Winnie to fill.

Mama cut in then. "Benjamin was here on a Sunday? You should have told him to leave."

I bit my lip. "Ben comes when he can. His visits don't always coincide with your schedules. And you're so ill these days, I think I would always be turning him away for lack of a chaperone."

It was painfully quiet for a second or two, as everyone in the room stopped what they were doing and stared at me.

Hector broke the silence. "You should have called on me at the hotel. I *am* almost an official doctor, you know."

She looked at Hector apologetically. "I've been wanting to tell you, Hector. And your father as well. I'm expecting a child."

Hector's pink lips curved upward. "My gracious! That's wonderful news!"

Charlie and Martha bounced up and down in their seats at the revelation.

Charlie said, "I hope it's a boy! I'm sick of girls."

Martha said, "If it is, let's name him Benjamin!"

Hector blinked maniacally for a second, then smiled flatly.

Mama looked down at her plate with a wormy smile. She murmured, "Girl or boy, I can't tell. But I've never been more ill, I declare."

Hector was all business. "No wonder you don't care for seafood! Well, don't fret. I have just the remedy for morning sickness. Father uses it, so I'm sure you've taken it before. I'll have my man bring the syrup over tonight. It should do the trick."

After big slices of apple cobbler, Hector asked to speak with me alone, and Mama and Daddy readily agreed. We walked out to the eastern porch, where just a couple of hours ago Ben and I had sat. The memory of him working over the paper with quill and ink, the way he had stroked the book when I gave it to him, made my full stomach lurch.

We sat down on the rocking chairs, facing out to sea. The light was fading gradually, a candle slowly running out of wick. But the evening held on to the heat of the day.

Hector said, "This cottage does have quite a view. You must be enjoying it."

"I am, most of the time. It is very isolated, though."

"Yes, I've noticed that. Maybe too much so."

His face to the dark ocean, he said sternly, "I don't think it's a very good idea for you to tutor this Benjamin anymore. He seems to be taking advantage of the situation here, and I cannot tolerate it." I shook my head and tried to interject, but he pressed on. "Your mother seems *very* ill, your father is never here, and you are entirely too kind a person to tell this man no. This Benjamin is no gentleman, Abigail. You must send him away the next time he calls."

I cried out harshly, "I hardly think it's your place to tell me what to do."

He looked surprised at my outburst. "I'm sorry, Abigail, if I upset you. But I called on you tonight to . . . I have been courting you for months. I'm sure you are aware of my intentions by now. And it doesn't make me feel good about my chances with you when you're entertaining a man at your home, and your parents aren't even aware of his presence! I'm starting to question your judgment!"

"I'm *teaching* him, not entertaining him. And my parents are the people who wanted me to tutor him in the first place. Question their judgment, not mine."

He turned his head slightly but still wouldn't look at me. "You've changed since you've been out here."

I quickly looked out to the dark sea.

He asked, "Did you think I wouldn't notice? You used to have a certain warmth, a certain affection in your smile when I called on you in Edenton. Your letters were full of encouragement. After a couple of weeks out here, your demeanor shifted markedly. I could not even attempt to guess why. But this indifference to me was the reason that I decided to sacrifice a month of my summer to stay here in Nags Head. I wanted to try to win your affections, if I could."

There was nothing to say that wouldn't ruin me forever.

He stepped over to my side and got down on one knee. His eyes were opaque tide pools in the night. He said quietly, "Tell me, am I succeeding?"

I bit my lower lip hard, trying to think of what to say. "I certainly understand your wanting to be assured of returned affections before offering a proposal of marriage. And I am flattered by your attentions. There are many women more worthy of them than I am. But I can't give you satisfactory answers at this time, Hector."

He simply gazed at me, his eyebrows knit together. "What has happened to you out here?"

Unexpectedly, hot tears bled into my throat. "It's the change from solid earth to shifting sand, I suppose. A lack of solid footing."

He slowly stood up. "I see. Perhaps you'd do well to return to Edenton as quickly as you can. You're a bit homesick, in my opinion."

Edenton seemed far away, a forgotten city buried beneath generations of rubble and water. Going back there seemed almost impossible.

Before he departed for the stable, he said, "Think on Edenton in September, Abigail. And perhaps an autumn wedding. The cooler weather will be a nice change for you, I imagine."

⚭

After watching Hector ride off toward the hotel, I stumbled back into the house. I feared I might get sick before I made it to a basin.

To my surprise, Mama was still downstairs, sitting up straight in a ladder-back chair. And Daddy reclined on the sofa, his boots cock-eyed on the floor below him. They were waiting up for me.

"You like teaching Benjamin, don't you?" Mama asked casually, as I tried to hurry to the kitchen.

I stopped in my tracks and closed my eyes, my belly churning the seafood stew up to the base of my throat. I choked out, "I like teaching."

She spoke to Daddy when she mused, "She always did care more for the barnyard animals, remember?"

Daddy said, without amusement, "Them and her uncle Jack."

He looked at me from an upside-down position and said, "And now Ben. Makes sense, at that. He's a bit of Jack, and a bit of animal, all rolled up into one sandy Banker." I ground my teeth back and forth, and Daddy said calmly, "He should have known better than to show up here on a Sunday. And he damned well should have known better than to discuss my business with you. After all I've done for him, he shows me disrespect like that."

"What business, Daddy? He didn't say anything about business."

Mama cut in. "Benjamin has learned a good deal from you. You've done your duty well, Abigail."

"He's learned his letters, for sure," Daddy said thoughtfully.

Mama went on, "And now we must concentrate on what really matters. We mustn't put off Hector."

"You will no longer tutor Ben. Is that understood?" Daddy boomed. "Enough is enough."

I bit the inside of my cheek so hard that I tasted blood. I made myself nod as the tiny room spun around me.

Mama smoothed her skirt and folded her hands in her lap. Her blue eyes were smudged under with shadows, but they glittered with excitement. "Now then. Hector spoke with your daddy this afternoon. He has asked for your hand. Tell us, did you receive a proposal this evening?"

I shook my head, no longer able to hold the vomit in. I ran outside and leaned over the porch railing as the hot stew roiled through my mouth and landed thickly in the drifts of sand below. Cries of every emotion, some years and years old now, came out with the mess. Tears fell from my eyes and water poured from my nose. I even felt a warm trickle of urine escape and run down my leg.

I couldn't hold *anything* in.

<hr />

Ben's skiff was so tiny that I could do nothing more than sit on the small wooden bench and peer over the side into the swishing sound water. But it appeared to be a well-constructed, hardy little boat, and it was so clean and neat that I had a hard time believing it was Ben's. The reddish-orange skiff had a mast outfitted with a small sail, for breezier weather.

He worked the oars with strong, steady pulls as I sat clumsily on the low seat with my skirts bunched up around my ankles. As we moved rapidly over the Roanoke Sound, I watched his brown arms flexing and stretching from under the secrecy of my parasol.

It was a hot, stagnant morning, and the unmerciful sun reflected off the Roanoke Sound. But the gulls glided, and the fishing boats meandered along, in no particular rush to get anywhere.

I was jealous of their easy summer pace, and wished Ben and I had more time together. With a calmer demeanor than I had imagined myself capable of, I had told Mama that I was going to the island for a day trip with the Edenton folks, and that I would return for supper that evening. Winnie even packed a hamper of food for me. So, with the lie hanging over my head, I felt an intense desire for speed.

And too, I had made up my mind that I wouldn't tell Ben the bad news until the end of the trip. I didn't want what could be our last day together to be spoiled. And instead of feeling sad, I was as loopy as a drunk. My head, heavy with lies and secrets, felt unattached to the rest of my sun-warmed body.

Not more than half an hour after we set out, we docked the skiff on the eastern side of the island, and Ben rushed around to help me out of the boat and onto the rickety pier. "Watch your dress, now. That's fish guts right here," he warned, and actually pulled the hem of my dress off the ground so that it wouldn't drag in the filth.

"I can't feature why I'm not boatsick today," I said, unfurling my parasol in front of me. My insides felt all of a piece, in spite of the heat and the rowing.

"I reckon you're growing your sea legs. Getting used to the movement of a boat on the water. It just takes time is all," said Ben.

"Sea legs," I said with a grin. I pictured my legs with scales and fins, like a mermaid's tail.

Near the end of the pier, we borrowed a cart and horse from an old man Ben seemed friendly with. He clambered up to us through the sand, limping severely with every right step. "Well, well, Benny, whatcha doin' with the likes of this pretty lady? He didn't grab you 'gainst your will, did he, missy?" he cackled to me. His scraggly gray beard was stained a reddish brown around his mouth, and his eyes were so blue they glowed white in the light of the day.

"He's showing me around the island today," I said, eager to be off. The man bulged with undisguised admiration.

"You couldn't get a better guide with all the gold in the world. But I 'spect he ain't chargin' you money, now, is he? A pretty lady always rides for free! Hee, hee, hee!" He slapped his hand in amusement against the side of the little stable.

Ben said, "Settle down now, Rufus, you're beside yourself. We'll be back before the sun goes down."

Ben helped me onto the small cart while the old man hovered, making little comments on my hat and parasol. None too soon, Ben sat down next to me and gave the reins a little shake, and we pulled away.

The old man hollered after us, "Benny, don't you give your pap no more to bend my ear over now! I'm plumb tuckered from hearing 'bout your disrespectful ways."

Ben just snorted and shook his head.

I turned in surprise to Ben and asked, "What on Earth is he talking about?"

He was unnaturally quiet, as if he didn't want to discuss it. "I got me a new job. At the construction site down yonder at Hatteras, to be exact. I'm gonna help build the tallest brick lighthouse in the world."

"That's wonderful news! Isn't that what you wanted?"

He smiled, but sadly. "It is, at that. I didn't want to pull nets for Pap for the rest of my days."

"And I gather your daddy isn't pleased with you?"

He shook the horse's reins extra hard. "You could say that. He's pretty sore about the whole thing. I told him it was something good for the both of us. Bring in more money, easier days and all. But he don't care 'bout that."

"I suppose he wants you both to be together. It's nice, in a way. To have your daddy want to be with you."

He huffed. "Shackled to him, is more like it. Well, I say that life's too short to be the underdog forever. A man's got to strike out on his own, or he's nothing but a coward."

We were silent then. Birds twittered in the bent trees and squirrels scurried underfoot as the small Banker pony trotted along the sandy pathway. Ben's arm occasionally brushed lightly against the sleeve of my dress, but neither of us acknowledged it.

Soon he was back to his old self, his eyes twinkling with humor. "The table's turned on you, Abby. It's my turn to play the teacher."

"I suppose I can tolerate that, if it's only for a small while. Do go on," I said sweetly.

"Up north just a ways we'll see what remains of the Lost Colony at Fort Raleigh. Three hundred years or so ago, man named Walter Raleigh thought Roanoke Island was a dandy place for his colony of English folks. Only they didn't account for the Indians and the rough winters and the lacking of food. They disappeared, no trace of them. Likely killed off or starved before anyone could come from England to help 'em."

"That was nicely put, Benjamin. You've done this before, I suppose?"

"Only for the gals in need of the most learning," he joked.

He stopped the horse in a heavily wooded area near the Roanoke Sound. The water twinkled in white patches through the pine and cypress trees, and the air was ripe with the smell of fresh bark and salt, the smell of promise.

Ben got out of the cart with an easy jump and walked over to my side. Because it was so hot, I had earlier removed my gloves, so I was able to touch for the first time his calloused, slightly damp hand.

His grasp was tender yet secure, and as I stepped down into the sand strewn with pine needles, I found to my surprise that I couldn't let go of his hand. I held on for a second too long to be considered appropriate, and then I hastily uncurled my fingers. But I could still feel the warmth of his hand in mine when it was gone.

I could feel him gazing at me, could even feel on my cheek the light of the water reflecting from his eyes, so I ducked under my parasol and walked ahead through the trees.

Ben kept a respectable distance between us as he showed me what appeared to be the remains of a moat around the centuries-old fort. He outlined roughly where the original fort had stood. He said he'd been here many times as a young boy, and that he had brought Eliza here once when she wanted to run away from home. They had set up a makeshift camp and stayed for over a week, their own little colony.

The thought of Ben and Eliza sleeping under the stars and sharing meals in this very spot made me unexpectedly jealous. I could feel the arteries in my neck pumping green blood. Eliza and Ben were bound forever by their history together. I was nothing next to all that.

"The Yankee troops pilfered some souvenirs from this area during the war. Even found some old bricks the colony used in their houses and forts. The military had to bring in armed guards to keep folks away. So there's no telling what's been taken and what's been messed with. Seems a shame what folks will do for amusement."

I walked around and around the perimeter, trying to imagine the colonists' loneliness and isolation, their fear of the unknown, and their hopes for the future. It soon became too devastating to think of their failure, after such a mighty effort.

At noon the heat was almost unbearable. I fanned myself under my parasol, and Ben periodically wiped his face and neck with a filthy rag as we rode toward the western side of the island.

I saw that the land had to a large extent been cleared of trees and underbrush, and former Confederate and Union army barracks were strewn here and there along the path. Soon I could see the Croatan Sound, shimmering like a mirage on the other side of the island. Far across the water was the mainland of North Carolina.

Ben directed the horse toward a small village with neatly designed streets and avenues. They were lined with crude log cabins, with little gardens in between. Black women were hanging their wash to dry on clotheslines strung precariously between short trees, and children, dogs, and chickens all ran happily around the sunny plots of land.

Ben then told me about the Freedmen's Colony, which I had heard very little about, for being so close to it geographically. He said that it had held a lot of promise for a few years during the war, but that over the past couple of years most of the freedmen had left for the mainland to find work.

"What happened to it? Why did everyone want to leave, after being given so much?"

"The white folks fighting in the war came home to find the freedmen living on their land, and they wanted them off quick. All they had to do was prove their property ownership, and the government sent the freedmen on their way. And from what I've heard, the rations were cut off, and they weren't getting paid for the work they did for the Union government. They couldn't survive with no money, no food."

"Seems to me there are lots of things to do, though."

"It's a hard life out here, Abby. There are skills to learn. It ain't easy to teach a man how to fish or hunt if he's never done it before."

"They could farm," I offered. "Our field hands were hard workers and knew the land right well."

"There ain't much farming to do out here. The soil ain't the greatest, and most of the land down south is covered in swamps."

"Surely they can learn a trade, though," I said. I thought of the hundreds of thousands of this country's former slaves milling around with no education and no opportunity for free labor, and it was terrifying. "If they can't learn, what's to become of them?"

"I reckon they just need some good teachers, for a start. Which reminds me, I got something to show you."

When we found a place to water the horse, we got out to walk farther down the avenue. It seemed more than strange that we had seen two different kinds of settlements in one day. Both focused on new beginnings, but for two different races of people. Unfortunately, it seemed that the Freedmen's Colony was going the same route as the English one.

Ben beckoned me over to a lopsided wooden barnlike structure with a couple of closed windows on each side. He opened the rickety door and the smell of stale sweat and mold hit me strongly.

"This here is the only Negro schoolhouse left on the island." The light was dim, and big flies buzzed lazily against the windows. "Used to have missionary teachers in here, but they left a couple years ago."

The room was mostly comprised of ammunition boxes, which I imagined served as chairs and desks. There was a well-used blackboard and a table with a broken leg in the front of the room, but other than that, it was mostly hot air.

"This is a sad little room," I said. "I can't imagine anyone trying to learn in here."

"Well, it ain't as fine as the porch of a house on the beach, but . . ."

His eyes flitted to the door, where a large black man and a handful of black children were crowding closely, staring at us. The man was tall and barrel-chested and wore a suit of well-made, but mighty worn, clothes. The children were thin and barefoot, and their clothes were nothing more than rags sewn together.

"Can I help you?" asked the man in a commandingly deep voice.

"I'm Miss Abigail Sinclair, and this is my friend Benjamin Whimble. He thought I'd like to see your school."

He just stared at me, silent and vaguely menacing. I added apologetically, "I hope we're not intruding."

A very small girl with bright brown eyes and grains of sand in her springy hair grinned at me. "You're to be our new teacher?"

I softened slightly, grateful for the childish intrusion. I hated to disappoint her. "No, I'm sorry. I'm not. I'm just visiting today. I'm living over in Nags Head for the summer."

I pointed east, somehow aware that this group of children wouldn't know where a resort town was located.

The little girl's brow folded. "I thought sure you was the lady. You ain't joking me, are you?"

The man patted her head and said, "Luella's been on the lookout for a new teacher. She's got education on her mind all the time these days."

He put a stack of Bibles and books on the old table. "I am Elijah Africa. I'm the preacher at Sheltering Oaks Baptist Church, but I've been teaching the children here every afternoon while their parents are out working."

Ben looked pale all of a sudden, and didn't utter a word.

"We're pleased to meet you, Elijah," I said for both of us, with a quizzical look at Ben.

Elijah, too, gazed at Ben. "Haven't I seen you somewhere before?"

Ben said defensively, "More than likely. I'm a Banker from birth. I'm out here a good bit, fishing and trading."

Elijah nodded slowly. "Well, you're just in time for our lesson, and the students like to show off what they've learned. You're welcome to stay for a while. "

I smiled. "That would be wonderful."

But Ben blurted, "Sorry to put a damper on, but we should be going. Time's a-ticking. Ain't that right, Abby?"

I put my hands on my hips and shook my head at him. "No, we have time yet."

Ben huffed impatiently and went to stand near the door with his arms crossed and his foot propped up on the thin wall behind him. I took a seat on an ammunition box and pulled up an old barrel. The little boys and girls giggled, ran for their own boxes, and pulled them up to sit near me. Elijah pulled out a handful of Bibles and passed them out to the class. He also handed out a few battered copies of an instructional reading textbook called *The Freedmen's Reader*.

He began the lesson with a passage from the Bible, Paul's Prayer for the Ephesians, a prayer for knowledge and understanding. The children took a while to find the particular passage, so I helped the youngest ones locate it, as they squirmed and fidgeted.

Then Elijah began to read, his voice reverberating off the shabby walls of the room.

"Wherefore I also, after I heard of your faith in the Lord Jesus, and love unto all the saints, cease not to give thanks for you, making mention of you in my prayers; that the God of our Lord Jesus Christ, the Father of glory, may give unto you the spirit of wisdom and revelation in the knowledge of him: The eyes of your understanding being enlightened; that ye may know what is the hope of his calling, and what the riches of the glory of his inheritance in the saints, and what is the exceeding greatness of his

power to us-ward who believe, according to the working of his mighty power, which he wrought in Christ, when he raised him from the dead, and set him at his own right hand in the heavenly places . . ."

He was credible. Years of trampled emotions were threaded through his drawn-out words. I had never heard a voice so complex.

"Far above all principality, and power, and might, and dominion, and every name that is named, not only in this world, but also in that which is to come: And hath put all things under his feet, and gave him to be the head over all things to the church, which is his body, the fulness of him that filleth all in all."

"Amen," he said, gazing at the cobwebbed ceiling, rendered important in the aftermath of the words. He closed the Bible, so small in his large hands.

He then began to sing a hymn, and motioned for the children to sing along with him. And it was as if their lives had been set to music. I heard each agonizing minute of their days in the rise and fall of the notes, saw innocence in their sweet, toothy mouths, their pink tongues. I pretended to pick a stray thread from the sleeve of my dress so they wouldn't see the tears welling in my eyes.

The children then recited the alphabet in a singsong chant. In response, Elijah asked them if they had been practicing their letters and numbers.

"I practiced at 'em 'til my stick done broke!" said a small but muscular little boy. From that, I gathered that they were to practice their letters with sticks in the sand.

"Do you have no slates or chalk? No paper or quills?" I interrupted.

Elijah raised his eyebrows at me. "We have no money for those kinds of items. We are lucky to have the books that we have here, this building, these boxes. These children barely have food to eat. We make do with what we have. You can understand that?"

I heard Ben snicker from the doorway.

I blushed, and stammered, "I-I'm sorry. I didn't mean to sound insensitive."

As he wiped at his forehead with a handkerchief, his dark eyes studied me. "Miss Sinclair, *why* are you here?"

I didn't know how I had found myself in this dank, stifling room on this strange little island, but it felt like I had come home to something. I spoke, the words slowly forming on my tongue. "I think I can help you. I can get you some supplies, things that can help with their learning. Slates, books, chalk, paper. If you want them."

He paced back and forth across the rough floorboards, his large boots making the entire floor of the room vibrate. He finally said, "We need a teacher, too, for adults as well as children. Might you know of someone who could take on the task?"

My stomach dipped, as if I had jumped from a great height. I said firmly, "I could do it, but only at night."

Ben stared at me. And he appeared to shake his head, just barely left to right.

Elijah looked unfazed. "That would be fine. The adults prefer night sessions, since they work during the day." He crossed his arms. "Do you have any experience in the field of teaching?"

"I do. I tutor my younger sister and brother."

Ben gave me a brief smile, but his voice came out pinched. "I can vouch for her. She's been teaching me reading and writing this summer, and I've learned more than I ever thought I could by her. She has right much insight into the book of *Robinson Crusoe*."

Elijah actually smiled at that. "Oh, yes, that's one of my favorite novels. Savages and the civilized man. When I learned to read, it was the first novel that I read in one day."

"One day! Good Lord, it's taken us the whole summer to get

through it, and that's with Abby reading it to me! I wouldn't be able to make it through ten pages on my own, without Abby here."

"Practice, Mr. Whimble," Elijah said good-naturedly. "Daily practice."

"You read a lot, I take it?" asked Ben, tightly.

"Every time I get the chance," said Elijah. "When would you like to start, Miss Sinclair?"

"Is next Monday too early?" I hadn't even thought about the possibility of sneaking out of the cottage, or how I was to get to the island and back.

His face was determined. "We'll see you then, around nine o'clock. Plan for three hours of learning time, for around fifty students."

At that, the children shouted with glee and got up from their boxes to gather around me. They giggled among themselves and jumped up and down. But Luella just stood in front of me, staring. "I knew you was the lady, didn't I?"

"You must be very bright indeed," I replied. I tried to offer Luella a confident smile, but the notion of teaching a group of fifty students—people of all ages and abilities—was overwhelming. I hoped Elijah would be there to help out. And Ben.

Walking out of the school building into the blazing afternoon sun, I shaded my eyes. "Were you all right in there, Ben?" I asked. "I guess the actual schoolhouse set you on edge."

He kicked at the sand and then laughed heartily to himself. "God does have a sense of humor, don't He!"

He seemed lost in thought for a while, and then he smiled at me, nodding his head to himself. He went on, but more peacefully. "I was just taken aback is all. I wasn't expecting all that. Lord almighty, a teacher for the freedmen. If only your pap could see you. My, he'd be so proud."

"I thought it was time for me to stretch my wings a bit. A lady can only teach one person for so long. I needed a new challenge," I said airily, unfolding my parasol.

"Ho ho! Mighty sorry if I bored you with my simple mind. You've got your work cut out for you now, though. Fifty freedmen, women, and children all looking to you to teach them. You sure you want to come over here every night? It's a risk you might not be willing to take, come light of tomorrow."

I stopped to look at him. "You'll come with me, right?"

"Well, I'm not free, you know. What'll you plan to give me in return?" He looked away from me, but I could still see the smile on his face.

"Ah, the old barter system, still alive and well on the Outer Banks. The pleasure of my company is all *you'll* receive."

"Whatever you say," said Ben, suddenly serious. "We just need to be real careful. There's something about that schoolhouse that I don't like, not one bit."

I laughed. "I knew it."

We returned the horse and cart to the old man Rufus, who fortunately was snoring away in the afternoon heat. Then we walked down the small pier to where Ben's skiff was rising and falling with the water, begging to be untied. Ben pulled hard on the rope to bring the boat close to the pier, then held out his hand to me.

But I couldn't get in. I stood there, looking down into the boat. The heat swam almost visibly in front of my face.

Ben looked amused. "Abby? Helloooo? We better get going if you want to make it back by supper."

I fought down a sob that had bubbled up, and I shook my head stubbornly.

"Lord God, what's the matter with you?" He moved close to stand in front of me. The way that he braced himself, I think he thought I was about to faint.

"Ben." That was all I could get out.

He whispered, "Yeah?"

I forced my mouth to work. "Are you going to marry Eliza Dickens?"

He exhaled deeply. Then he reached out and put his hands gently on my forearms. "Not if you don't want me to. See, I broke it off with her a while ago."

Tears of confusion spilled out of my eyes. "You did? Why? I thought she was your childhood sweetheart, the only one for you. You told me you were going to marry her."

He nodded his head a bit. "I know. I was planning on it. Until I met you."

The Earth seemed to stand still for a moment. "Me?"

He laughed, squeezing my arms gently with his coarse hands. "Yeah, you. Can't you see how much I care about you? You're supposed to be the smart one here! I don't do this kind of touring-around thing just for any gal, you know."

I laughed and stammered at the same time. "I-I wasn't sure. I didn't know. I mean . . ." My throat closed so that I could hardly speak. "It's a good thing we're going to be seeing each other at night now."

I couldn't go on. I could hardly bear to see his disappointment.

"Why's that?" His eyes clouded a bit.

"Because I'm not allowed to tutor you anymore, Ben. That Sunday visit of yours put Mama and Daddy over the edge. It's done."

Ben looked as if I had punched him in the gut. "Oh."

"I'm so sorry."

He ran his fingers through his hair and shifted his stance in agitation. "Your daddy cut me off, too?"

"Yes. He was adamant about it."

He shook his head slowly. "It don't take much to get on his bad side, does it? You think he'd be more grateful to folks that help him."

I shook my head. "He never has been. He forgets."

He smiled rigidly. "Well, I'll just have to get my learning at night, then." He took my hand and squeezed it. "I don't want to lose . . . everything we've worked for this summer."

"No. Neither do I," I said.

I looked back at the island, the little inlets of clear blue water and marsh grass and the tree-lined sand. Then I looked across the Roanoke Sound, to the blur of sand dunes a bit north of Nags Head Woods. I thought of that tree on Run Hill, and whether she was finally dying, right this very minute.

Quickly I matched my lips to his, and he grabbed me very tightly around my back, pressing the corset bindings into my spine almost painfully. His lips were a bit chapped, and he tasted of salt water and sunlight, sweet grass and soil. Just as I expected.

I stepped back to look at him and he rubbed the tears from my cheeks with the meat of his ragged thumb. Then he held my face with both of his hands and just looked at me, his eyes searching and darting from feature to feature.

And I looked at his face, too. I knew it so well now, its flickers of confusion and bursts of pride. Instead of eyes and a nose and cheeks, I saw water and a boat. A boat that was sailing somewhere.

He picked me up by my waist and twirled me around on the pier.

Then he gave a great shout that echoed over the Albemarle Sound. A flock of Canada geese took off anxiously, without even honking, water pouring from their wings as they climbed into the air.

He said, "I'm glad we got all that cleared up."

My measured steps clunked loud and purposeful as I walked quickly along the planked railway back to the cottage that evening. The Earth had started spinning again, but in a new and different direction. The heat had dissipated a bit, and violet and pale pink clouds splashed across the sky above the ocean. My spine stretched as straight as a pine tree.

Hunger raged in my belly, as if I hadn't eaten in days. But I had hardly gotten inside the cottage when Winnie came out of the kitchen with a wooden spoon in her hands. Dread crept into my limbs like a kind of paralysis.

"You want to look in on your mama before supper," she said, nodding her head up in the direction of her bedroom.

I whispered, "Is she angry with me?"

Winnie looked concerned. "No, she ain't angry. But she ain't her own self a-tall. She been asking for you."

With more relief than annoyance, I wearily climbed the creaking steps to Mama's room, my day with Ben and my decision to teach fading into the close air the higher I went.

She was in bed, covered up to her thighs with a quilt and staring into the nothingness of the dim, musty bedroom. She hardly looked at me when I walked into the room. Her lacy white nightdress was stained around her chest, and her long hair hung in greasy locks around her propped-up head.

I sat down in a rocking chair. I glanced at the open white Bible on the bedside table, at the gold-rimmed pages reflecting the candlelight. "How are you, Mama?"

She ran her hand over her belly. She said softly, "I could lose this baby."

"Should I send for a doctor? Perhaps Doc Newman could pay you a visit out here. I'm sure he would, if we called for him."

She reached her fingers out into the air. "I can touch the specter of death, he lingers so closely. I can smell his rancid breath, his rotting skin."

She grabbed for the bowl she kept beside her bed and dry-heaved into it. When she was satisfied that nothing was left in her stomach, she sat back and looked at me with wild, strained eyes. "Can you smell him, too? He stinks."

I shook my head, fighting the increasing urge to scream. "That's just the smell of the ocean. It's not death."

Intricate cobwebs of perspiration stuck to her forehead. "I'm not afraid to die."

I began to perspire, too. It was so warm up on the second floor; I didn't know how she could spend her days up there. Maybe the heat was addling her. "Mama, you're not going to die. Now stop that."

Her breathy laughter caused the candle beside her to flicker and dance. "When I was younger, I believed that there was a divine purpose for me. I clung to life. I was afraid that I would disappoint God if I died too soon."

I had never heard Mama talk about her childhood before. Daddy had once told me that her father had been an immigrant stevedore on the bustling wharves of Edenton, and that she had grown up dirt poor on the waters of the Albemarle Sound. But I had never pictured her as a young girl, just like me. Afraid of death, clinging to life.

She spoke in a low, rasping voice, so that I had to draw my chair closer to her bedside. "Did you know that I was reading and writing at the age of three? Speaking words an adult would speak. My parents . . . they feared for my life. Simple people. They were told by the town's most respected doctor that I was probably afflicted by a malignant growth in the brain.

"This doctor was intrigued enough to send me to various kinds of medical specialists. All across the East Coast, I traveled. Oh, they all found me highly interesting. But not one could diagnose a problem with my brain, so I was sent home as a curiosity, something to be studied."

She paused to adjust the pillow behind her head. The sound of the clock's gears clicked steadily through the small room. I wondered if she was making this story up, in this disconnected madness. Anything seemed possible in there.

I waited on the edge of the rocker for her to speak, perspiration wetting the creases behind my knees.

Finally she continued. "A few of the psychology experts periodically traveled all the way to Edenton to visit me. I was a lonely, quiet little girl, always did as I was told. So I would answer their questions, write their essays. They would scribble madly in their notebooks. They crafted pages and pages of reports to take back to their universities."

"What did they find?" I asked, my curiosity overpowering the closed-in chaos.

She chortled. "It finally became obvious to them that I possessed the most superior intelligence. It took them a while to figure it out, you know, because I was a girl." She twisted her fists into her bedcovers. "I was only five years old at the time. I remember feeling blessed, like I was carrying a bright light inside me. But my parents thought me cursed. I think they would have been happier if

I had a tumor in my brain. They could understand maladies of that nature."

"What happened to you?" I asked softly.

Her eyes closed, and she didn't answer me for a few moments. Then she went on. "I was forbidden to read and write. I was not to attend school. If your father hadn't seen me sitting in the seamstress's shop window, I would still be there today."

The story of Mama and Daddy's meeting and courtship was never discussed in our house. I had gleaned from various sources that Daddy was originally supposed to marry Penelope Critchfield, a rich planter's daughter in neighboring Bertie County. But when Daddy saw Mama, it was love at first sight. Penelope Critchfield was forgotten, at least for a time. But now the husband of Penelope Critchfield, Amos Drumwright, was one of the richest men in the eastern Albemarle, having invested the majority of the family estate in railroads.

Two spots of pink grew on Mama's white cheeks. "When I saw the Sinclair library, I wept. I had never seen so many books!" she whispered, waving her hand through the air above her head. "The library shimmered—the dust motes twinkled in the beams like stardust. It was a message from God." She grabbed for my hand and seethed, "You see? He was rewarding me, finally, for my struggles. For my faith in Him. He was answering my prayers."

"Oh, Mama," I whispered. Her grip was hurting my hand, but I held on to her.

She giggled a bit. "The low-class stories I'd heard growing up were good for something, as it turned out. I became pregnant with you, and your daddy and I married. The library was mine. Your daddy never cared for those books as I do. He hardly even reads."

She let go of my hand, finally, and it throbbed, the blood pushing back into the veins again. It seemed that my appearance was necessary to Mama only as a way to gain access to a well-stocked library.

She hadn't married for love or wealth or power. She had married for education. And she had borne children for it as well.

It wasn't a completely bad reason for marrying someone, I supposed. Our library was somewhat famous in Edenton. Mama had informed us a few years earlier that there were 1,700 books in it. 'Course, she had accrued many more treasures since that counting.

I asked, "Why are you telling me this? Why now?"

She didn't answer me. Instead she wailed, "And what good came of all my gifts, in the end? I have not distinguished myself. I have failed God."

I asked tentatively, "What did you want to do?"

She sighed, a gust of resignation. "Something . . . else."

I was annoyed, suddenly. "Your life isn't terrible. Most women would gladly change places with you."

She blew her nose into her handkerchief and looked at me as if seeing me for the first time in her life. "Your face, Abigail. You look like a fishmonger, with those freckles and brown skin. What will Hector think?"

Then she began weeping into her nightgown sleeve, but I couldn't think of a thing to say or do to comfort her. As I watched her, I recalled how Mama zealously guarded the library. We were not allowed in the room unless we had permission from her. Mama often spent entire days in the library, and she didn't care for intrusions.

From her, I learned to see books as golden treasures, forbidden fruit. When I was small, I remember physically aching to open one, to crack the old covers with the smallest flicks of the wrists and read the carefully chosen words.

Mama—now bitter and worn down by life—had once been as eager to learn. I imagined her as the quiet little stevedore's daughter with the quick mind, and my heart wept for that child, for her lost potential. As much as she'd grown, she still seemed stunted.

But I admired her courage, and her cunning, her ability to completely disregard what was expected of her. Opportunity had presented itself, and she had taken it, boldly and without apology. It was a powerful lesson for me.

I saw glimpses of myself in my mother, and I was comforted, in a way.

CHAPTER THIRTEEN

Abigail Sinclair
August 10, 1868

"You do great deal much good," says he; "you teach wild mans to be good sober tame mans; you tell them know God, pray God, and live new life."

"Alas! Friday," says I, "thou knowest not what thou sayest; I am but an ignorant man myself."

"Yes, yes," says he; "you teachee me good, you teachee them good."

—ROBINSON CRUSOE

HANNAH UNTIED THE SATIN LACES OF MY CORSET AND I FOLDED IT AND placed it in the trunk, now full of unwanted underthings. Throughout the summer the pile of stockings, garters, crinolines, and petticoats had grown bigger and bigger, discarded for their frivolous uselessness. I pulled on my most common gray dress, with nothing but a thin chemise between that and my skin.

Then I stretched out on my bed, pretending to go to sleep. I waited for Charlie and Martha's chests to slow into sleep, their breathing keeping time with the measured crash and sweep of waves outside.

My own breath was shallow, in the face of what I was about to do. Thick clouds had endeavored to block the light from the heavens tonight, so the sky was uncommonly obscure. And the air was humid and motionless. Flies buzzed in and out of the windows, checking on me.

After a time, I felt the creaking house ease into its slumber. I climbed carefully through the window and swung my feet softly onto the porch.

I looked at Hannah and Winnie, slumbering peacefully in the hammocks, blankets wrapped loosely around them. Keeping an eye on them, I tiptoed down the sandy porch steps, as quiet as a ghost crab.

But as I made my way toward the hotel, I felt someone grab my upper arm and pull on it. I tried to scream but a hand clamped over my mouth, a hand that smelled of cooking spices and lye.

Her voice whispered, "Oh, Miz Abigail. You going crazy as your mama."

My heart pounded, but relief spread like butter through my limbs. "Winnie, you scared me to death!"

"You *need* some scarin'! Get back in the house now, and I won't tell your mama you're out prowling 'round like a cat in heat."

I found that it was much easier to be honest in the pitch dark. "I can't. I'm teaching at a school over on Roanoke Island. A school for the people of the Freedmen's Colony."

She didn't speak for a few seconds, as her grip on my wrist loosened. "Who in their right mind would put you up to that foolishness? I'll give 'em a hunk of my mind and a foot up their—"

"It was mostly my idea. I decided that I could do it, and I am. I thought you'd understand."

"How you getting all the way over there? I know you ain't rowing a boat your own self."

"Ben is taking me."

She clamped a hand to her heart. "Oh, Lord, I knew I ain't heard the last of that boy. Yes, I knew that glint in your eyes. Had it when you was nothing but a baby girl."

She started wringing her hands. "Your daddy gonna whip you and then me and probably ever last soul in that house for letting you out. And what would Mr. Hector say? More's the pity, is what he'd say, and move on to the next young gal. They likely waitin' in a line for him, right this minute. And here you are, acting crazier than a fly stuck in sugar."

"I don't care about Hector."

She sucked in her breath. "You should care about him, is what I'm telling you. Nice doctor man, with a nice family, too. That fishing boy don't have two pennies to rub together."

"Out here, money doesn't mean as much. It's different."

"Oh, I know you. You'd miss all your nice things, all your learning books. Come on, come back inside, and I won't say one word."

She started pulling on my elbow, but I stood my ground. "You should come with us tonight, Winnie. You'll learn more than you do by eavesdropping through an open window. Tonight is my first lesson. I met a few of the children already, and the preacher of a church who teaches them during the day. I think you'd like it over there."

She sighed deeply. "I *must* be gettin' along in years, to hear you say such words to me. The baby becomes the teacher, ain't that how it goes?"

She dropped my arm and looked to the house, which seemed to be watching us conspire. She closed her eyes and muttered to herself for several minutes. Then she said tightly, "All right, then, teacher. Show me this schoolhouse."

We woke up Hannah to let her know where we were going. She didn't want us to leave, but I could tell that the notion of being in charge overpowered her objections.

Hand in hand, Winnie and I strode quickly through the silent village of Nags Head. When I saw the shadow of Ben, waiting for me at the soundside pier, I almost cried with relief. He smiled at the two us, but none of us dared speak.

He helped us into the skiff, and I saw the box of teaching materials on the floor of the boat. After the meeting with Elijah last week I had hurriedly sent a letter home to Edenton requesting a box of chalk, slates, and our old instructional books to be sent to me at the cottage. Last night Ben had fetched the heavy box from its place in the chicken crawl space under the cottage.

Ben maneuvered the boat with the steady hands of an expert, even in the darkness, and as I watched him, a sense of calm draped over me. He must have made this very journey many times, at just this very time of evening, hoping for a good haul as he wearily staked the nets.

After docking on the western part of the island, we made our way down the dark, quiet streets to the school, Ben huffing over the box of supplies.

We knocked on the door when we arrived, and Elijah was there to open it. I saw beyond his placid face that the room was packed to overflow, students lured by the prospect of a qualified teacher. I estimated that about a hundred people had crowded themselves into the schoolhouse, a number far more terrifying than the fifty Elijah had prepared me for.

Ben whistled softly and looked at me with amusement in his eyes.

I saw that a few lamps had been lit and set on boxes, but they hardly threw off enough light to give an illusion of daytime. It was so dark in the room that I wondered if they could even read their books.

But the room breathed with life, the whites of many eyes dancing in the lamplight. They called out exuberantly when they saw us, and many of the children—some of whom I recognized from last week—came running over to greet me.

Luella, with her bright smile and skinny arms, was one of them. She pulled me by my hand over to meet her round-bodied mother, Ruth, whom Luella greatly resembled, more in attitude than in appearance. Her mother embraced me right there on the spot, pressing me into her fleshy bosom.

Her mouth opened wide when she cried, "Luella's told me all about you, and I'm sorry to say I thought it another one of her tales. But here you are, all of sixteen, seventeen years old if a day, ain't you."

The other adults—some of whom were beyond elderly—stood up and smiled at me gratefully. But I just stared, with no words to offer them. I couldn't believe so many people had chosen to spend their evenings in this dark little room. Most of the country was likely sound asleep, but here these people were, making light of the darkness in their lives.

A cold current of fear washed over me then. What would these hopeful people think if they suspected my family of owning over a hundred slaves a mere three years ago? Did they wonder why a black woman in an apron and head scarf accompanied me tonight?

Trying not to tremble visibly, I made my way to the front of the room. "I'm Miss Abigail Sinclair, and I want to learn *your* names before we begin. So if you would, call out your full names as I point to you, and try to keep your present seats from now on so that I don't mix you up."

I pulled out some paper and my quill from the box and made ready to write. Then I gestured to the first man in the front, a man of about thirty with strong arms, but he didn't say a word. I smiled encouragingly at him, thinking he was shy of me. He looked over to Elijah with a plea in his eyes, but Elijah just stood there, his hands clasped behind his back.

So the man said quietly, "The reverend wanted us to fashion out some new names, instead of carrying on with our slaving names. So you want us to give our new names, or our old ones, or both maybe?"

Elijah said to me, "Most slaves had no surname at all. If they did, it was their master's."

The man said, "The massa called me Cupid. He liked to tell me it was for a god of love, then he laughed and laughed. But my mama named me David."

Elijah said, "Their slave names had no dignity, you see."

A thin gauze of sweat stretched across my forehead. "Oh, well, I'd like to hear the new ones, then."

Everyone present breathed a collective sigh, surprise and happiness on their faces. Some of the students hollered out their names with force and pride, and others barely whispered their names or didn't speak them at all. And some took great pleasure in explaining the meanings of their names, reciting lists of ancestors and places where they'd lived.

There were mostly Kates and Williams and Marys and Johns, names given to them by their parents. But their surnames were unique. Many were pulled from the languages and cultures of western Africa and were difficult for me to spell. *Isabel Ibo, Edward Bakango.*

But there were just as many Lincolns and Washingtons and Jeffersons and Union general surnames. *Sampson Grant, Ellen Burnside.* Some honored nature, taking the names of flowers, medicinal herbs, trees and mountains, rivers they'd traveled, and boats they'd escaped on. *Lucy Neuse, Peter Champion.*

Some took the surnames of missionaries and officers they had known and loved in the colony itself. *Isaac James,* after the superintendent of the colony, Reverend Horace James. *Penny Roper,* after a well-loved teacher named Ella.

And some were simple and strong. *Elias and Sallie Freeman.*

When I got to Winnie, I spoke for her. "This is Winnie. She raised me from a baby." I stopped then, I realizing with a shock that I really didn't know a thing about her.

Had she ever been in love? Did she ever want children of her own? She had come to our household as a wet nurse, which meant that she already had a supply of milk in her breasts. The terrible realization hit me hard, and I reached out my hands to steady myself on the desk.

Winnie shook her head at me, smiling. Then she spoke in a voice that seemed to come from deep within her gut, a wise sort of voice I had never heard from her before. "My name is Asha, Miz Abigail. I never did tell you that. Your mama named me Winnifred when I came to be your mammy. 'Course, I never did take to it. Sounded like a real good name for a hoss."

The whole class laughed loudly. One woman sitting next to Winnie got up and hugged her warmly, as she would a good friend.

Winnie went on. "*Asha* means 'life.' It's an African name. And I still call myself by it, inside my head."

I whispered, "Okay, then. Asha." I could feel the entire room of students appraising me, wondering if I was going to work out after all.

I looked to Elijah, fighting my emotions, and said, almost apologetically, "I brought some things for you. More books will be arriving this week."

He nodded, gazing at the boxes of chalk, books, and slates, not even asking where I had gotten them. I explained that a group of five students must use one slate among them, but that each student could keep a piece of chalk. The children let out whoops of joy and scrambled up to get their hands on a piece.

As the students set to experimenting with the slates and chalk, my eyes roamed around the airless room, taking in the boxes and barrels and bare boards, the floors littered with clumps of mud and sand and mouse droppings. Every so often I'd hear the noisy chirping of a nearby cricket. Wispy spiderwebs laced the corners of the room.

I recalled the room in which I had tutored Charlie and Martha back in Edenton. It was set apart from the busiest parts of the house. Trees grew outside the many long windows and served to filter the sunlight in the early afternoon so that the room always wavered with shades of white and gray. The only sound we heard was the rhythmic ticking of a grandfather clock.

But the students here didn't care about the appearance of the schoolroom. They didn't care about the noise and the chaos and the barrels and boxes. Only learning mattered to them now. Nothing could have kept these people from this room on this night.

Golaga Grant, a teenaged boy with a thick white scar on his forehead, asked, "How long you plan on learning us? You ain't gonna up and leave, like those missionaries did, is you?"

I stumbled for words. "I'm not entirely sure yet. But I plan on being here every weeknight this month."

At that, every face turned to regard me with an expression of disappointment. There were only three weeks remaining in the month.

Luella piped up, "That ain't quite good enough, Miz Abby. That ain't near enough time for all the learnin' we need to do." She pointed to the book on her lap and said, "Can you come over here, now? Mama 'n' me can't make no sense of the words in this book you brung."

It was difficult to keep Luella focused on the book, however. She kept touching my hands with soft little caresses while I was pointing to the words in her book, and it was distracting me. Finally I had to cock my head at her. "What are you doing, Luella?"

Ruth, holding the book only an inch away from her eyes, said, "Oh, don't mind Luella none. I don't think she ever touched white skin before today."

Luella marveled, "You got you the whitest skin I ever seen. But I was trying to figure why you got so many brown spots all over your hands. Is you got a bad sickness?"

I laughed. "They're freckles. I was born with them all over my skin."

She climbed onto my lap. I couldn't stop her. But I could feel everyone eavesdropping on us. She looked at me as if she were committing my face to memory. "You got loads of 'em on your face, too. All over your nose and your cheeks. Where you come from, Miz Sinclair? 'Cause I'd like to go there and see about getting me some freckles."

"I'm from Edenton, North Carolina. Where are you all from?"

Her face fell, and she said, "Over yonder in Hertford. My daddy . . . he got shot by the massa when we was crossing the water. He was bleeding all over us and saying sorry. Then he died, and I still had a hold of his hand. Miz Abby, I peed in my sleep ever night after that." She paused to wipe a tear from her cheek. Then her face broke into a smile. "But now we're free, just like the massa! And my britches are dry again."

"Amen to that!" said Ruth, raising a hand into the air.

That Luella had shared such a painful story with me humbled me into silence. I had the urge to apologize for her lost daddy and her fear and suffering, but she didn't want an apology from me. She wanted admiration.

I reached for her hand. "Luella, has anyone ever told you that you have the most beautiful skin in the world? It reminds me of a shell I found almost buried in the beach sand, not too long ago. It's the size of my thumbnail, very small and round, and the smoothest ebony. It's so soft, from being battered by the ocean for so long. The sunlight doesn't even reflect off its surface. It just seeps inside it. I always thought if I could see inside it, it would glow like a holy light."

The whole room had grown quiet. Luella inspected the skin on her bare arm and rubbed her hand up and down a few times. Then she grinned at me. "I guess I don't need no freckles after all."

After that, everyone set to learning with intensity. I could just hear the relief in the squeak of their chalk and the turning of their pages. They were ready to move on, and so was I.

CHAPTER FOURTEEN

Abigail Sinclair
August 16, 1868

But now I began to exercise myself with new thoughts. I daily read the Word of God, and applied all the comforts of it to my present state. One morning, being very sad, I opened the Bible upon these words, "I will never, never leave thee, nor forsake thee." Immediately it occurred to me that these words were to me. Why else should they be directed in such a manner, just at the moment when I was mourning over my condition as one forsaken of God and man?

—ROBINSON CRUSOE

I SHOULD HAVE FELT GUILTY ABOUT SNEAKING OUT OF THE HOUSE. I should have felt remorseful about spending time with Ben. But nothing felt wrong in the least.

I missed tutoring Ben, but the nights on Roanoke Island made up for the lack of daylight with him. If anything, I had grown to like teaching more since I had been going to the schoolhouse.

But the work was exhausting, and the Sunday afternoon by the ocean was hot and buzzing with insects. I put my feet up on the porch railing and closed my eyes. After dozing a while, I heard some awkward splashing nearby. I opened my eyes a bit, and to my surprise I saw a herd of Banker ponies meandering along the shore. They walked knee-deep in the surf to ease the sting of the flies that swarmed their legs.

The stallion was imposing and almost all black, except for a white splotch in the shape of a handprint on his chest. He kept a close watch on his mares, who weren't doing much except enjoying the feel of the water splashing on their legs.

In their midst I saw the little red horse, and I was so excited to see her again that I walked down the porch steps into the sand. I gave a little whistle, and all of the horses raised their heads to find the source of the sound. I watched as she left the group and plodded through the surf toward me. The stallion let her go, and I smiled, thinking that she likely wasn't a member of the harem at all.

She came up to me without fear and snuffed at my empty hands. "I don't have any treats for you. But I know how much you prefer cord-grass."

She lifted her head to nuzzle my face. She smelled powerfully of ocean water on horsehair. I ran my hands over her smoothed-up coat and scratched behind her ears.

"So you charm wild horses, too. Is there anything you won't do?"

It was Hector's crisp voice, cutting through the lazy air. I turned around to see him, too well dressed in a dark gray suit and black vest and holding his black top hat. His black shoes were half visible beneath the sand.

His voice had sounded sarcastic, but I saw that he was amused.

With great difficulty, I arranged my face into a smile. "Good afternoon. You surprise me, calling on me in such an informal location. It isn't like you."

He arched an eyebrow at me. "I do apologize. I thought you, of all women, would appreciate the lack of decorum in my visit."

I laughed shallowly and wrapped my arms around my chest. "You seem a bit overdressed·for the occasion, if I may say so. Beachcombers don't usually feel the need of a top hat."

He shrugged. "Perhaps my choice of ensemble would seem overdone, if one did not suspect the reason of the visit."

My smile collapsed. Of course, Hector had come with a distinct purpose in mind. I doubted sincerely that he had ventured onto the beach during his entire month on the island.

He held out his arm for me, a perfect ninety-degree angle to his body. "Let's promenade."

As we strolled slowly down the beach, my head pulsed in panic. I couldn't say a word for fear of encouraging him to reveal the purpose of his visit. But thankfully, Hector seemed preoccupied with the sand in his shoes, and practically let out a yelp when the surf threatened his feet.

After a few minutes of self-conscious trudging, though, he seemed to remember himself. He stopped walking and let go of my arm. "It's time to face the facts, Abigail. The summer is almost at an end, and your family will be returning to Edenton."

I felt small and helpless, like a crab that has lost its hole in the sand.

He continued, "Although what you will be returning to in Edenton is far from ideal. Your father's plantation is struggling mightily, as I'm sure you know. He may not be able to keep it. And I'm not sure what will become of you and your family if you lose your land."

I turned my head away from him to see the red horse continuing on her way through the surf. I watched her hindquarters jealously. "We're not going to lose the plantation. Daddy has been working hard this summer to avoid that. He says we are going to have a bountiful crop this year."

He patronized, "But who will harvest it? You? Charlie and Martha? Who will pay the sky-high taxes on the land? The whole of Edenton knows your father's situation by now. He is no longer the planter king, I'm sorry to say." The facts, as Hector presented them, sounded as fearful as a rocky cliff. I felt tears begin to prick my eyes, but he kept on talking. "And you are of marrying age. You aren't a little girl anymore. And it's time for you to take yourself, and your family's situation, more seriously."

He took my hand in his strangely cool one and gazed at me. He said softly, "I have always considered you to be the most beautiful girl in Edenton. In fact, I have had trouble finding any women that rival you, even in the Northeast. You are splendidly radiant."

The tears spilled down my cheeks, and I swiped at them with my free hand. I couldn't stop myself from trembling.

He got down on one knee, slowly, arthritically, and still gripping my hand. He looked up at me. "Abigail, I would be honored if you would consent to become my wife."

I stared at him, at his too-soft lips that many women would die to kiss, and wished powerfully for the sand to swallow me whole. I couldn't speak for fear of sobbing.

He smiled, apparently thinking I was emotional with happiness. "I'll wait until you can answer me with words."

I wrenched my hand away from his covetous grip and covered my tear-stained face with my hands. I said through clenched teeth, "I can't marry you, Hector."

He got off his knee abruptly, his eyes bulging with fury and his hands twitching, as if he wanted to hurt me with them.

"*Who do you think you are?* You will have no more marriage proposals, Abigail!" he raged. "You are too unconventional—quite peculiar, if you want to know the truth. And no one will want such a wayward woman, with no family estate! Your parents have spoiled you with too much leniency. The tutoring of Benjamin Whimble! Failure to chaperone you! And this cottage by the sea! It's the most ludicrous structure I've ever seen! I believe your parents have quite lost their minds!" He was spitting, he was so angry. "You WILL marry me, Abigail. There is no question about that. Your parents will insist. Even they know the state of things, you can be sure. I am to be a doctor soon! A refusal would be madness."

The angrier Hector became, the calmer I grew. "Why would you want to marry someone who doesn't want you?"

He sniffed grandly. "Of course you want me. Giving me the mitten is just another one of your silly charades, to keep me interested in you."

"As a matter of fact, I hardly know you well enough to say that I want you. And you don't know *me*. From everything you've said today, I'd think you would find those proper Northeast beauties satisfactory enough. I'd have thought you'd have run for Yankee territory weeks ago."

He frowned. "I know you well enough, I think. I know you like lilies, horses, sand dunes, and chocolate cake . . ."

I bit the inside of my cheek to keep from laughing. "But you don't really *know* me, know what makes me happy or sad, or thrills me or scares me. I will never understand the desire to spend your life with a person you don't even really know. It seems like a great, pointless waste of time."

He stared at me uncomprehendingly. "I'm sorry to bring you to reality, but that is what marriage is, in the end. It is no parade, no vacation at the *beach*, for heaven's sake."

I shook my head. "It's what I want, Hector. Perhaps I *am* too unconventional for you."

He reached down for his top hat and placed it carefully on his head. "I plan to call on you only once more, but back in Edenton. This god-awful place has mottled your brain. Perhaps back at home, surrounded by sadness and ruin, you'll reconsider your answer."

Then he stumped back up the shore, cursing the sand with every step. I watched him go until his top hat was a very small black smudge.

The night air in the room hardly moved at all, although the windows were wide open. The bed linens were damp and stuck to my skin, making it itch. Even with my nightgown hitched up to my thighs, I felt pressed down, uncomfortable.

I was doomed now, for sure. When Mama and Daddy heard that I had refused a proposal of marriage from Hector, I would likely be disowned and cast out of the house. I thought of myself wandering the beaches of the Outer Banks, with scraggly hair covering my naked breasts, shucking oysters and milking cows for my sustenance.

I turned my head on the pillow, my hair sticking to my neck in the heat. Charlie's and Martha's sleeping faces were flushed, their cheeks slick with spit. At least *they* slept well here, in Nags Head.

I thought of what it might feel like to submerge my body in the cool, quiet depths of the Fresh Ponds, to forget the whole world for a few moments and let my body drift and sink amid thousands of years of rain water.

I stroked the insides of my thighs, savoring the imaginary feel of the water groping along the curves. And I saw Ben's face, felt his strong arms helping me through the water. Just settling my mind on the essence of him made my breath quicken and my calves tingle. And I knew what it was that I now wanted.

I wanted Ben to teach me how to swim.

⌒

The next evening, Ben agreed that I needed to learn how to swim in a depth of water deeper than a bathing tub, so the following morning I climbed the steps to the warm upstairs bedroom, where Mama was curled into a hump under the bed linens.

"I'm off to the Fresh Ponds with Maddie and the rest. I'll return for supper."

Her voice came out muffled. "And will Hector accompany you?"

"I believe so, yes," I lied.

She unfurled herself and turned to me, and poking her head out of the covers, she actually smiled, a slight blurring of her scarlet lips. "I imagine he'll be proposing to you soon, Abigail. Wear your best dress today. That skirt and shirtwaist aren't appropriate at all."

I looked down at my old brown skirt and the white shirtwaist that I thought would be perfect for a quick walk in the woods before swimming.

"All right, then."

She just lay calmly in bed, watching me. It didn't feel quite right, leaving her up here all by herself.

I asked, "Do you want any other books to read? I've got plenty downstairs."

She reached for the Bible beside her. "Oh, no. This is the only book I need now."

I nodded, thinking she already must have read it hundreds of times through this summer. Before I left, I walked to her and kissed her lightly on her warm cheek, trying to imagine the spurned daughter of immigrants buried deep inside her.

I went to my bedroom to change into one of my best day dresses, a pale pink, short-sleeved cotton and silk piece with little embroidered rosettes along the hem. I forgot the corset and hoop, though, so the dress didn't look quite right. But I hardly cared. I tied a bonnet onto my head and left for the Fresh Ponds, carrying a basket with my heavy flannel bathing costume and some corn bread, apples, and a canteen of water.

The cool woods were empty of visitors so early in the morning. Without the incessant chatter of human voices, the air was still and clean. The towering greenery made its own kind of noise, a vibrating hum that was felt and not heard. Great cumulus clouds roamed the skies, occasionally blocking out the sun.

In the reflection of Great Pond, I saw myself, my red hair and pink dress garish next to the serene greens and blues around me. As I stood looking into the clear water, I heard Ben crack through the leaves that had fallen dry onto the sand. His brown face appeared beside mine in the pond.

"Where's the parade?" he joked, grabbing a handful of skirt.

Hector's proposal lingered unknown in the air between us like a bad odor, so I hurriedly removed the bathing costume from the basket and looked around for a place to change my clothing. I walked over to a nearby cedar tree, but its circumference was too thin to hide me completely. "Turn your back."

"Can't I just close my eyes? You don't trust me not to look?" he said playfully.

"No, I don't. It'll only take a minute."

He turned away from me. "All righty, then. Let me know if you need any help."

I first removed my shoes and stockings. Then I unfastened the closures along the back and slid the sleeves down. With some awkwardness amid the branches and leaves, I stepped out of the heavy dress and draped it over a low branch. Then I slid my chemise over my head, baring my breasts. Finally I unfastened my pantalettes and, with some hesitation, bunched them down to my ankles and stepped out of them.

And there I stood, naked for any passerby to see. I felt the cool air caress my buttocks and tease the hair between my legs.

With one eye on Ben's back, I stepped into the gray Turkish pants. Then I pulled my arms through the sleeves of the paletot and buttoned it up the front. The entire costume hung on me like a blanket.

"Okay. What do you think?" I said, holding out the material of the dress on either side of me.

He turned around to look at me. Then he started laughing until the tears pooled in his eyes. He couldn't even speak.

"I'm so glad that I amuse you," I said, a blush washing over my face.

He doubled over, clutching his midsection. "I'm sorry, Abby, I really am. But how in tarnation do you expect to learn how to swim wearing all that cloth?"

I sighed and looked down at the hideous thing whose fibers made every inch of my skin itch. I hated everything about it. "I suppose I could just wear my underthings."

He straightened up quickly, all the laughter gone. "Okay by me."

So I retreated back behind the skinny cedar tree. I changed out of the bathing costume and put on the chemise and pantalettes again. Then I loosened my hair and tucked the pins into the basket.

When he turned to me and saw my bare arms and calves and hair hanging down my back, he breathed in audibly and looked away.

He said, "Much better."

Then he unbuttoned his shirt and removed it, and I could see his muscular brown chest and thick shoulders and arms, so real in these quiet woods. He started walking to the edge of the pond in his frayed trousers. He held out a hand for me, and I took it with tension stiffening my fingers.

"Don't be afraid, Abby. I'm not going to let anything happen to you," he said. He looked into my eyes, steadily, without blinking, and I knew it was true.

We waded into the cool water, so that the surface skimmed the skin around my knees, and then he stopped me. "All right. Now I have to put my arms around you. We'll go where it's just a little deeper."

I nodded, and he came close to me and put his hands around my middle. His flexing hands almost spanned the entire girth of my body. His arms moved with assurance, with knowledge of water.

He drew me out into the pond a few more yards, where my feet couldn't touch the leafy bottom. My legs dangled in the open water. I kicked them a little, enjoying the way the water reached all the way up my flanks.

My chest was now submerged up to my neck. My chemise floated around my breasts, and my pantalettes twisted around my thighs.

Ben's arms pulled me out lengthwise, so that I was floating on my back, arms and legs stretched out in the water. I felt my hair sway heavily next to my face, weighing my head down. His forearms held me under my back.

"You can open your eyes, you know," Ben said.

I unscrewed my eyes and saw his face. He was gazing at me with such love, I felt my throat squeeze.

I said softly, "You're a good person, Ben."

His face hardened. "There are things about me that you wouldn't care to know."

I laughed. I just knew that Ben didn't have a bad bone in his body. I said, "I wouldn't want you to be *too* perfect."

I closed my eyes again, listening to the sounds of the woods with under-water ears. I felt Ben's hand move to hold my thigh, his other hand still holding my back. His palm wound up through the leg of the pantalette, so that his hand rested on my bare skin. He rubbed the wet flesh with his thumb.

I breathed in deeply of the woody air, a smell of life. I just floated with a mix of dark and light playing over my lids.

Then I felt his mouth on the nipple of my breast, through the cloth of the chemise. He sucked it gently, while his hand moved even farther up my leg. My breath quickened as if I were hurrying somewhere, but all was fluid and stillness. He took his mouth away and the air cooled my nipple into a pebbly peak. He rubbed it softly with a thumb.

Ben took his other hand from beneath my back, and just like that I was floating on my own. I smiled, my eyes still closed.

He whispered, "I don't know what I'm going to do without you, Abby."

I felt a little drop of water fall on my face then, and I looked up half expecting to see Ben crying. But the clouds through the arch of trees were gray with rain. The drops fell on my face and chest and pattered about us on the water. With the sun gone, the water began to cool.

He took my hands again and pulled me up. "Hold your breath, now. We're going under."

We both took deep breaths and went under the gray water. I could now feel the leaves and twigs on the bottom of the pond. I could taste their little souls in the freshwater.

I forced myself to open my eyes. I saw Ben's face through the murkiness, and he was smiling at me, little bubbles traveling from his nose to the surface. The raindrops speckled the water above us, and I felt so safe, under the world above. I never would have thought it possible, before Ben. He held my hands tightly.

We came up for air, and my head dripped water down my back and chest. Ben's clean face was chiseled stone. And still the rain came down, a gentle shower.

He let my hands go then and said, "Just be still. Feel your body in the water. Move your arms and legs around just a little, and keep your head up."

He demonstrated treading water, and he made it look so easy. I kept my eyes on his face as I fought down the fear. But the feeling of being alone in the water was too tempting.

It was just me, moving alone. Only me, keeping myself afloat. I managed to tread water for a few seconds before I started sinking a bit. He grabbed me, laughing. "Don't drown on me, now."

"I wasn't going to drown," I said, slightly offended.

"Now, kick your legs." He held me at arm's length and I started kicking my legs, making big splashes in the rainy water. Then he let me go and I put my face in and swam with my arms up and out of the water while kicking my legs, as I'd seen the men doing in the ocean surf. And I was swimming. Not very prettily, but I was swimming!

He hollered out, "Now you got it!"

He swam over to me with four easy strokes and kissed me with wet lips. And I felt a part of this woods, like I was meant to be here and no place else.

I thought briefly of Uncle Jack, when he was saddling up Ace of Spades for one last ride over the plantation before he left for the war. He had breathed in deeply, filling his lungs with breaths of barn air, and said, "I sure will miss this smell when I'm gone."

I had joked, "What, essence of manure?"

With his face more serious than I had ever seen it, he had answered, "Yes, indeed. Smells like home to me."

I had laughed sarcastically, and he had abruptly left me then, riding off on Ace with a stony look on his face.

Now I knew what he had meant. Nags Head, with all of its different textures and layers, had become a home to me, and it felt as serious and as important as a dirty barn did to Uncle Jack. I somehow knew that Uncle Jack would have been proud of me for saying so. He would have been proud of this new Little Red Reb.

"I better put my dress in a dry spot," I said, looking over at the pile of fine pink cloth fallen onto a duff of leaves.

"Too late for that," Ben teased. But he sighed and made to help me out of the water, gazing unabashedly at my body in the wet underclothes.

We sat down beneath a live oak tree with a thick, gnarled trunk, and he wrapped his moist arms around me. We were silent, listening to the sound of the rain pelting on the leaves of the wax myrtle trees beside us.

He said, "The only thing left for you to do is climb Jockey's Ridge. Then you've officially lived in Nags Head. It's the tallest sand dune on the East Coast."

All summer the dunes had gazed down their sloped noses at me like elderly relatives. I had taken them for granted. I suddenly was filled with a feeling of urgency. "Let's do it today."

"You sure you can stay away that long? It might take a while. Won't your mama miss you?"

I snorted, then took the corn bread, water jug, and fruit from the basket. We ate and drank for a while under the live oak, and soon the rain stopped and sunlight shone through the trees once again, shards of jade shimmering in the rain's remains.

But I found myself missing the rain when it was gone.

Nags Head Woods stretched north to south along the sound side of the dunes, with Run Hill perched to the north of the woods and Jockey's Ridge anchored on the southern end. It would be a short walk to the dunes through the dense maritime thicket.

We navigated a sandy trail, used mostly by locals, that wound its way beneath a curly arch of tree limbs. Ben made no attempt for my elbow, as Hector would have done. I knew that he'd offer his assistance if I really needed it, but for the most part he just let me walk.

The farther east we went, the more sandy the terrain became. Scrubby live oaks, loblolly pines, and clumps of cottonbush and beach heather were scattered over the gentle hills. I knew that this was where the gray foxes and possums and raccoons lived, out of the sea spray and northeast winds. This was where the mainland men liked to hunt, guiding their sweating horses over the sand hills. Every few seconds, lizards darted across our path, leaving thin snaky trails in the sand with their tails.

Here the trees were forbidden to grow tall. The land quickly began to resemble a desert, where nothing but sand existed. The farther east we went, the more I saw that only sporadic clumps of beach grass had managed to anchor themselves into the shifting sand.

We soon reached the base of one of the three tallest peaks of sand and looked up. It would be a hard climb, even for someone like Ben. I hadn't fully realized how high the piles of sand were. It must have taken thousands upon thousands of years to create them, and here I was, about to try to climb one.

"Believe it or not, this here slope is the best place to start," he said, looking up. We began to climb, Ben staying to the back of me. My feet immediately sunk into the yielding sand, so I hardly seemed to move in my damp skirts. The ridge was steep, much steeper than Run Hill.

I got surprisingly winded after a few minutes of climbing, and abruptly sat down, my legs pointing straight down the slope of the dune. Ben, hardly breathing at all, sat down with me and said with a grin, "You've got me worried, gal! Too much activity for one day, I reckon."

I could hardly speak. "Don't worry about me."

"Whatever you say, schoolmarm," he joked, grabbing my hand and kissing the sandy palm.

I huffed, "Tell me this, you braggart. Why doesn't this sand ever blow away?"

"Well, I'll tell you, since you asked so nice. In the winter, the winds usually blow out of the northeast, and in the summer, they blow out of the southwest. So the sand is constantly blown to and fro, never disappearing," he said. "Plus, just below this dry stuff here, the sand's wet. Helps the dune stay put."

The top layer had dried quickly in the afternoon sun. The sand was as fine as powdered sugar, quite different from the pebbled, clumpy beach sand, which scrubbed my feet raw. This sand made me want to lie down and sleep on it, bury myself in it for a hundred years. I scooped up great innocent handfuls and watched it pour like honeyed dust between my fingers.

After a while, I caught my breath and stood to continue. Ben stood, too, and said, "Follow me, now." He started to climb.

I said, offended, "Why is that? Am I too slow for a Banker?"

He laughed. "It'll be easier for you, following in my footsteps."

And he was right. The sand was more forgiving once it was broken up a bit by his hardy feet. Inside the skirts of my dress, sweat trickled down my burning thighs. My legs hurt so badly that I started to use my arms to propel myself upward. I grabbed at the sand in front of me, as if it could offer me any sort of leverage.

But soon I could see the crest of the ridge in front of me. With a few more lunges, I was at the top.

And there was nothing between me and the sky, which had been painted with the golden oranges and pinks of a stained-glass sunset, as reverent as a view from a church pew. With the light of the sun to the west, the ocean was bluer than I ever recall seeing it from the beach. The brownish-blue sound rocked contentedly on the other side of the dunes. And the wind whipped freely up here, with no obstructions.

From this vantage point, everything looked temporary. The Banks looked so skinny, as if the webbed water could just cover them up forever and no one would know they were ever here.

From far away, everything fell into its correct place with such clarity that I was sure this was the view that God must have. There was the sand, there the ocean, and there the sky. It all fit like a perfect puzzle. The only thing out of place were the cottages. I could see our house, tiny and burdensome.

I covered my face with my hands as sobs lodged in my throat. Ben quickly drew me to him, and I buried my face in his tattered shirt. I inhaled his scent of sweat and sand and pond water. I felt his hard chest beneath my cheek.

With closed eyes, I imagined the house, down below, waiting for me. The cottage porch was probably empty right now. The table was missing the weight of books. The chairs lacked their occupants.

I ran my hands through Ben's stiff hair, rubbed his strong neck and shoulders and back with creaking fingers. He placed both hands on my neck, thumbs resting on my jawbone, as he kissed me. My mind emptied of all thoughts. I was a substance of air, of ocean, of sand. Not even human.

But Ben suddenly pulled away from me. Some climbers had just bumbled onto our dune. With goose pimples of irritation popping on my neck, I turned around and saw a handful of young children, exploring after their supper. They all gazed about as if they had suddenly found themselves on the moon. I breathed with relief, seeing that Charlie and Martha weren't with them.

Biding our time, we sat down on the sand. The wind eased giant locks of my hair from the pins. I took off my shoes and banged the sand out of them.

Ben watched me with liquid eyes the color of the ocean. He said, "Has anyone ever told you that these sand dunes reminded a man of a place in England called Nags Head? The name caught on with folks, and has stuck ever since."

I shook my head. Apparently there were many theories regarding the history of the name of Nags Head, but I doubted anyone knew for sure anymore.

"It's also magical. It's said that any couple that's engaged to be married on top of this sand hill will live a long, happy life together. And it always comes true."

I looked at my hands, the word *engaged* smoldering in my brain. I said, "That's just a Banker myth."

He shook his head. "Can't always explain everything away, Abby. Don't you believe in anything that you can't see or read about in your books?"

I raked the sand through my fingers and across my open palms. It was so soft, I almost couldn't feel it. "I used to. I used to think that animals could talk to me. I used to hear the trees speak to me."

I remembered when I used to conduct one-sided conversations with the horses. I paused after every question and sentence, to give the horses time to respond to me. In the summertime, before the war, I used to sneak out of the house and sleep in the tobacco fields, with the green stalks swaying above me. I would talk to the ripe shoots and compare stories of youth.

"But after the war, after my uncle died, I couldn't hear anyone or anything. The only things that made sense were words in books," I said.

He nodded. "You could escape for a bit, I reckon. Go to your own deserted island."

I said, "It's strange, though. Every time I pick up a book now, I can't seem to make my way through it. I don't want to escape anymore."

He smiled at me. "All I know is, when I'm with you, I believe in something magical. It's like the feeling I get when I hook a fish on the line. I still can't believe it happened to me."

Finally the children ran wildly down the sound side of the tallest dune. I could hear their screams—of fear or delight, I couldn't rightly tell—grow fainter the lower they went. I hoped they wouldn't care to climb back up again.

Ben mumbled, "It's just us up here again."

"Then why do you look so downhearted?"

He looked in the direction of the cottage. "I reckon we don't have much time left this summer."

I ran my finger along his strong chin and jawbone. The gingered stubble scratched my finger like a cat's tongue. "Then let's just live up here. Our very own sand dune."

"Now, I've been thinking on this a lot. You don't have to go back. You could stay here on the Banks. With me . . ."

I faced away from him abruptly. "Hector proposed to me two days ago."

Ben spluttered, "What did you tell him?"

"I told him I couldn't marry him. But the word *no* seemed unsatisfactory to him."

Ben stood up, spraying sand all over my dress, and crossed his arms tightly across his chest. He didn't speak for several long minutes.

Then he looked down at me, his eyes wild and desperate, like a man awaiting the plank on a pirate ship. "I could provide for you, Abby. You may not think as such, but I'm moving up in this world. Won't fetch what a doctor could bring home, but we'd get by. We could be together."

He spoke rapidly, without looking at me. "We'll have enough to buy as many books as you want! Big fat ones with the longest words you've ever seen! We could read together, all day and night. Escape the world together."

I stood up, wanting to calm his agitation. I caressed his fevered face, and he closed his eyes. I ran my fingers over the lines that branched out from his eyes. I paused to lay my finger in the crease between his nose and lip.

I said, "Remember when you told me I'd grown my sea legs?"

He nodded, exhaling slowly.

"I haven't been able to get the notion out of my head since then. I felt stronger, like I'd learned how to walk again, but in a different direction than everyone else."

He stood still. A gentle wind blew sand over our feet.

I said quietly, "I've got to see where my sea legs carry me."

With his eyes still closed, tears trickled down his cheeks.

The sky seemed too close now. It smothered me. I struggled to get my bearings, but the sand had blown and blown, covering my path completely. It was disconcerting to realize that I couldn't go back to where I had started. And I had no idea how I had gotten here, my footprints long gone. The only way forward was down a sucking slope.

I breathed deeply and held the breath for as long as I could. The sky was a deep purplish gold, a healing bruise. I closed my eyes and I could hear every particle of sand skipping along the dune and flying through the air, endlessly connecting with one another.

I pulled Ben down onto the sand. He propped himself up over me and his weathered face was set against the backdrop of the fading sunset. I pulled his damp shirt over his head and ran my hands over his back.

He gently lifted the hem of my dirty pink dress, and the night air cooled my legs. He stroked my sandy toes, one by one. He kissed the freckles on my knees. I lay back in the sand and closed my eyes, his fingertips drizzling over my body like ocean spray. As he caressed my thighs, the insides of my arms, I thought of summer strawberries, ripe tomatoes, sugar and honey.

But then he pushed himself inside me, as strong as an arm pulling in a net. I gasped with the tearing of flesh. My hands dug far down into the sand in a strange agony, trying to reach the cold, damp layer below.

But with one glance at his face, the pain went away. I rolled my head back and forth in the soft cradle of sand. He drove in and out of me, a fierce lullaby.

I could see the beginnings of the stars in the graying sky. His warm tears slid onto my skin. He sobbed out my name until darkness descended. I whispered to him of the love in my heart.

'Round and 'round we all went. Life, and death, would spin and spiral forever, taking and giving. But time stopped on the dune that night. Life suspended herself, like the full moon in a dark, dark sky.

⌀

Daddy had finally called Doc Newman to the cottage. He had taken a special packet schooner from Edenton, incurring an inflated rate of passage. His clothing was disheveled and his white hair stringy when he arrived at the western door, but he still had the twinkle in his eyes that I remembered from when I was a small girl. I almost expected him to reach into his pocket for some sweetmeats.

He greeted me more affectionately than he had in the past. "Hector tells me that Nags Head was right beautiful this summer. Hot, and every inch covered with sand. But beautiful nonetheless. He seemed quite taken with it."

He winked at me, making his bushy white eyebrow plunge over his dark gray eye.

I smiled tentatively and said, "Yes, it has been hot, but more pleasant than Edenton has been this summer, I imagine."

"Oh, it has been a swampland, to be sure."

Winnie led him upstairs and I followed along, wondering what, if anything, Hector had told his father about me.

Mama was in bed, her bowl propped on her middle. She looked so downright awful I hardly recognized her. But when Mama saw Doc Newman, she brightened up immediately and handed the bowl to me. It held what appeared to be spit-up watermelon.

Doc Newman sat down in the rocker by her bed and placed his big black medical bag right on top of her white Bible on the bedside table. Mama flinched at the affront, but said nothing.

He smiled at her. "I heard you've been feeling under the weather, Ingrid. That baby in your belly giving you some trouble?"

Mama waved a limp hand. "Oh, no, not too much trouble. It's to be expected."

"Nolan indicated you've been experiencing some mood swings. Not feeling yourself. *Not leaving this bedroom*. Ingrid, you need fresh air. It's too stuffy up here. Defeats the purpose of living by the sea."

He raised the windows and propped open the shutters with sticks. The ocean air filled the room.

Mama's face darkened at the mention of her husband's name. "What does Nolan know about carrying babies? Even when he's here, he's gone. He's got other things on his mind this summer."

"I imagine he does. *Your* job is to carry this baby."

"My body doesn't want this baby. I'm so sick, I can't even get out of bed. And the smell of the sea makes me ill. I can't stand it."

He said rather sternly, "If your body didn't want the baby, it would have rejected it a while ago. You're going to have to carry the baby, Ingrid. You're going to have to try harder."

Mama's eyes welled with tears at his advice. "I can't," she whispered. "I don't want to."

Doc Newman and Mama looked at each other, likely thinking on the many years of blood-soaked, bedridden hardships they'd weathered together. His furry eyebrows knit together in a V.

"You can do it, Ingrid," he said softly, but without conviction.

She said, "I've been reading the Bible. There is one verse that I can't get out of my head. It comes to me in my sleep. Book of Luke, chapter six, verses forty-six to forty-nine. Do you know it?"

He shook his head. "Not off the top of my head. What is it?"

Mama didn't even reach for her Bible. She began reciting from memory a passage that I remembered from Sunday school.

"And why call ye me, Lord, and do not the things which I say? Whosoever cometh to me, and heareth my sayings, and doeth them, I will show you to whom he is like: He is like a man which built a house, and digged deep, and laid the foundation on a rock: And when the flood arose, the stream beat vehemently upon that house, and could not shake it: For it was founded upon a rock." She paused, then spoke in a whisper, *"But he that heareth, and doeth not, is like a man that without a foundation built a house upon the earth; against which the stream did beat vehemently, and immediately it fell; and the ruin of that house was great."*

Doc Newman said with interest, "What does that passage mean to you, Ingrid?"

She put her hands over her eyes. "It fills me with fear."

She took her hands from her face and glanced at me, a brief look of motherly regret. "I have scorned Christ's prophecies. I have cared only for myself. *I have not loved.* And look! Now I am living in a house upon the sand! A house built expressly for false Christians! I am surely doomed to hell for eternity. *God is telling me this,* I know."

Doc looked alarmed. "Now, Ingrid, that's taking things too far, indeed. You're an upstanding Christian woman. I've never seen you miss a day of church. I think you need some more fresh air, move around a bit. Staying up here all day isn't doing you a bit of good."

With that, he told Winnie and me to leave the room so he could examine Mama, who was sobbing into her pillow. Half an hour later, Doc Newman clomped slowly down the narrow staircase. Winnie and I both greeted him expectantly at the bottom of the stairs.

Without meeting our eyes, he dispensed his favorite prescription. "She needs fresh air, and lots of it. That room is making her loopy. Quoting scripture, indeed."

This hardly satisfied me. "Dr. Newman, pardon me for saying this, but it seems to me she needs more than just fresh air. She is unwell . . . in her spirit, too. And you led us to believe that she couldn't get pregnant again."

He shrugged as he snapped his doctor's bag shut. "I've been known to be wrong in these kinds of cases. Things do happen."

I dared to ask him, "Will she survive the birth?"

He fiddled with the rim of his hat. "It's hard to tell. Everything appears to be moving along normally. But as you know, her pregnancies and births have been hard on her body. I can't say for sure what will happen."

I stared at him, wanting more of an explanation, especially one that freed her and the baby from death sentences. He just kissed my hand with his papery lips. "Rest and fresh air, Abigail. Oh, and I'll see you soon, I hope."

With a slight tilt of his flossy head, he donned his hat and headed straight through the sand toward the hotel.

As soon as the screen door banged shut after him, I heard Mama call me upstairs. Her voice sounded strangled, as if she were set to retch, so I hurried up to see her. She was out of bed and standing in the middle of the room in her dirty nightgown. I had forgotten how tall she was.

"*Refusing* a proposal of marriage?" she spit, her white face contorted. "Are you trying to kill me with your willfulness, Abigail?"

Doc Newman must have known more about the situation than he had let on. I couldn't believe that he had mentioned it to Mama, especially in the state she was in.

But I could still feel Ben's kisses on my thighs from earlier in the evening. I could still feel my sore flesh rubbing against my pantalettes when I moved. I couldn't think about anything else.

I uttered the only words that came to mind: "I don't want to marry him, Mama. He's not the one for me."

She began to pace the floor, her heavy breasts swinging against the cotton of her gown. She muttered violently to herself and pulled at her long hair. "You didn't think you could keep the refusal a secret from us, I hope?"

I shook my head pathetically. "I didn't think you were up to hearing about it right now. Have you seen yourself lately? You're losing your mind up here, Mama."

She moved quickly to me and slapped me hard across the fleshy part of my cheek with her bony fingers. "Do you think I like worrying about you? Do you think I *enjoy* planning for *your* future?"

Her voice was laced with a dormant Swedish accent. I had heard it only once before, when she was delirious after one of her miscar-riages. "Do you know that you have always been like this? Ever since you were a baby, I have felt your desire for independence like a hot poker in my belly, and it has caused me no end of anguish." She grabbed her breasts and squeezed them hard. "You flatly refused to take my nourishment. Oh, I tried to hold you just so, forcing your mouth toward my breast. But you would cry, your little fists screwed tight.

"I was forced to bring in Winnifred. Of course, you drank from her breasts like the milk contained the sweetest sugar. You never wanted me to hold you. You wiggled away from my body and lay facedown down in your cradle. From the time you first walked, you wanted to do everything by yourself, and do things your own way, never listening to my instructions. Roaming the fields, talking to the horses.

"And your laugh! You barked that laugh all day long, the most ir-ritating sound, like an animal in heat."

I remembered, suddenly, that it was Uncle Jack who had triggered all the laughter. I certainly didn't inherit the habit from my parents. I tried mightily to imagine the advice he would give me right now, but all I could hear was Jack's own belly laugh, a sound that I always as-sociated with unconditional love.

In spite of the tension in the room, I stifled a smile, thinking of him at his happiest, and as the tickly warmth spread into my throat, threatening to erupt, I realized with clarity that some of Uncle Jack's best qualities lived on in a Banker named Ben. And the two of them made me stronger, encouraging me.

Mama went on, oblivious to my straightening posture. "Messy rib-bons dripping down your back, hem always dragging in mud. Noth-ing ever vexed you, except when you couldn't do what you wanted. But I'm tired of your tantrums now. Worn out by your willfulness.

You will marry Hector. I will arrange a visit myself, upon our return to Edenton."

And down came the cage, with wooden bars, pilings in the sand. I asked reasonbly, "Do you want me to end up like you, Mama?"

As irrational as she had become this summer, when she looked at me, her eyes were as serious as a tombstone. "I see that you have dreams for yourself. You wear them all over your sunburned face. Learn to live without them, Abigail. Trust me, they will hurt you badly."

She removed the sticks from the shutters and shut the windows, encasing herself in the oppressive heat once more. Then she lay calmly back down on the bed, pale and spent. She reached for her Bible, free from the weight of the medical bag.

With all thoughts of laughter gone, I walked quietly out of the room, my thoughts already skipping to the night of teaching ahead of me.

CHAPTER FIFTEEN

Benjamin Whimble
August 23, 1868

I cannot express what a satisfaction it was to me to come into my old hutch and lie down in my hammock-bed. This little wandering journey, without settled place of abode, had been so unpleasant to me, that my own house, as I called it to myself, was a perfect settlement to me compared to that; and it rendered everything about me so comfortable that I resolved I would never go a great way from it again while it should be my lot to stay on the island.

—ROBINSON CRUSOE

I SWUNG THE AX SO HARD IT WENT HALFWAY THROUGH THE OAK TREE ON the first blow. With a few more cracks, and a holler from my throat, it set to falling down into the dirt with a crash. Then I moved right along to the next one. I couldn't think about nothing except Abby, and trying to show her that she could stay here with me.

After Jockey's Ridge, I went straight over to see old Mrs. Barker about cutting some of her timber down. She'd been after me a while to do it, on account she needed the money from the wood right much, ever since her husband had died a couple years back.

As payment, she told me I could have some of the wood for my own use. It wouldn't be much, after she had sold what she needed to, but it would be a good start, maybe just enough to build a house.

I featured Abby laughing that open-mouth laugh when she saw the tiny thing it would surely be. It would be near to about as small as her outhouse on the beach. But I was powerful hoping she wouldn't care.

I kept thinking on the feel of her heavy hair, the bones of the back of her skull under my hands. And I couldn't stop seeing that thatch of red hair between her legs, as unlikely a sight as a tangle of scarlet seaweed floating in a green ocean. I still felt what it was like inside her. The memory of it was as warm as a summer evening spent sitting on top of Run Hill, thinking on all the good things that nature offers up for free.

I wanted that feeling for the rest of my days.

The summer sure had been a higgledy-piggledy one, the best of heaven 'n' hell all back to back. The thoughts of the weeks previous, what I'd done for Mister Sinclair, were still weighing me down like a ton of bricks. When I wasn't thinking about Abby, those memories haunted me all the time.

I took an extra-hard swing at the tree in front of me and it cracked loud as thunder as it fell, right in line with its fallen comrades. I stopped to wipe my forehead with the tail of my shirt and looked on the broken trees.

For many long years, those trees felt pretty good, thinking they were out of harm's way. But there was no safe place on the Banks, for no living thing. Something was bound to get you, one way or another. Sooner or later, you were cut off from the roots you'd spent long years growing.

But those trees—so strong and proud—looked just like my future home. They would be put to some good use, even still.

⚭

After one last haul of wood to the building site, I rode tuckered old Junie back to Pap's to wash up. And it was with a hopeful heart that I went to the weddings in Nags Head Woods.

Two couples I'd known for a coon's age were uniting in matrimony, having finally gotten a bona fide preacher to do the honors.

By the time I got there there was already a big boodle gathered in a clearing near the sound side. There were tables and chairs set up for a wedding feast, and flowers and vines were strung from the branches of the trees as a decorative touch. Pap stood with the other old-timers, likely sharing fishing yarns they'd told over and over through the long years.

I bet he had a mouthful, since he didn't talk with me anymore. So much was different for me now. Seemed like I needed to talk to Pap about it to make it all seem real to me. But none of it was what he wanted to hear.

My buddies were still glad to see me, though. "Where you been?" Jimmy hollered. He looked me over close. "What'd you do, wash yerself?"

Harley said, "I'll bet you been off with that teacher gal. What she been learnin' you now, is what I want to know." He slapped me on the back.

I grinned, not being able to help myself. Just the mentioning of her made me want to scurry 'round the sand like a jackrabbit.

Harley whispered, "Better tell you now, Eliza is here, and none too happy at that. She's acting more 'n' more like her mama every day."

I caught sight of her with some of her friends, laying out the fixings. She looked right nice, her hair pinned up again and wearing what looked to be a new blue dress. But her face was gray and ornery. She never was the grinning kind of gal, though.

I doubted I should go talk with her right now. She'd rightly yell at me in front of the wedding guests and ruin the frolic. Just then, little Genny Harper came running through the woods, hollering that the preacher was coming. Sure enough, a wagon came rolling through the woods, carrying the reverend.

The crowd whooped and the wedding couples appeared. Their brown faces told of only happy thoughts. They held each other's hands and wouldn't let go.

I thought of Abby, and how I'd like to marry her in these very same woods. Maybe she'd wear that yellow dress of hers. It lit up the woods like sunshine, but she didn't really need a dress to do that. I thought of her pink nipples poking through her wet undershirt, soaked with water from my own Great Pond, and almost swooned right there in the sand.

Soon a peace settled over the folks, which is really saying something, since us Bankers aren't known for our soft voices. I heard an osprey's call and the quiet slap of the sound water. And I heard the preacher's words ring out loud and clear, giving me gooseflesh all over my arms. He married the two couples in about five minutes flat, and then the feast began with shouts of glee.

The ladies had plumb outdone themselves. There was more belly timber than I'd ever seen in my life: savory venison, hams, sea bass and grouper, cuts of beef, all manner of chicken, biscuits and gravy, and cakes, custards, jellies, and pies. I for one ate like a swine on holiday.

When the sun started its setting, Jacob fetched his fiddle and began to scratch his bow on the strings. Harley and Jimmy joined in, and then all the folks commenced a double shuffle dance right there. Bare feet kicked up sand like a hurricane wind. Then a barrel of beer was rolled out, and everyone quit their dancing to get a cup full.

At candle-lighting, couples started their pairing off for more dancing. But I just sat in the sand, drinking beer and soaking up the good will. In the shuffling group, I saw Eliza dancing with Abner Miller. The man had had his eye out for Eliza for a long time, but she never took no notice of him, he having a lazy eye, buck teeth, and a limp.

Eliza twirled 'round in her blue skirts, her hair coming loose from her up-do. She hadn't so much as looked at me all night. But she wasn't looking much at Abner no how. She kept trying to move a different way than he was, and with him limping along, they looked like a three-legged donkey chasing its tail.

A while into the dance, Eliza shouted about something and went off to sit on a log. Abner just stood there, a-looking over at her like he'd lost his dog. Then Elena and Iola—her two best friends—broke off from their partners, too, one of who was a gangly-legged, pimple-faced boy named Willy. The girls sat talking like little old biddies behind their hands.

Willy came over and said, "I never knew Eliza to be so highfalutin. She told us we can't dance proper and to go get ourselves lost."

Before I could wonder a thought, Eliza came strutting over. She smiled at me, but the gesture made her look mad instead of happy. "You look slicked up tonight, Benjamin Whimble. What's the occasion? Surely you didn't get all primped up for a wedding. I *know* how little you care about such things as weddings."

I tried my best to be natural. "A man's got to wash himself ever once in a while. Man alive, I must have been dirtier than a pig's snout, the way you all are acting tonight."

She reached out and touched my face with a finger. "Well, I think you look right handsome. Hey, and what do you think of *my* looks?" She curtsied for me. "I made this dress myself. Ordered the fabric from a fancy store in New Bern. Cost me a pretty penny, but some things are just worth it."

Before I could say a word, she grabbed my hand and said, "I want to talk to you. What say we walk over to the water and leave these drunks to their dancing, if that's what you call it."

She started pulling me toward the sound, away from the carryings-on. Willy just stared and shook his head at us real sorry like as we left.

We reached the water's edge and stood in the wet sand looking at the round moon. Eliza wouldn't let go my hand, and I didn't have the heart to let go myself. I breathed in deep. "How you been, Eliza?"

"Not so good, Ben, if you want to know the truth. But I hear *you've* been having a grand time with that Abigail. Folks have been spotting you all over the Banks with her. That's nice of you, to play tour guide with her before she leaves for the mainland. Must be any day, and she'll be catching that steamboat for home."

At that I pulled my hand away from her, but it took some wrenching to do it. "Is this what you wanted to talk about? 'Cause I don't want to discuss her with you. It ain't right, given our history."

She looked so sad then. " 'Our history,' says he! Don't that cap the climax! You know, I always thought we'd live our lives together, right here, in sight of the woods and the sound, like you wanted. I know this place ain't much. Nags Head ain't much better than a pile of sand stuck in the middle of the sea. But it's *us*, Ben." She sounded like she was going to have herself a good cry. "I can't see myself here without you. And I sure can't see you with that Abigail. Her family ain't right for this island. They never will be. They don't have the guts to stick it out here, year after year, storm after storm. They ain't made of the same stuff we are." She crossed her arms over her chest.

"And everyone agrees with me. You shouldn't go mixing with the weaker kind of folks. It'll bring down the island, make us soft. We need to stick together, us Bankers."

At first, I'll allow, I thought the Sinclair house was the craziest sight I'd ever seen. And I still thought that way most days. But sometimes I caught myself wishing for a window to the sea, so that when I awoke in the morning I could look out and for miles and miles see nothing but water. Raging waves or lapping curls, it wouldn't matter. It would be like having a friend who never left your backyard, a friend with a temper sometimes, sure, but also a merry friend, a true friend, one who was always there through thick and thin.

"I miss you, Ben. That's all. I just miss you." Her eyes were wild and her breath was quick and loud. "I can be a lady, too, just like Abigail. I can make you love me." She grabbed my face hard with both her hands and kissed me rough. She tried to poke her tongue in my mouth, but I pushed her away.

"Stop it now, Eliza. I've got nothing else to say to you." I turned and walked back to the party, closing off my ears to her gut-wrenching sobs.

I felt so sorry for what I'd done to her. But the love I had for Abby would never go away. Even if she did leave me for Edenton, I would always want her. And Eliza could never be enough for me again. That was just the way it was.

⚭

The party was dying down when I got back, but Jacob and Jimmy and Harley were still there, getting soused on the beer. I joined them in the sand. They all looked at me but didn't say a word about Eliza.

"Well, well, Benny. I been noticing you haven't told us much about your new job. I *heard* that you were set to work construction down in Hatteras," said Jimmy.

I grabbed Jimmy's cup of beer from him and took a deep pull. "You heard right. I'm a bona fide member of Mister Stetson's crew. How's *that* make you feel?"

They all stared at me like I'd grown fins and gills. Harley hollered, "I think it's way past high time you told us how you got that job, and if there's any left for us! You've got to look out for your friends, you know!"

Jimmy gulped the rest of the beer and waved his empty cup in my face. Then he asked, "That big bug you guiding for have anything to do with you getting that job?"

"And what if he did? I deserve that job, fair and square. And I'm helping my pap retire. Just shut pan about it."

I noticed Jacob not saying much a-tall. He just sat there in the dark, smoking a pipe and watching me. "I hope you not getting in too deep with that Mister Sinclair," he finally said. "He ain't of no account."

I should have known Jacob would have more information than most. Being a waterman, he went all over the rivers and sounds and swampy inlets of northeast Carolina. He talked to all kinds of folks, black and white and yellow, rich and poor. He was naturally good-natured and helpful, so folks trusted him to keep their secrets.

"It ain't none of your beeswax, none of you. And if you know what's good for you, you'll keep out of it."

I was starting to feel like the surrounding trees were set to fall down on top of me and crush me into bits and pieces.

Jacob stood up then. He glared down at me, like all possessed. "The Freedmen's Colony *is* my business. I brung some of them over my own self, back during the war. Hid them in the swamps with the snakes and gators. Snuck 'em past the blockades. Got them set up in the colony. It was the least I could do, being born free."

Jacob had also saved my life, lugged me from the sea like ship's wood. He said he'd help my pap out when I left for Hatteras without even clearing his throat. He was just that kind of man.

"I didn't know that," I said. "I knew you were friendly with some of the colony folks, but I never knew you helped them like that."

"Ben, you been my friend many long years, and I never had nothin' but the most friendly feelings for you. But I been hearin' the craziest yarns lately—I couldn't even make 'em up my own self. One day you're in the freedmen's schoolhouse. Another day you're in the hotel having whiskey with Mister Sinclair, and sailing back and yon to the island at all times of day."

He lowered his voice to a whisper. "Mister Sinclair, who rides on the ship of a bona fide Ku Kluxer, a newspaperman with a Negro-hating pen. On top of guiding for Mister Sinclair and getting learned by his daughter, I think to myself, he sure in the thick of it! It don't look good." He looked away from me, as if through talking. But he wasn't yet finished with me. "I can see you're up to the devil's work. I don't want you messin' with those folks on the island. Just mind your business."

Then it hit me. Under his anger was fear. I could smell it on him, like rotten eggs. I whispered, "You know about Mister Africa, don't you?"

Jacob breathed out slow and long.

I said, "You know what he did. Damnation, Jacob."

Harley and Jimmy sputtered, "What in tarnation are you all yammering about? Who has done what in Africa?"

Jacob's face looked peaceful, though. "I wasn't more than a boy when I brung him down the Chowan, when word got out what he'd done. Most every Negro wanted to help him out, but the difference was, I could do it.

"What I heard was, he hid out for a few months in the attic of a freedman in Windsor. That friend set me up with him. Back then I was fetching folks and sailing them to Union land. I met him in the swamps near the river late one night. He was dirty and skinny, looked like he'd break if the wind knocked him down, and weak as a baby bird from hiding in that little spot. Had nothing 'cept a ratty old Bible, and he was just holding on to that Bible for dear life. He slept with that thing bunched up in his hands every night I was with him. You ever see anything like that? It'll squeeze the blood right out your heart."

He stopped for a minute, then lowered his voice.

"I hid him in a barrel during the day, case the boat got searched. He never did complain against it. He never talked of what he done to get in the spot he was in, and I never asked. He knew trouble was in it, for both of us.

"What I didn't know was how much I'd get on with him. We spoke about all manner of things those long days. Got to know him right well, good enough for my uncle to book him passage on a whaling ship, take him out of here for good. But he come back, you see. He wanted to help his people." He whistled low and shook his head. "I never met a man like him in my life, and I doubt I ever will."

"He's a killer, Jacob. You can't just close your eyes on what he did."

"I don't forget, and I *know* he don't. But now you can see he's helping those folks on the island. Somebody's got to do it, and he's the best man for the job."

I shook my head. "He's done bad, Jacob. He's got to pay."

"Oh, he paid all right. He been paying up his whole entire life."

I stared at him, trying to find the right words. "I'm sorry, Jacob. I don't want you to take it personal. I . . ." This was just too much for me. I rubbed my face with sandy hands, dirtying myself up again. "There are things I just had to do."

He laughed. "You didn't have to do nothin'. That whole entire family got you all mixed up. You need to square yourself, or you never going to be right again."

Then he left us there. I thought about what he said as Harley and Jimmy peppered me with questions. I knew that what I'd done went against my better feelings on the matter. I couldn't think about that brand on the preacher's shoulder without getting sick to my stomach. I couldn't smell the leaves of yaupon bushes without getting a pain between my eyes.

But I had good reasons for doing the things I did. Least *I* thought they were good reasons. And the man had it coming. You just can't kill folks and expect to get away with it, even if you did happen to turn preacher.

That is what I would keep telling myself, in the heavy dark, with the shadows of trees watching me squirm like a dying goose.

∞

Abby didn't nurture the slightest notion I was building her a house, even though I was covered in sawdust and riddled with splinters every night. I wanted to surprise her someday soon. I wouldn't think about her leaving the Banks, not anywhere near it. And I sure couldn't think of her marrying that Hector.

At night, when we sailed back to Nags Head after long hours of teaching, she kept up her reading of *Robinson Crusoe* by lamplight, and the closer we got to the finish, the slower she read. Words dripped off her tongue like hot butter.

I was happy, on account we had finished the book. Abby gave it to me for keeps when she closed it up for the last time. I figured I might be able to make a go of it on my own, and I never would have thought such a thing at the start of it.

But I didn't want to make a go of it on my own. I wanted her there with me, every little book I read in the coming years. Even if she wasn't sitting right next to me, I wanted her there, somewhere close by.

Old Robinson and Friday got rescued at the end, twenty-eight years after the shipwreck. Can't feature going back to a country full of highfalutin folks after that. Must have been a real shock to their systems, living like they had.

Likely wished for the little cave house, after a while of being sur- rounded by too many comforts. Thought of the dwelling as a home, even though it was just a cave with some wood built over the door. It took him over six months to make, and by his own hands at that. Had all of his worldly things in there, lined up neat and pleasing. It wouldn't be easy to leave a home like that.

But I reckoned *home* was one of those words with lots of different meanings. To me, home was where I found myself most happy. Could be a boat, could be Pap's shack, could be a porch by the sea. Now I'm featuring it to be this house of oak.

It was mighty peculiar, the place where I found myself raising the dressed logs. It was in a space clear of trees, and much closer to the ocean than to the sound. I put all the windows and a little porch on the side of the ocean. I planned to make two chairs and a table for us, but I didn't have time to do all that just yet.

I did pick out two strong oak trees in back of the house, where I hung the old hammock. Used to be my ma's, that she never used the whole time she was living. Had too much work to do, said Pap. I thought that was a shame. The hammock spot had sight of the ocean and the sound through the trees. I thought of Abby a-laying there reading a big book, then maybe fixing cooter stew for our supper.

And if you've never looked up and seen a cloudless blue sky through the green leaves of trees, then you haven't seen much. The view of the world from a hammock is just about the best there is.

When the house was more or less done with, doors hung and gaps chinked, I walked around and around it, trying to find weak spots in the floor boards. Didn't take me long to cross the breadth of it. It was a small thing, only one little square room. But I had built it strong, and the front windows would let in plenty of sunrise.

It had the makings of a happy house. With the roof and porch just so, it looked like it was smiling.

CHAPTER SIXTEEN

Abigail Sinclair
August 31, 1868

"Well," says Friday; "but you say God is so strong, so great, is he not much strong, much might as the devil?" "Yes, yes," says I, "Friday, God is stronger than the devil, God is above the devil, and therefore we pray to God to tread him down under our feet, and enable us to resist his temptations, and quench his fiery darts." "But," says he again, "if God much strong, much might as the devil, why God no kill the devil, so make him no more do wicked?"

—ROBINSON CRUSOE

THE EVENING AIR WAS STAGNANT IN THE SCHOOLHOUSE. THE DAY'S temperature had reached nearly a hundred degrees, and the room still bore the aftereffects, smelling powerfully of body odor, mine included.

But the students were oblivious to everything except the work at hand. I now knew how to harness the power of literature. I had begun *Uncle Tom's Cabin*, at Elijah's request. He had handed his own copy to me, with both hands, as if handing me a dead loved one's personal effects. The day after he gave it to me I read it through from cover to cover, with a sticky pit in my stomach. Suffice it to say, it wasn't a popular book in Edenton when I was growing up.

Winnie, or I should say Asha, was enjoying the novel when I read it at the end of the lessons. I watched her more than I watched anyone else. She was easy to find in the sea of brown faces, for she still wore her white head scarf.

Already twice tonight I had called her Winnie. Everyone turned about, wondering who it was that I had called on. And Winnie refused to even look up until I called her Asha. Then she would laugh.

To begin the night lessons, Elijah led the students in a spiritual, the same kind of songs they sang in their church. Luella told me that their singing and chanting were more subdued in the schoolhouse. She said that everyone really let loose in church, and I had a hard time featuring it.

Hold your light, Brother Robert,
Hold your light,
Hold your light on Canaan's shore.

What make ol' Satan for follow me so?
Satan ain't got nothin' for do with me.
Hold your light,
Hold your light,
Hold your light on Canaan's shore.

It was a beautiful song. Dark night on the water, lanterns pushed out, hopeful people looking for the promised land before Satan lured them away. The students repeated the simple song over and over, clapping and stamping their feet.

Elijah sang last. His soulful tenor caused many of the students to stand and sway, eyes closed and hands in the air. I stood, too, and Ben. We looked at each other and smiled at ourselves, standing in this extraordinary place.

With a final ruckus of feet on the floor as we drew out "shore" on the last verse, the rickety door to the schoolhouse, already propped open with a brick to bring in the coolish night air, smacked all the way back against the wall. I thought perhaps it was a student, running late.

But when I turned to see who it was, I gasped in confusion. Two broad men wearing costumes and sandy boots clomped in. Long red robes that buttoned up the front covered their bodies up to their necks, and their masks looked to be dark red cloth painted with grotesque white noses and mouths. They both had pointed horns twisted atop their heads. And they each carried a long rifle.

The students jumped up in panic and scattered to the walls, but all I could do was stand at my post in the front of the room. I looked over to where Ben stood, but he remained queerly motionless, almost as if he had been expecting them.

The squattier devil said, "Well, well. Lookie what we have here. A schoolhouse full of niggers. Never thought to see that in my lifetime. But here it sits. Sure does reek in here, though. Reeks like niggers."

He walked around the front of the room, breaking pieces of chalk and throwing books and Bibles to the floor. He smashed two of the oil lamps, casting the room into almost complete darkness.

The other devil looked to me. "And a white schoolmarm, to boot. She must be a Yankee transplant."

The short one walked over to me and sneered, "What's your story, gal? Why you learning these darkies?"

Ben hollered out from the back of the room, "She's got nothing to say to you! Leave her be!"

He drawled, "What do we have here? You her beau or something? Ain't that sweet." He walked over to Ben, reared the rifle back casually, and hit him in the gut with the butt. I watched in shock as Ben slumped to the floor, coughing in pain and holding his stomach.

I squeaked out a "no" through my fingers. The taller, less vicious man standing next to me peered into my face through the darkness. "You look familiar to me," he said.

The short one snickered. "After a few minutes outside, I'll *make* her familiar."

"Lay a hand on her, you bastards, and you'll live to regret it!" cried Ben from the floor.

The squat devil cocked his head back and hollered, "I thought I told you to quit your ballin'!"

The other man looked at me again. "No, I've seen her before, I'm positive of it. What's your name, darlin'?"

I couldn't speak. My eyes started squeezing out tears but my body was as immobile as a tree buried in sand. I didn't understand what was happening. The stewing apprehension I'd dragged around during the war felt like a silly game compared to the hot fear I now felt.

He placed his hand on my arm and squeezed. "I won't ask you again."

"Abigail. Abigail Sinclair." I had no control over my voice. It was much louder than I meant it to be. And it trembled like a gull's wing in the wind.

"Dear God," he said flatly. The devils looked at each and backed out the door. I heard them murmuring anxiously to someone outside.

Then the door banged again, and another masked man walked in, stooping a bit to get through the door. I could see his shiny leather boots peeking out from the bottom of his red robe.

The man took one look at me and stopped short. He rasped, "Abigail?"

And I recognized his voice. It resounded through my entire body. My mouth said, "Daddy?" even though it still didn't make sense to my head.

He spoke through the cloth over his face. His voice sounded strangled. "What in God's name are you doing here?"

The other two men skulked in the doorway, watching. I reached out for the wall, to brace myself. For the briefest of moments I questioned what I was doing here. Seeing myself through Daddy's eyes, I made no sense at all. I was a traitor to the Southern force. But the moment passed, with the wave of pride I now felt.

I said calmly, "I'm teaching the freedmen."

He was silent for a while, as he regarded me. He was terrifying in that costume, in the flickering darkness. He shook his head back and forth, waggling the horns.

He began pacing. "Who did this? Who put you up to this?"

Ben was standing up now, one hand gripping his torso. He said, "I did, Mr. Sinclair. I brought her over here."

Daddy turned toward the voice and barked, "Ben? What in the sam hell is going on here?"

"It's all my doing. I talked her into coming here—"

I interrupted, "No. That's not true." I looked at the cowering horde of people in the room, at the weeping children. I couldn't see Luella or her mother, or even Asha.

I said, "I want to be here. These people deserve an education."

Daddy started laughing, a whiskey-laden snicker I had heard many times before. His horns jiggled with amusement. The other two men started snorting along with him. "I can't believe what I'm hearing. My own daughter, a teacher of the darkies! What ever happened to Little Red Reb? What would your uncle Jack say?"

I responded angrily, "He'd likely ask you what you're doing here, dressed like that. And carrying a gun."

He looked directly over to Elijah, who was standing quietly in the back of the room with two of the children who had lost their parents in the war. "We came for Elijah Bondfield. Or Elijah Africa, as you know him."

We all looked at Elijah with fear in our eyes. Then the students cried out and rushed to him, blocking him from view. I could name each of them, both their first and last names. But I still could see how they must look to Daddy and the men. Black, and in the way.

One of the devils let a shot out of his rifle. The bullet blasted through the thin wooden ceiling with a crack, scaring everyone into silence.

Daddy warned, "Back away from the reverend. He's coming with us. Anyone in the way gets a bullet to the brain."

But no one moved an inch.

I cried, "Why are you taking Elijah? He's a good man! He's not the one you're looking for, I'm sure of it. Daddy, please!"

Daddy said bluntly, "Abigail, you aren't as smart as you think you are. It's time to keep your mouth shut now." He turned to speak to the entire group. "Your good Reverend Elijah here is nothing more than a murderer. Took us a good long while to find him, but we tracked him down eventually. He was easier to locate when he started getting uppity. And don't you all forget that." He pointed his index finger around the room. "See, we never forget cold-blooded killings in North Carolina. The coward killed his master and mistress in their sleep and took their money when he left. He can't deny it now, being a man of God like he is. Why don't you tell them, Elijah?"

Elijah looked straight ahead at no one in particular when he said, "It's the truth. I killed the Bondfields, but I stopped calling them my master and mistress long before that. They were cruel— no respect for humanity whatsoever. They weren't fit to live on God's Earth. And as for thievery, I took what was owed me, for my labors."

The tall man raised his rifle and pointed it evenly at Elijah, but Daddy whispered something into his ear, and he lowered it reluctantly.

Daddy said sharply, "Now, listen up good. This is no longer a place for 'freedmen.' This island belongs to us now. You're going to pack up your things, all your voodoo dollies and drums and Africa herbs, and get off this island. If you don't, you're going to be seeing an awful lot of us. All over your sorry little streets, up inside your rotten shacks and churches. And if you think we look spooky tonight, you're going to know what hell is if you breathe a word of this to anyone. You forget the name of your teacher here"—he looked over to me with utter disapproval in his cut-cloth eyes—"or we'll hunt you down like turkeys."

I had never seen Daddy so angry before. My God, he used to be such a strong man, so prideful, so important. He had been a pillar of Edenton society. Now his pride had molded into hate, foully putrid. He had sunk so low he wore a costume to hide himself.

The men tried to get to Elijah, but the crowd refused to part for them. They screamed, "No, don't let them through! Not the reverend!" The devil men started butting people's heads with their guns, and Daddy stood looking on, fingering the trigger on his rifle. The same rifle that he used to kill wild animals.

I was vaguely aware of Ben striding through the room to us. His face was filmed in sweat. He pleaded, "Don't do this, Mister Sinclair. Turn him over to the authorities."

Daddy gripped the back of Ben's neck with his large hand and said quietly, "You, son, are a disappointment. Why would you bring my daughter here, knowing what was going to happen to the reverend? Why the hell would you put her directly in harm's way?"

"What is he talking about?" I asked both of them.

Ben wouldn't meet my eyes. He said bluntly, "With all respect, Mister Sinclair, your daughter is a good teacher. Fact, you were the one who hooked us up, remember? And *these* folks happened to be in dire need of a teacher. How was I to know you were going to ambush a schoolhouse? There's little children here, for God's sake. Innocent people."

He snorted. "Abigail is my daughter, and I say what she does and where she goes and who she sees."

"I reckon we knew what you'd say about her coming out here," Ben said. He went stubbornly on. "Elijah's a good man to be around. He lifts you up, you know. *Those* kind of men are in short supply these days."

Daddy nodded thoughtfully, then looked to me with malice in his eyes. "Ben's not as sweet and simple as he'd like you to think. He's been helping me this summer, above and beyond his guide work. I can't imagine how, but he identified the brand on Elijah's back. Made our lives a lot easier."

I shook my head. I whispered, "I can't believe that."

Daddy shrugged dramatically. "He couldn't turn down a government job."

Ben put his hands over his face and moaned softly.

"Is this true?"

Ben nodded slowly, with his fingers over his face. My head pounded in shock, and I felt my heart wilt inside my chest, brown and jagged as an old apple core.

But I couldn't even think anything through, with Elijah's voice booming through the room. "It's all right, people. Move away. I've been expecting them, although I will say I wasn't expecting men in costumes. Know that I've made peace with God for my actions. I'm ready to go."

The weeping students moved away, slowly, reluctantly, revealing the reverend, who had never looked as imposing as he did now.

As the men moved to grab him, though, Asha stepped out from the crowd to stand in their path. "You should be ashamed," she said through a clenched jaw.

"Good God in heaven, what next? The circus come to town?" Daddy barked, his chest heaving. "Abigail, you better have a damned good reason for dragging Winnifred out here, and behind your poor mama's back, too!"

I breathed in deeply, then said, "She came for an education, obviously."

Asha spat, "Just look at you, all dressed up, doing the devil's work. You all say you follow Jesus Christ, but it's the devil hisself that got you on his leash. This ain't *right*!" Her face was wet with silvery tears, and she could hardly speak. "I won't be coming back to Edenton with you all."

She didn't look at me when she said that.

Daddy, for just a moment, was at a loss for words. But he soon hardened himself to her, to all her years of service to us. "Good riddance, then. Don't come crying to me when things turn bad. And they will, Winnifred."

The men pushed her away, tired of waiting. But they didn't have to pull and push the reverend. Elijah walked out of the room with his head held high.

As he made to leave the schoolhouse, Daddy said with quiet fury, "I'm just real sorry you had to see all this, Abigail, but you never should have snuck over here. Go on back to the cottage with Ben. And we won't speak of this night again, to anyone."

Then the schoolhouse was as dark and quiet as church on Tuesday. No one moved or spoke or even cried. Everyone must have sensed that it would be their own death if they ventured out of the schoolhouse. We stood still, staring at one another's feet.

I could actually smell the fear in our labored breaths. But soon I couldn't tell if it was urine or cold sweat that I smelled. I was afraid to look at the students, scared of what I would see in their faces. How my own daddy had made them feel. They would never trust me again.

The silence stretched out, a cold, glassy blackness that wavered on and on for long minutes, and then we heard a rifle shot in the distance.

And the silence shattered into shards. The entire group rushed for the door and ran outside screaming. Ben, Asha, and I followed the students down the dark street, since everyone seemed to know where they were going. And with my senses heightened, I smelled something burning and quickened my pace.

Then I saw the source of the fire, and I had to walk closer to confirm my first thought. It was, incongruously, an enormous pile of books, burning in the middle of the street. The fire lit up the night, so that I could see everyone's panicked faces as they took in the ugly sight.

Ben moaned, "Oh, God, not his books. They've burned his books."

There must have been hundreds of books in the pile. Their covers were melting and curling in the blaze.

Some of the students ran into the house across the street, and then, over the spitting fire, I heard several people wailing. Ben tried to grab my arm but I slipped through his grasp and ran up the steps into the house. Ben followed at my heels.

The inside of the house was empty except for a rope bed and a table and chair. But I sensed the commotion in the yard behind Elijah's house. I walked out the back door, and Ben again tried to pull me back. But I had already seen the tall wooden cross driven into the dirt. Elijah hung from it, as if crucified. Nails had been driven into his hands and overlapped feet.

But he hadn't suffered too much on the cross. He had been shot straight between the eyes. The hole where the bullet entered was jaggedly dark and oozing, a tiny pocket of hate. His white shirt had been removed, and he had been whipped all over his chest, and likely his back as well. Blood dripped from the slashes down onto the dusty ground.

But even worse than all that was his face. On both cheeks were freshly burned brands of the letter *B*. His handsome black face was almost unrecognizable.

Ben tried to hug me to him, but I pushed him away. I stumbled through the house and back out into the street again, where the fire was growing even higher, feeding on the knowledge inside it. And through the smoke I saw a glint of white over the sound. It was Mr. Viceroy's fine schooner, sailing across the water. In the pitch-black sky, its white sails glowed like a malevolent ghost. The *White Storm*.

The truth of the night was slowly bubbling to the surface. *My daddy is a murderer, full of hate. Ben is a liar, full of secrets. The Reverend Africa, a murderer himself, was killed in cold blood. Nailed to a cross, branded, and whipped.*

I faced Ben and looked him straight in the eye. In a voice void of all emotion, I said, "I would like to go home now."

And by home, I meant Edenton. I was done with the Outer Banks for good.

CHAPTER SEVENTEEN

Abigail Sinclair
August 31, 1868

> *. . . conscience, that had slept so long, began to awake,*
> *and I began to reproach myself with my past life, in*
> *which I had so evidently, by uncommon wickedness, pro-*
> *voked the justice of God to lay me under uncommon*
> *strokes, and to deal with me in so vindictive a manner.*

—ROBINSON CRUSOE

BEN ROWED US SLOWLY NORTH THROUGH THE CROATAN SOUND. THE OARS wobbled pathetically through the water, as if he were deliberately trying to delay me. An angry grief accumulated in my throat like lava.

We had left Asha with Pearl Jefferson, a stout, loquacious woman with whom she had gotten friendly at the schoolhouse. She would not come back to the cottage with me, and I didn't blame her. I thought I would cry, saying good-bye to her. But no tears had come, even when she hugged me tightly to her heaving chest.

We crossed the northern edge of the island, and Ben raised the sail to catch the strong southwest wind. Once we were moving along at a brisk pace, Ben choked, "I'm so sorry, Abby."

I shook my head violently. I couldn't speak a word to him.

"I've done wrong, I know. I got all caught up in the idea of being a person of some account, and I couldn't get free. Your daddy . . . he knows how to work people over, get them to do things."

"No," I said, turning my head from his pleading eyes.

I suddenly recalled Ben's mysterious warning about Daddy, for me to "be careful of him." Ben had known *something*, even as far back as Independence Day. And the more I thought, the more I re-membered—his sour feelings about Roanoke Island, his fits of downheartedness, his strange reaction upon meeting Elijah, and even Daddy's abrupt cancellation of Ben's tutoring sessions.

I was so furious my hands twitched. I rasped, "You deceived me. You deceived Elijah."

He sighed deeply, and continued to row without responding.

"You could have warned him," I spat. "Every night we went to the schoolhouse, every night you sat there, knowing what you knew."

He shook his head stubbornly. "He killed those people. Even you heard him admit to it tonight. He wasn't all he made himself out to be, Abby. *He* was the one fooling *us*."

My throat made a queer little choking sound, and then closed up completely. I couldn't wait to be off this little boat, far away from this person I'd thought I knew so well. I scrubbed my forehead hard to block out the pastel memory of making love to him on Jockey's Ridge.

Yet as soon as that thought retreated, it was replaced by the image of Elijah on the cross. It was hard to reconcile with the image of Elijah bending over in the glittering darkness to help someone sound out a word. I began to sob and squirm around on my seat, desperately trying to see land.

Ben pleaded, "I didn't kill the man, Abby. I just helped uncover the truth is all."

But I clamped my hands over my ears and forced myself to watch the water flow beside the boat. The more water that went by, the closer I would get to Nags Head. Yes, we were almost there.

My thoughts settled on Hector, and how I would likely be married to him by the winter. I could forget all of this ever happened and live a quiet, easy life. Supervise a garden of orange lilies and eat chocolate cake after every supper. It sounded good enough to me.

∞

Breathless from running all the way from the docks, I climbed through the bedroom window and wearily made my way to bed. I sat down and stared at the children, sleeping soundly. Even in the darkness, their red hair gave color to the white linens beneath them.

In the face of so much vivid innocence, I began to cry silently. I didn't even undress. I just curled up in a ball and sucked on my knuckles. I listened to the rise and fall of the ocean and wished that I were smack in the middle of a wave's crest, right before it hit the undertow beneath it.

I couldn't think, I couldn't see past the hateful things that men could do to one another, the excuses they made for their evil. I tossed on my bed like a ship in a storm for the remainder of the night.

And the next day came, in spite of itself. I couldn't believe it, when

I saw the sunlight streaming into the room. In my mind, it was still dark and cloudy, no moon or stars to light the gray matter.

The children came immediately back into the room after rising.

"Abby, wake up!" Charlie said, shaking my shoulder.

I tried desperately to make my mouth work. "I am awake."

"Winnie is gone, and the breakfast isn't even made! We can't find her anywhere! Do you know where she's gone off to?" asked Martha, a look of worry on her face.

I sat up, trying hard not to remember Elijah's branded face. I said softly, "Winnie has gone to stay with a friend of hers over on Roanoke Island. She might . . . She wants to stay there for a while."

"You mean she's not coming back?" Martha cried.

Tears filled Charlie's wide green eyes. "She left us *alone?*"

I tried to explain. "There's a good school over there, and Winnie likes it very much. She wants to learn how to read and write, just like you. You know how she was always bragging about you two."

Charlie nodded, agreeing with the notion of his exceptional abilities. But his voice shook when he said, "But she didn't say good-bye! That's not how you're supposed to leave somebody. You're supposed to give folks a big hug and a kiss on the cheek and shake hands and cry and all that."

I nodded numbly. "A friend of hers needed her very much. She had to leave in a hurry."

"Can we bring her things to her, at least?" Martha asked, trying hard not to cry.

"Perhaps," I said carefully, although I knew the island wasn't a place for them right now. And Asha didn't have many possessions at all. She had only one calico skirt and shirtwaist, one starched white apron and head scarf, one worn pair of boots. She was wearing it all when I left her.

But we walked out to the porch, anyway. A thin blanket with about a dozen patches sewn onto it was folded neatly in the center of her hammock.

Martha lifted it to her nose and inhaled. "It smells so clean, just like Winnie. She'll want this blanket, I bet."

Her face turned into itself then, and she began to cry. I hugged her to me, the blanket in between us a poor substitute for a lifetime of Asha's comfort.

Hannah, lonely and overworked, agreed to stay with the children that afternoon. With the sun blazing through my bonnet, I rode Mungo to the one place in Nags Head that still held good memories for me. I knew that poor old horse would never make it up the dune itself, so I hitched him to a scrubby pine tree next to one of the fresh ponds and made my way up Run Hill.

The tree was still there, of course, buried up to its middle in sand. I ran my hands over the rough bark of a low branch.

I clenched and unclenched my jaw, then said loudly, "You're still alive."

Then I sat down in the sand and looked across the tops of the trees and the Roanoke Sound to Roanoke Island. The students were likely burying Elijah today, and mourning the loss of their only leader. I didn't know how they were going to get by without him, in the face of so many threats. I supposed that was the point of Daddy's costumed violence.

I groaned, fighting tears, and from my reticule pulled out the Prayer of the Ephesians, copied onto a piece of paper that I had carried along with me. It was the first Bible passage I had heard Elijah read to the class.

I read it to the tree slowly, remembering the way Elijah's voice had pulled me outside myself. With the students, I had learned that there was no *us,* no *them.* We had been one group, united with a common purpose—fighting off the encroaching sand.

I took Elijah's copy of *Uncle Tom's Cabin* and walked a few yards down the dune to where the sand was in the process of drifting. I buried the book in the soft sand so that when the dune finally moved on, maybe even hundreds of years later, Elijah's book would reappear, resurrected.

Daddy returned to the cottage the second day after Elijah's murder. I was in the kitchen, helping Hannah with a tomato pie, when I heard his boots stomp into the house. My hands paused on the tips of the crust, my heart hammering. Hannah glanced worriedly at me and took the pie to finish herself.

He hollered to the house at large about supper plans at the hotel, his ugly tenor raising the hairs on my arms. "We've got things to celebrate! Get dressed, and don't dillydally!"

I heard Charlie ask, "Why are we celebrating, Daddy? Winnie has gone off and left us."

Daddy paused for a few moments, then said jovially, "Oh, well. People come and they go, son. You'll survive."

"Mama's been ill today. I don't think she wants to go to the hotel," said Martha petulantly. Martha had been grumpy with Daddy ever since Ben had stopped coming for his tutoring sessions.

"Oh, she'll go all right. I'm making an important announcement tonight." I heard him stomping around the rooms. "Abigail? Where are you?"

I walked slowly out of the kitchen, my hands wrapped in a

dishrag, eyes everywhere except on him. When I did finally raise my eyes to his, my whole face tightened in protest. I would never be able to look at him again without seeing him in a red robe and a devil mask.

"Wear your best dress tonight," he said. And from the flatness in his eyes, I didn't think he would ever be able to look at *me* again with-out seeing me as a teacher in a schoolhouse for freedmen.

Then he galloped up the stairs two at a time, to see about Mama. Mama had been hollering for Asha for two straight days, even though I had told her the same thing that I had told Charlie and Martha. But she kept forgetting, I suppose.

Apparently Hannah couldn't make toast nearly as well as Asha could. That morning I had found two burned pieces of bread half buried in the sand, directly under Mama's bedroom window.

That evening we all arrived at the hotel with long faces, except for Daddy. He wasted no time in grabbing a waiter and ordering a bottle of champagne. When the bottle arrived at the table, Daddy insisted on popping the cork himself, and the final crack made me flinch.

He stabbed the flute into the air victoriously, yet his voice sounded as hollow as the now empty bottle. "I want to make a toast, for I am the happiest of men tonight. My daughter Abigail has accepted a pro-posal of marriage from none other than Hector Newman, whose name speaks for itself here. Our family will soon merge with the Newman house, and we couldn't be more pleased."

Mr. Adams hollered, "To the lovebirds!"

Daddy finished, "To North Carolina. As we all remember her."

I hadn't even corresponded with Hector since he'd proposed to me. My face flushed with five different emotions, and I put my hands on the edge of the table, ready to push my chair back.

But the way that Daddy wasn't even looking at me caused me to

stay seated. The air around him vibrated with malice and manipula-
tion. This was my punishment.

I forced my hand to take a glass of champagne and tap it against
Maddie's and her mama's. The air resounded with the clinking of
glassware and a boisterous "Hear, hear! To Abby and Hector!"

Maddie sipped her champagne, gazing at me. Then she cupped her
little hand to my face and whispered, "For a while there, I was wondering if it wasn't going to be Mrs. Abigail Fisherwoman." She
raised her voice and asked, "Do you love him?"

Everyone turned to me, even Daddy.

I murmured, "Oh, Maddie, hush now. Don't embarrass me."

I began to butter my roll, but Maddie wasn't done with me yet.
Thankfully, she lowered her voice this time. "I liked him. He had
some honest quality that you just don't find in a lot of beaux. Dirty as
all get-out, and I declare I've never smelled such a stink!" She giggled
and drank the remainder of her champagne. Then she said, "But I
knew you best of all, Abby. I knew you could fall for a man like that."

I shook my head. "You're wrong. He was my daddy's guide, an ignorant Banker. That's all."

She scolded, "You can't hide it now. You've got that look about
you, even while you're denying it. You love him still."

I suppressed the urge to cover my face with my gloved hands. She
was so wrong. I hadn't even been able to think of Ben without getting angry all over again. My idea of him was now entwined with
brutality and secrecy, and I couldn't separate them to save my life.

Daddy's voice distracted me then, when I heard him say quietly to
Mr. Adams, "Got my *Old North Statesman* today. Did you see Zeb's
editorial yet?"

Mr. Adams grinned from ear to ear. He said under his breath, "Oh,
yes. Read it first thing this morning. Made Patience's burned-up bis-
cuit taste just like heaven."

"Best one Viceroy's ever written," Daddy said, his eyes glowing malevolently.

Mrs. Adams picked up on their mutterings, too. "I declare, I can't believe that man was living just over on Roanoke Island! Imagine, a cold-blooded killer in our midst! My precious Madeleine visited the island quite often this summer. I shudder to think of her crossing paths with that murderer."

Maddie squealed, "And how positively awful, pretending to be a preacher. Those darkies will follow just anyone, I guess. I'll bet they knew all about his murderous past but didn't see fit to turn him in. They're all so sinful."

Mrs. Adams nodded. "I hope they all crawl back to wherever they came from. They should just leave that island alone and let things settle down. Those island folks haven't seen a moment's peace since the war started."

I put my knife down carefully and took a deep breath. Then I said evenly, "Mr. Africa wasn't *pretending* to be a preacher. He *was* one. A good one. And that island is a perfect place for those people. I hope they stay."

Everyone stared at me openmouthed, silverware and glasses poised in midair. Daddy said calmly, a torn-up roll in his hand, "Don't speak of things you don't understand, Abigail."

My anger made me reckless, and the ignorance of the present company spurred me on. But my voice trembled when I said, "Our country does still have a legal system, I believe. He didn't deserve to be killed like that."

"Sure he did. He got what was coming to him," Daddy said. Then he smiled at the table apologetically and crooned, "Come now, Abigail. Let's talk of weddings, things you know more about than *this* ugly business."

Mrs. Adams's eyes were still round with surprise when she whispered, "Yes, Abigail. I'm just dying to discuss your plans."

I got up calmly and made for the exit. My sea legs were stronger than they'd ever been. I could feel them flexing under my hoops with determination. Maddie smiled hugely at me, enjoying the spectator role for once, and even Mama, who'd remained silent the entire time, looked curiously at me.

"My, my, Hector sure does have some work to do! Proper doctor's wife, indeed!" I heard Mr. Adams muse as I walked away. "Takes after her daddy. I always did say that."

◌

That night I couldn't sleep, even though I was bone-tired. I felt cool and hardened, as if I had started the summer as a squishy mound of clay and had come through the furnace, strong and ready for work.

My heart hadn't cooperated during the process, though. It was still soft and warm with life. I could feel it beating childishly in my chest. But I would be a doctor's wife soon. I tried to harden my heart, too, and forget how it felt to swim in a pond of freshwater.

I had closed my eyes tightly, hoping that the cries of the gulls would lull me to sleep, when I heard Mama's footsteps padding lightly down the stairs. I heard the screen door nearest my bedroom squeak slowly open and close quietly. My breath caught in my throat—perhaps she was ill and needed a doctor. Maybe, in a fit of madness, she was going out to look for Asha! Asha, the one person who could help me with Mama. It was up to me now to care for her.

I got up hastily and, still in my nightdress, followed her into the darkness. I saw her quite clearly, standing at the ocean's edge, her white nightdress already soaked up to her knees. Her long yellow hair blew wildly in the ocean breeze.

I hurried over to her through the sand. Over the sloshing of the waves, I said loudly, "Mama, what on Earth are you doing?"

She turned her head slightly to me. "I had to get out of the cottage," she called. She sounded surprisingly rational, for someone in her current situation. "It's evil, Abigail."

The darkness seemed to close in on me, disorienting me for a moment. Fighting panic, I asked, "But why are you standing in the surf?"

She replied calmly, "I haven't so much as touched the ocean since we arrived here in June." She paused, then said slowly and succinctly, "It doesn't smell nearly as bad when you're standing in the midst of it."

I could see the outline of her slightly rounded belly through her gown. The wash swirled and frothed around her feet, causing her to lose her balance every now and then. I called, "You're making me nervous, Mama. It's too dark out here to save you if you get sucked out to sea. Come on back to dry sand now."

She turned to face me. "Your daddy . . . he's still not home. He's at the hotel, drinking with some men." She paused and gave me a peculiar smile. "They're celebrating."

She looked at me for a long time, her back to the waves that marched toward her. Her face was ghostly white, surrounded by so much darkness. She finally asked, "What happened over on Roanoke Island?"

I had thought that with all of her health problems this summer, she hadn't a notion of what was happening under her very nose. But I knew now that I had underestimated her.

"Oh, Mama," I cried.

She spoke carefully now, each word heavy with meaning. "Your daddy was involved in something over there, something terrible. You know what he did."

I nodded slowly, my long hair blowing into my eyes.

"*How* do you know?"

I couldn't lie to her anymore. I was beyond that now. I waded into the warm, slapping surf to look her in the eye. "I was teaching at a school for freedmen at night. I was there when it all happened."

She put a hand over her mouth, then looked back out to sea.

Then, with tears running down the back of my throat, I told her about the school, about the students, about the nights of teaching. I told her about bringing Asha with me, and about her decision to stay on Roanoke Island. I told her about Elijah Africa and his many gifts. I told her that Elijah had been murdered "by some bad men bent on revenge," and she covered her face with her hands.

And then I couldn't stop myself. I told her about the pile of burning books in the middle of the street. She moaned out loud and doubled over, physically affected by the crimes.

And confessing those things to her lightened me of the burden. I filled my lungs with the salty breath of the sea, and the ocean washed over my calves. I could just make out a handful of stars, peeking through the silver night clouds.

"I'm sorry that I lied to you, Mama. I haven't quite been myself this summer. And so much has happened to me, I don't think I'll ever be myself again."

She nodded slowly. "Yes" was all she said. She didn't seem angry at me in the least.

We both stood knee-deep in the ocean, staring at its vastness, lost in our troubled thoughts. After a while, she said, "I'd like to see this school. Will you take me there tomorrow?"

"What?" I gasped. "I don't think the students would like to see me. They know that I'm . . . associated with Daddy."

"Abigail, you have an obligation to explain yourself to these peo-ple. You were their teacher."

Cold fear swept powerfully over me, putting this warm, sloshing water to shame. "You'll come with me?"

"Yes, although they may not take kindly to me, either."

But I couldn't feature her going anywhere in her condition. She hadn't been anywhere except the hotel all summer long. "Are you feeling . . . up to it?"

She looked down at her body, gently rounded now. She nodded. "I am. I feel better, somehow."

We struggled back up to the cottage in our wet nightdresses. Then, while standing on the porch steps, we squeezed the remnants of ocean out of the cloth. The water dripped and puddled into the thirsty sand below, returning home.

⬦

Early the next morning, I arranged for Hannah to stay with the chil-dren and to keep an eye on Daddy, whom I had heard clamber up the stairs late in the night. Over a quick breakfast Mama told me that he was still passed out cold and wouldn't likely awake until the after-noon.

Justus hitched Mungo to the cart, and Mama and I rode over to the hotel docks. The desk man there helped us to procure a boat to the island. And together we sailed across Roanoke Sound with our guide, a red-faced old man who still seemed half asleep.

The sun was rising over the east, and the morning was still a bit cool. I never in my wildest dreams thought that I would be sailing in a boat with Mama like this, but she seemed as natural as you please, with her bonnet tied in a perfect bow under her chin and her white parasol fluttering in the wind.

We docked at the old Union port on the western side of the island and strolled side by side to the school through the dusty roads of the colony. Mama walked slowly, as if she had recently recovered from a long illness. She gazed about her curiously at the simple cabins, at the old barracks, but I was sweating with nerves. All I could see were the burning books, the cross bearing Elijah's abused body. And I felt eyes watching us from the windows of the buildings.

As we neared the schoolhouse, my feet trudged as if through the stickiest of mud. Tears collected in my eyes, and I grabbed Mama's gloved hand. "I can't," I whispered. "I can't go in."

But she pulled me forward with a surprising amount of strength. "Yes, you can. You must."

Mama pulled back the screen door and we stepped into the school. It looked the way that we had left it that night, with the books and slates I had given the students strewn all over the boxes and barrels. Bits of chalk and broken lanterns lay crushed on the dusty floor.

My heart started to pound too quickly, and I feared I might faint. I stumbled out the door and forced myself to breathe the fresh air. I walked slowly around the grassy yard behind the schoolhouse, remembering the day that Ben and I first met Elijah. It had been oppressively hot, but Elijah's teaching had quickly made me forget it.

As I turned to go back to the schoolhouse, I noticed several bunches of purple wildflowers and blue hydrangeas over a fresh mound of dirt, somewhat hidden beneath a grove of dogwood trees.

I closed my eyes for a few moments, listening to the flow of the Croatan Sound a few hundred yards away, and then walked closer to peer at the dirt. There, beneath some of the flowers, was a small, rough-hewn cross. On the horizontal branch were the words REVEREND ELIJAH AFRICA, FREEDOM IN HEAVEN.

I covered my face with my hands. The students had buried him near the school, instead of in the freedmen's cemetery near the church. I nodded; it was a good decision. I tried to imagine the students singing a mournful hymn and reading a Bible passage, or a bit of a book, before placing him in the ground.

I untied my bonnet and removed it, to feel the breeze in my ears. Suddenly Mama was in front of me. I stared at her numbly. I couldn't remember why we had come here in the first place.

She put her hands on my cheeks and said, with a twinge of awkwardness, "It's all right, Abigail. I'm here now."

I began to sob, my tears running directly onto her gloves. "He's dead, Mama. Elijah is dead."

"But the school is still here. Think of that." She looked at me with something like pride in her eyes.

We walked back into the schoolhouse, and I sat down on a barrel. Mama walked around the room, picking up chalk and flipping through the books, likely recognizing the supplies that came from home.

After a while I heard the screen door open and saw Luella and her mother, Ruth, step through the door. Luella ran over to me and buried her head in my lap.

Surprised, I put my hands on her curly hair and said tenderly, "I'm so happy to see you, Luella. Have you been well?"

She nodded solemnly. "I'm okay, Miz Abigail. Just sad is all. Where you been? You didn't come to the funeral for Mr. Africa."

I looked to Ruth, my tears still wet on my face. "I wasn't sure I was welcome here."

Ruth smiled kindly and said, "Oh, please, Miz Abigail. Don't be so hard on yourself."

Luella said sternly, "You is still our teacher. We wanted you to read from *Uncle Tom's Cabin* at the funeral. You was the only person who could make it sound right. "

"How was the funeral, then?" I whispered, my belly in a knot.

Ruth twisted her hands in her skirt and replied, "It went well as could be expected, I s'pose. It's been quiet since then. Nary a lawman has ventured out to see about all this. Like it never done happened."

I nodded, my face burning with humiliation, and glanced over at Mama, who had sat down unobtrusively on a barrel. But I felt her eyes watching me.

Ruth went on. "It's a real shame. I never *heard* so many good things spoke of a man at a funeral service before." To Mama, she said, "He tried hard to help us, you see."

Mama just nodded.

Luella exclaimed, "Oh, I saw Mr. Benjamin at the funeral. He was hiding in the trees, but I saw him with my eagle eyes. I waved over to him, but he just put his finger to his mouth like 'Shhh!' He was gone when it was all over with."

Just then, a few more students stepped into the classroom, and then a few more, and a few more. My mind swam in apprehension as I greeted them, but still the squeaky door kept opening, closing, opening, closing, as more and more freedmen, women, and children came into the room. Soon I saw Asha and Pearl Jefferson in the crowd.

Everyone smiled at me as if it were my birthday party. "I can't believe this," I choked. "You're all here."

Asha came over and hugged me fiercely to her taut body. "Don't no one forget what you did for us this summer, Miz Abby."

I smiled, speaking over the lump lodged firmly in my throat. "I'll be returning to Edenton soon, but I want you all to know that I'm going to find a good teacher for this school. I promise you."

Asha said, "We'll be here waitin'." Everyone voiced their agreement.

Tears were pouring from my eyes, but I hardly noticed. They *forgave* me. They were strong enough to look beyond my history, strong enough to stay on such an uncertain island, even after the threats. Perhaps this colony would survive after all.

I took my time moving from student to student, squeezing their hands and exclaiming over the many things they had learned.

At long last, I walked over to Mama, still watching us from a barrel. "This is my mama, Mrs. Ingrid Sinclair. She wanted to see this special schoolhouse before we go back to Edenton."

I saw their eyes take in Mama. I knew what they were thinking, that she was married to a terrible man, a murderer, that she had been a part of the slave-owning system. I half expected them to push her out of the schoolhouse and put her on a boat directly.

But Golaga Grant surprised me, murmuring, "You sure is fine-looking, Mrs. Sinclair."

Some of the students gasped in embarrassment, and some reached over to swat him over the head and shoulders. But Mama just said, "Thank you. And what is your name?"

He said shyly, "My name is Golaga Grant."

"Golaga. Is that an African name?"

"Yes'm."

Mama nodded and breathed in deeply. Then she slowly stood up and took Asha's strong, callused hands in her white-gloved ones. Her pale face had become splotched in purples and reds, and her voice was tight. "I'm . . . sorry. So very sorry. Tell me your name again. I've forgotten, after all these years."

Asha smiled her big toothy grin. She whispered, "It's Asha. Just Asha. Thank you, Miz Sinclair."

Mama shook her head, but didn't speak. Asha laughed, with tears pooled in her brown eyes. "I'm a-coming to see the baby, now. I'll see you all in about six months. You tell Master Charlie and Miz Martha

I'll see them again when they's the big brother and sister, and not to worry."

Luella came over then and grabbed my hand. "Miz Abigail, what do you think of calling this school 'The Elijah Africa Freedmen School'? I done thought of it myself, and I think it's right good."

Before I could say anything, though, Mama said, "I'll have a placard made up." We all followed Mama outside, where she examined the blank space above the door. "How about here?"

The students nodded their agreement. It was a perfect place for a placard, and with strong nails and quality wood, it would last a long time, even on this island.

And when I looked at Mama's face, at her red nose and at her bloodshot eyes, gazing at the schoolhouse, I saw what Golaga Grant had seen.

Soon after a dinner shared with some of the students at the home of Pearl Jefferson, Mama turned a nasty shade of green and expressed her desire to get back to Nags Head.

A quiet thirty-year-old student named Leopold volunteered to row us back across the sound, so we all rode in a borrowed buggy to the docks on the eastern side of the island. Leo helped us out of the cart, and as we walked down the planks I saw Benjamin, lit by the afternoon sun and instructing two freedmen in the raising of a sail.

My heart flipped inside my chest, suddenly alert. Like it was yesterday, I remembered kissing him on these very docks. I could still recall the grassy saltiness of his lips. We watched him unnoticed for a while as he went over the rules of the waterways. And of course, he was a very good teacher.

Finally he looked up, surprise in his blue eyes. "Well, if it ain't the Sinclair women."

I smiled at him tentatively.

He blinked at us in utter confusion, standing there on the docks with our parasols. "You all out for some sightseeing today?" he asked, fiddling with the sail again.

I stammered, "M-Mama wanted to see the school today. We saw the students while we were there. I told them good-bye."

He stopped messing with the sail and stared from me to Mama, taking it all in. After a few moments he said, "You're leaving soon, I reckon."

"Yes, in two days."

He stood up straight then and spoke to Mama. "I want to say thank you, Mrs. Sinclair, for making it possible for Abby here to teach me this summer. She is one heck of a natural-born teacher. You should be real proud of her."

But Mama just nodded, perspiration droplets along her upper lip.

Ben said, "You doing all right, Mrs. Sinclair? You look like you need to get out of the sun, if you don't mind me saying."

"We're heading back to the cottage. Mama isn't feeling well."

Just as I said that, Mama swayed and reached out for my arm. Leo jumped out of the little rowboat and grabbed Mama's other arm, and together we helped her into the boat.

"We have to go," I said reluctantly. I bit the insides of my cheeks, unsaid words ricocheting inside my mouth. "It was nice to see you again."

I saw him swallow before he said, "Yeah, and you, too. Take care of your mama, now."

I sat near Mama so that I could hold the parasol over her on the trip back to Nags Head. But I turned my head just enough so that I could see Ben, standing on the end of the dock, a hand shading his eyes. We watched each other until I couldn't see him anymore, until Roanoke Island was a long, greenish smear.

As Leo rowed us quickly across the sound, Mama slumped onto my shoulder, warm and heavy. My mind raced, recalling in vivid detail the last two months. The more Mama slept in the shade of the parasol, the more easily I could picture Ben's silhouette, still standing on the end of that dock, still waiting. He always tried so hard; he always wanted to please.

This cool, forgiving water that flowed beside the boat could take me back to him. I could swim. I could swim all the way back to him, the way he had taught me.

But we had almost arrived in Nags Head, and I was needed. Suddenly Mama spoke, likely stirred awake by the slowing of Leo's oars. "A young woman named Eliza Dickens came to the cottage a few days ago. She returned the dress that you soiled, the first of the summer."

"Oh?" I said, ripped completely from my reverie. I couldn't believe that Eliza—the offspring of the rude market woman—had harbored my dress the entire summer. "Did you see her? Did she speak to you?"

"The poor creature came all the way upstairs, to my bedroom. From the sound of it, she pushed Hannah to the floor." Mama's eyes were tightly closed, and speaking seemed a great effort for her, yet she went on. "She was difficult to understand, with her blubbering. But the manner in which she threw the dress on my bed left no room for interpretation."

She paused for a few moments. I watched her chest fill deeply, watched her exhale the used-up air through a small oval between her lips.

She whispered, "She believed that it was a mistake, our coming to Nags Head this summer. She hopes that we don't return again."

I nodded my understanding. My arm ached from holding the parasol just so, and my forehead pounded painfully. I asked tentatively, "Do you think we will? Return again?"

She sat up and opened her eyes, finally. She gazed at me for several minutes, lost in thought. Then she said, "Yes, I do believe this place suits you, Abigail."

CHAPTER EIGHTEEN

Abigail Sinclair
September 4, 1868

Besides the pleasure of talking to him, I had a singular satisfaction in the fellow himself. His simple unfeigned honesty appeared to me more and more every day, and I began really to love the creature; and, on his side, I believe he loved me more than it was possible for him ever to love anything before.

—ROBINSON CRUSOE

CHARLIE, MARTHA, AND I MOVED SLOWLY AROUND THE BEDROOM, FOLDING clothing and throwing stockings, books, and underthings into several cases propped on our beds. We were leaving Nags Head the next day, and packing a summer's worth of belongings was the last thing any of us felt like doing.

Charlie and Martha were dreading the return of routine and discipline back at home, but I was glad to be leaving the cottage. Everywhere I looked now, I saw too much. Every time I glanced at the table on the porch, or at the shell chime dangling in the breeze, I wanted to cry. The empty hammock caused me so much grief that I took it down.

I would miss the ocean air, though, and the solitude of the beach, especially now that most of the vacationers had called it a summer. Just as I was thinking of taking one last walk down the shore, there was a knock on the eastern door of the cottage. My heart jumped, and I realized I was expecting Ben.

I listened carefully as Hannah answered the door. Soon after that, she popped her head into the room and said, "There a old man here to see you, Miz Abigail. A Banker man."

My face drooped like a hound's as I walked through the house and peered curiously through the screen. And I had to look twice, because there stood a man who resembled Ben, but many years aged.

I could see that he and Ben had the same startling blue eyes, the same stature. But Ben's features were more subdued. The man had a bulbous red nose and layers of leathered skin around his eye sockets. His ears stuck out from the sides of his gray-frizzed head, and his blue eyes were bloodshot and watery.

"You Abby?" he croaked, looking past me into the house. A black Labrador sniffed around the porch, keeping half an eye on us.

"Yes, sir. You're Ben's daddy," I said.

His forlorn eyes blinked.

I glanced around the side of the cottage, hoping to see Ben lurking somewhere close by. "Where is Ben? We're leaving tomorrow, and I'd like to give him a proper good-bye."

He rumbled, "Ben's up and gone, down yonder to Hatteras. He's set to work the construction down there, and he won't be back for a long spell, I reckon."

Fighting tears, I whispered, "Oh. I didn't know he'd left already. I just saw him yesterday."

He eyed me for the briefest of seconds, then said gruffly, "I got something to show you. Come along with me for a pace. Won't take long."

"Let me get my shawl," I said quickly.

"Suit yourself," he mumbled.

As I grabbed my shawl, already packed in a case, I told Charlie and Martha that I was going for a walk, and then hollered up to Mama that I would be back in an hour. When I emerged from the bedroom, Ben's daddy had already started walking south, away from the house through the sand, surprisingly fast for his age. The dog ran right next to him, his tongue lolling up and down. I hurried up and down the sand hills to catch up with them.

He grumbled, seemingly to no one in particular, "I says to him, you're a fisherman. Simple as that. Only trouble can come, fiddling 'round with figures and books and such. And now look."

"Ben was the fastest learner I've ever seen."

"You don't have to tell me my boy was bright. I raised him up, you know. Point is, he don't need that kind of learning out here."

"But it made him happy."

He stopped in his tracks and looked to me with dislike in his old eyes. Then he swatted the air with a wrinkled brown hand and bawled, "Aw, shitfire. Ain't no use."

We trudged on in silence. We seemed to be winding our way down the middle of the island, along a sort of sand path that only the locals knew. We neared a slightly wooded area and he slowed his pace a bit.

Then he said, his voice low, "Almost here."

Soon we stood in front of a house, a crude little one-room shack in a clearing of woods. It looked brand-new, the split wood glowing in the daylight.

He said, "It's too near the ocean. But since he met *you* folks, he started waxing on about a house by the sea."

I gazed in surprise at the house Ben had built. I saw the porch, wrapped around the house lovingly. I saw the windows looking out to the sea. Then I saw the hammock, hanging around back between two strong oaks.

"Looks built good enough," he said, cracking the porch step with his knuckles.

Ben was always busy with so many things; I couldn't imagine when he would have had time to construct an entire house. "When did he build it?"

"Couple weeks ago. He didn't tell me what he was up to, but you can't hide nothing from no one out here. I found out soon enough."

"Will he live here? When he comes back from Hatteras?"

He shrugged. "If he ever *comes* back."

I walked up to the door and pushed it open, the black dog brushing past me, his tail darting crooked as he followed a scent. The room was so simple—four walls, fixed space. But the ocean breeze blew straight through the open windows, whipping my dress around my legs.

Love and hope resounded in every board and nail. I had told him I couldn't stay in Nags Head with him, but he went ahead and built an entire house, anyway. I started laughing, an odd, high-pitched whinny, and Ben's daddy looked askance at me.

"Something funny to you? Missy, most of us out here would kill for a house like this'un."

I straightened and said, "Your son is the most exasperating . . .

most prideful . . . oh, mercy." I crumpled to the dusty floor of the house. My eyesight goggled in and out; I was unable to focus on anything except the loss of Ben.

Ben's daddy thumped over and bent down to peer into my face. Tears glistened in his sunstruck eyes, too. He rasped, "Listen, what's done is done. But I wanted to show you what he'd built. He would have wanted you to see it afore you leave."

He wiped his face with a grizzled hand and exhaled deeply, spewing the sweet smell of chewing tobacco.

I started sobbing so hard I thought I'd retch onto the sawdust floor. He just looked at me writhing on the floor, never saying a word, never touching me. As if he were watching a fish gasp its last, still wrapped up in his net. He stood up, knee and ankle joints popping, and slowly hobbled out of the house, the dog following reluctantly after him.

After what seemed like a very long time, I sat up blankly and removed my suede shoes. I took one in my hand and looked at it. When I had first worn these shoes last spring, they had rubbed the backs of my ankles so hard I had biting blisters for two weeks straight. But Mama had insisted that I wear them despite the blisters because they had been costly.

Eventually calluses formed on my ankles, and the suede stretched a bit, making the shoes more pleasant to wear. Now the soles of the shoes were worn almost all the way through, and the soft suede was rubbed clean off the leather, from my time in Nags Head. The shoes were ruined.

I got up, leaving my shawl behind, and walked barefoot out into the sand. The ocean wasn't far at all, maybe four hundred yards away. The sunlight glittered on the water, as if a mass of souls were engrossed in happy conversation. It was peaceful and innocent, but I had seen it at its worst as well. It made me love it that much more.

I started to ask something of Uncle Jack, but I stopped before the words could take flight. I hadn't heard his voice for a long while.

I retrieved the reticule from my skirts and took out the letter, once as familiar as my own hand. Without even reading it, I gently crumpled it and tossed the ball of haunted, yellowing words into the frothing surf. I watched as the paper floated, and then melted, into the sea.

Then I walked back to the little shack to say good-bye. I sat down on a step, thinking I should go back to the cottage now. We had a steamboat to catch in the morning.

I rubbed the smooth boards under my feet and pictured Ben dragging the logs over and splitting and sawing and nailing them all together. He must have done it quickly, with hope in his heart.

I found myself sitting and sitting, unable to get up.

A gigantic seagull stared at me suspiciously from the beach. "Come on, get up, Abby," I said out loud.

The sea spray smelled potent and hinted at the autumnal. Cooler weather would arrive in a few weeks, rendering the summer heat a memory. It was back to a cluster of people for me. Back to a madman for a daddy, a sickly mother, two needy children. Back to a fiancé I didn't want.

Yet instead of going back the way Ben's daddy had led me, I walked over to the old gray hammock Ben had hung. I got in with some difficulty, then settled back and took in the view. I saw why he had hung it here. The branches arched over me, but allowed plenty of sky to peek through in patches.

I closed my eyes and a tear rolled down my cheek. It cooled on my face as it evaporated.

I dozed for a bit, and in a dream I heard cracking twigs in the scrubby woods, then the seagulls bickering. I heard the ocean folding its hands in prayer and moving up the beach in peace. I heard the sound's slapping in between the pulses of waves.

My heart pumped my blood like honey, flowing evenly.

I awoke to Ben's face, looking down at me. The sky behind his head matched his eyes perfectly. He wasn't smiling at me, but he had a look of serenity about him.

My sleepy mouth mumbled, "I miss you, Ben."

He touched my forehead with his rough palm, gentle as an angel's blessing, and the drowsiness fell away. I sat up quickly, making the hammock sway.

"Ben?" I cried. Light off the ocean blinded me so that I couldn't see.

He laughed. "You're not mad with me anymore?"

He tried to help me out of the hammock, but I fell into his arms with a crash. I hugged him for a long time. "I thought you had gone to Hatteras to begin work on the lighthouse. Your daddy told me you already left!"

"I did. But Mr. Stetson ain't ready for crews just yet. Men just standing 'round, breakfast and supper for the gallnippers."

"Oh." My smile evaporated.

"And too, I couldn't not give you a proper farewell. You rowing away with your mama was about all I could think on for two days straight. I stood there on that dock for hours, mulling over what I wanted to say to you. But nothing seemed good enough."

"So you came back to try again, after going all the way down to Cape Hatteras?" I laughed.

"Yeah, I did. Being away from it all made the words come easier." He smiled shyly at me. "I didn't reckon you to be *here*, though. See-ing you here, at this house, made me forget everything I planned to say!"

"Your daddy brought me here. He and a black Lab."

He shook his head from side to side and laughed. "I knew he was up to something. He's getting squirrelly in his old age."

"He loves you, Ben." I put my hands on his scruffy face and gazed at him as the curious seagull finally took flight over us. Ben was covered in mosquito bites, some of which looked to have been scratched at stubbornly. But his eyes were just as blue as they had ever been.

"And what about you, Abby?" he whispered. "After all that's happened, everything I did."

I couldn't speak just then. I took his hand and looked to the house in front of us. I could barely see the images, shrouded in salt mist. Two people, at ease on the porch, laughing and talking and reading the days away. A little red boat, sailing back and forth to Roanoke Island, to a schoolhouse for freedmen. A family in Edenton, forgetting their plans for an eldest daughter, looking at themselves instead.

He beamed as he looked at the little cottage with me. "This cottage is much better than your daddy's—none of that bad blood in it. It's fresh," he said. "Authentic Nags Head live oak. Won't do to keep secrets in this kind of a house." He asked, "Do you like it? Is it good enough for you to forgive me for all the hurt I caused you?"

"Yes," I said simply. With my hands still on his dirty face, I kissed him for a long time.

Once more I looked up through the trees to the sky, so vastly blue. It would cloud over someday soon. Rain would slant sideways on the innocent little Outer Banks house, and thunder would shake its pilings.

Sooner rather than later, the ocean would roar to life again and go to work on the Edenton pine. In the blink of the ocean's eye, Daddy's frontier claim would be as good as driftwood.

On the other side of the Banks, the great piles of sand would con-

tinue their march into the old forests, swallowing whole trees as easily as a red horse grazing cordgrass. Eventually the sand would move
on, freeing the roots from their oppression, and with any luck, they
would go about their growing again.

That was the risk, and the beauty, of living.

ACKNOWLEDGMENTS

I would like to thank my agent, Byrd Leavell, for taking an interest in the first few pages of an incomplete manuscript. Without him the novel would never have found its way home to my unbelievable editors, Lindsay Orman and Heather Lazare. Thank you, Lindsay, for loving the novel as much as I do, and for treating it with such respect. And thank you, Heather, for running the manuscript to the finish line. I consider myself doubly blessed to have two talented editors. I am also deeply indebted to the people at Crown for recognizing the novel's potential and for helping it along to its fruition.

I would also like to thank my husband, Sean, and my two brilliant children, Dorsey and Katherine, for encouraging me in my writing and for giving me the time and space in which to realize my dream.

Thank you also to my father, Norman Schnell, and to my late mother, Patricia Schnell, for having the foresight, creativity, and wherewithal to build a family beach cottage on the Outer Banks of North Carolina. It was here that my love for the barrier islands grew, and here that my ideas of unconditional love were reinforced.

Thank you to my family and friends for cheering me on throughout the entire writing process, namely my sister and brother-in-law, Suzanne and Jeff Gore, and my good friend Eliza Bosworth. By suffering through those rough early drafts and still managing to profess enthusiasm, you served as the platform from which I dove into uncharted waters. Thank you to my historian and friend, Mary Eberline, for your treasure trove of Civil War–era letters and my glove-free access. Thank you as well to the members of the Richmond writing community, especially the organizers and participants of the annual James River Writers Conference.

Numerous books were valuable in developing the cultural and historical background for the novel: *The Waterman's Song: Slavery and Freedom in Maritime North Carolina* by David S. Cecelski (2001); *Seasoned by Salt: A Historical Album of the Outer Banks* by Rodney Barfield (1995); *Time Full of Trial: The Roanoke Island Freedmen's Colony, 1862–1867* by Patricia C. Click (2001); *The Outer Banks of North Carolina: 1584–1958* by David Stick (1958); *An Outer Banks Reader*, edited by David Stick (1998); *Nags Headers* by Susan Byrum Rountree (2001); *Nag's Head: or, Two Months Among "The Bankers."* *A Story of Sea-Shore Life and Manners* by George Higby Throop (1850); *White Terror: The Ku Klux Klan Conspiracy and Southern Reconstruction* by Allen W. Trelease (1979); *Incidents in the Life of a Slave Girl* by Harriet Jacobs (1861); *Green Leaf and Gold: Tobacco in North Carolina* by Jerome Brooks (1975), *Agriculture in North Carolina Before the Civil War* by Cornelius O. Cathey (1966); and *North Carolina During Reconstruction* by Richard L. Zuber (1969).

Last but not least, thank you to the following musicians: Blue Merle, The Bees, Doves, Indigo Girls, Coldplay, Colin Hay, and Bryan Adams. The love story of Ben and Abby evolved as their music played in the background of my mind.

ABOUT THE AUTHOR

DIANN DUCHARME was born in Indiana in 1971, but she spent the majority of her childhood in Newport News, Virginia. She majored in English literature at the University of Virginia, but she never wrote creatively until, after the birth of her second child in 2003, she sat down to write *The Outer Banks House*.

Diann has vacationed on the Outer Banks since the age of three. She even married her husband, Sean Ducharme, in Duck, North Carolina, immediately after a stubborn Hurricane Bonnie churned through the Outer Banks. Conveniently, the family beach house in Kill Devil Hills, North Carolina, provided shelter while she conducted research for her historical fiction novel.

She has two beach-loving children, Dorsey and Katherine, as well as a border collie named Toby, who enjoys his sprints along the Outer Banks shore. The family lives in Manakin-Sabot, Virginia.